Praise for Portia MacIntosh

'Smart, funny and always brilliantly entertaining, every book from Portia becomes my new favourite rom com.'
Shari Low

'I laughed, I cried – I loved it.'
Holly Martin

'The queen of rom com!'
Rebecca Raisin

'This book made me laugh and kept me turning the pages.'
Mandy Baggot

'A fun, fabulous 5-star rom com!'
Sandy Barker

'Loved the book, it's everything you expect from the force that is Portia! A must read'
Rachel Dove

'Fun and witty. Pure escapism!'
Laura Carter

'A heartwarming, fun story, perfect for several hours of pure escapism.'
Jessica Redland

PORTIA MACINTOSH is the bestselling author of over 30 romantic comedy novels.

From disastrous dates to destination weddings, Portia's romcoms are the perfect way to escape from day-to-day life, visiting sunny beaches in the summer and snowy villages at Christmas time. Whether it's southern Italy or the Yorkshire coast, Portia's stories are the holiday you're craving, conveniently packed in between the pages.

Formerly a journalist, Portia has left the city, swapping the music biz for the moors, to live the (not so) quiet life with her husband and her dog in Yorkshire.

Website: portiamacintosh.com
Instagram: @portiamacintoshauthor

Also by Portia MacIntosh

Off The Record
Love on Tour
Always The Bridesmaid
Drive Me Crazy
Truth or Date
It's Not You, It's Them
The Accidental Honeymoon
Never The Bride
Here Comes the Ex

Marram Bay series
Snow Love Lost
Met Your Match

Honeymoon For One
My Great Ex-Scape
The Plus One Pact
Stuck On You
One Night Only
Faking it
Life's a Beach
Will They, Won't They?
No Ex Before Marriage
The Meet Cute Method
Single All The Way
Just Date and See
Your Place or Mine?

Better Off Wed
Long Time No Sea
Fake It or Leave It
Trouble in Paradise
One Wild Night
Ex in the City
The Suite Life
It's All Sun and Games
One of the Boys
You Had Me at Château
Wish You Weren't Here
Too Hot to Handle

Falling for You

PORTIA MACINTOSH

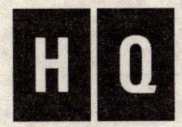

ONE PLACE. MANY STORIES

HQ
An imprint of HarperCollins*Publishers* Ltd
1 London Bridge Street
London SE1 9GF

www.harpercollins.co.uk

HarperCollins*Publishers*
Macken House, 39/40 Mayor Street Upper,
Dublin 1 D01 C9W8

This paperback edition 2025
1

First published in Great Britain as *Summer Secrets at the Apple Blossom Deli*
by HQ,
an imprint of HarperCollins*Publishers* Ltd 2018

Copyright © Portia MacIntosh 2018

Portia MacIntosh asserts the moral right to be identified as the author of this work.
A catalogue record for this book is available from the British Library.

ISBN: 9780008761974

This novel is entirely a work of fiction. The names, characters and incidents portrayed in it are the work of the author's imagination. Any resemblance to actual persons, living or dead, events or localities is entirely coincidental.

All rights reserved. No part of this publication may be reproduced, stored in a retrieval system, or transmitted, in any form or by any means, electronic, mechanical, photocopying, recording or otherwise, without the prior permission of the publishers.

Without limiting the author's and publisher's exclusive rights, any unauthorized use of this publication to train generative artificial intelligence (AI) technologies is expressly prohibited. HarperCollins also exercise their rights under Article 4(3) of the Digital Single Market Directive 2019/790 and expressly reserve this publication from the text and data mining exception.

Printed and bound in the UK using 100% Renewable
Electricity by CPI Group (UK) Ltd

This book contains FSC™ certified paper and other controlled sources
to ensure responsible forest management.

For more information visit: www.harpercollins.co.uk/green

For my amazing family

Chapter 1

Today is the first day of the rest of my life. Well, that's what the dog-eared copy of *The Guide to New Beginnings* currently poking out of my handbag on the front seat has been trying to convince me.

The last month has been a bit of a blur. It feels like just yesterday I was sitting at my desk, mindlessly yet happily going through the motions when one of my bosses perched on the corner of my desk, offered me a new job in a different location and, before I knew what I was doing, I said yes. A more exciting role in the company and a pay increase appealed, of course, but more than anything it was the chance to take my 8-year-old son out of life in inner-city London and raise him in a cute little coastal village up north. I've been worrying about a few things recently and getting out of the city seemed like the best solution – the only solution, really.

I was born and raised in Croydon, only moving closer to central London as I got older. My son Frankie has never known anything other than life in central London, living in a small flat, catching the tube to school every day. This isn't the life I want for him though. I want him to grow up in a small town, in a close community. Somewhere with scenery and fields with real grass, away from the pollution and commuting to school on busy trains, overflowing with unfriendly people.

I love my city and I'm proud of my roots, but after living here for all of my thirty-one years on this planet so far, now just feels like the right time to leave and try somewhere new.

I've always liked the idea of a fresh start, and I can't think of a better time for one than the start of autumn. It's September, and you can already see the signs of summer fading away, allowing the fall to blossom. I find the transition so gentle, as the weather cools down and the colours of the trees burst out of nowhere. It's sad to say goodbye to summer, but I can't help but welcome the cosy jumpers, the pumpkin spice lattes, curing up in front a warm fire with a good book. And now my life is changing with the season, I'm hoping it will be like a breath of that crisp fresh air, that everything will fall into place for me as sure as the leaves will fall from the trees. Here's hoping.

As well as the self-help book I've been reading to help me prepare for the change, I've also got my new planner, packed full of everything I need to know about my new home – and being a single mum, I've always found that my son's social calendar is even harder to keep track of than my own, so it's all going in the planner. Every last detail. I really want this to go well.

As our journey up north progresses, the concrete jungle we're so used to has slowly but surely transitioned to fields of green and wide open space, and it is exactly the breath of fresh air I've been gasping for. I'm too busy taking in the scenery to remember to change gear at a junction so the car stalls, giving us a jolt strong enough to wake Frankie up.

'Mum,' he whines sleepily.

I glance at him in my rear-view mirror and watch him rub his tired eyes.

'Sorry, kiddo,' I say. 'I'm not used to driving a manual.'

Frankie doesn't need me to tell him that; this isn't the first time I've messed up with the gears today. Well, living in the city, I've never needed a car, so I haven't driven one in years. The only car I have driven occasionally – my mum's – is an automatic. Still, it was so nice of my bosses to give me a company-branded VW Beetle to drive up here in and use as a run-around, even if it is an offensive shade of lime green. They've also rented us a cottage that looked positively picturesque in the photos they showed me. It feels weird, moving here without having visited, but everything happened so quickly. I'm sure there was time to do things properly, to come and scope the place out and make sure it was everything I hoped it would be, but I just really wanted to get out of town so that Frankie could start the new school year with everyone else – well, that's what I told them, at least.

'Are we there yet?' Frankie asks for the first time. I'm proud of him, for being so well behaved. Most kids would go bananas during a long car journey but my boy has only started to grow impatient in the last thirty minutes.

'We are,' I tell him with enthusiasm, although I can't help but notice that he doesn't seem as pumped as I am. 'You excited?'

'I guess,' he replies. 'It's gonna be weird.'

'It's gonna be *amazing*,' I remind him. 'I know you'll miss your school and your friends, but you're going to make new friends, you're going to go to a much better school. We're going to live in a big house and there will be fields where you can play, and we can walk to the beach – every day, if you'd like.'

'There's no McDonald's,' he tells me in a smart tone, as though he's sure I already knew that. In truth, I did already know that there wasn't going to be a McDonald's nearby, and that we were going to have to travel thirty miles to get my son a fix of his favourite chicken nuggets. Apparently, no matter how hard I try, I just can't make them as 'good' as McDonald's can.

'There is a McDonald's just a short drive away,' I tell him. It might not be the same as London, where there's a Maccies on every corner, but it's going to be fine. 'You're going to have everything you had in London, plus more.'

'Sam said he's been before to visit his nan and granddad, and he said it was boring,' Frankie informs me.

'Where?' I ask curiously, although I'm pretty sure his fourth favourite friend from school isn't the right person to be taking this kind of advice from.

'The north,' he replies.

I can't help but laugh.

'The north is pretty big. And maybe it was boring because he was visiting his grandparents' house – grandparents are boring.'

'Viv isn't boring,' Frankie insists.

'No, she certainly isn't,' I reply.

My mum, Vivien, isn't at all grandma-ish – she won't even let Frankie call her Gran, she says she looks too young, and, in her defence, she does. She's always been conscious of showing her age, insisting I call her Viv instead of Mum. She puts her all into being a cool grandparent and, to be fair, she's great at it. She was a cool mum too, much to my embarrassment. It's going to be weird, not being just a short train ride away from her.

After driving through nothing but green fields and dry stone walls for a while, Marram Bay is suddenly visible in the distance.

There are two ways we can go; one of them seems the right way, but the satnav insists we go the other, so I stick to what the map tells me and head for the town centre.

'We're here, kiddo,' I announce.

'It looks boring,' Frankie says with a sigh.

At the start of the trip he seemed excited. In fact, I think we spent the first hour of the journey singing along to the radio.

To try and distract my son, I flick the radio back on.

'. . . and I'm sure you'll all be pleased to hear that Rufus the Labrador is safely back at home now. And that completes today's breaking news,' a voice on the radio says. I make eye contact with Frankie in my rear-view mirror. He looks just as confused as I do.

'We'll be finishing the show earlier today, to join in with the festivities on the front. Tune in tomorrow to hear all about it. Ta-ra.'

'So I'm guessing that's the local radio station,' I laugh. 'Wanna go check out the festivities?'

Frankie sighs. 'OK.'

Marram Bay is such a beautiful place. It's small – even smaller than I expected. The town is cute, like something fresh out of a romantic movie – with ivy creeping up the walls and around the sweet little windows of the houses sitting at the top of perfectly tended gardens. Few houses look the same here, which I like. Everywhere has so much individuality and character.

It takes us no time to go from green open space, to farmhouses, to cottages, and finally to the seafront with its cute, quirky little shops.

'Erm . . .' I can't help but say, catching sight of the bizarre festivities on the seafront.

'Where are we?' Frankie asks.

'*When* are we?' I laugh to myself.

Upon closer inspection the town doesn't just look old-fashioned – it looks like the setting for a Second World War movie. The windows are covered with white tape, everyone is dressed in out-of-date clothing and the place is overrun with soldiers and army vehicles.

As we crawl along the road running alongside the seafront, we catch the attention of a woman in her late thirties. She's wearing a blue-and-white polka dot tea dress teamed with navy gloves, complemented by her brown hair that is neatly pinned into victory rolls. I stop the car at the side of the road, just as our eyes meet.

'Are we in the past?' Frankie asks.

Of course, I know that we're not – that we couldn't possibly be, unless we've wandered into some sort of *Goodnight Sweetheart* portal – but I don't really have an answer for him.

I smile at the pinup girl at the side of the road, only for her to cock her head in puzzlement. Why is *she* confused? I'm the one suddenly in the past. She calls over her friends – a land girl and an apparent member of the WRAF – who join her in staring over at us, chatting amongst themselves.

'Maybe we should go,' I say, but as I go to drive away, I – of course – stall my car again. Come to think of it, the lime-green company-branded Beetle is probably the reason everyone is staring at us.

After another judder, it occurs to me that my loud (both in volume and colour) German car is probably ruining the war-era aesthetic of the festivities.

'Ship, ship, ship,' I say repeatedly, until I finally get the car moving and drive off.

'Swears!' Frankie chastises me.

'I said "ship",' I point out. 'Remind me who is the kid and who is the mum?'

'I could ask you the same thing,' he replies.

Frankie is smart for an 8-year-old, however, as a by-product of this intellect, he thinks he is much smarter than he is. I know that I should probably be the one keeping Frankie in check but he's no bother at all . . . which is probably why he ends up keeping me in check instead.

'Let's go see the house,' I say cheerily. 'We'll meet the locals some other time.'

Like, I don't know, maybe this decade instead.

After spending the past few weeks – and a chunk of our journey here – trying to convince my son that we would be moving somewhere wonderful, I've driven him straight into some kind of weird place that seems to be literally stuck in the past. But in two minutes we'll be at the beautifully named Apple Blossom Cottage.

I glance quickly between my satnav and the road until we approach our destination. I spot the cottage of my dreams, hiding away behind a wall of leafy trees. Through the green leaves, the stone bungalow almost looks like part of the landscape. I'm so used to living in London, surrounded by either ugly old office blocks or new, ultra-modern sky-grazing skyscrapers. Outside the garden walls, Apple Blossom Cottage is enclosed by nothing but fields – this change of scenery is exactly what I need.

It's a small, but gorgeous cottage, just perfect for the two of us. The stone walls are covered with all different kinds of climbing plants, from ivy to roses, giving it a uniquely colourful beauty that I haven't seen before. The white-framed windows are small, peeping out from behind the plants. The frames look like perhaps they need replacing – not that I'm an expert, they just look a little tired. Then again, I imagine that's what you'd think if you looked at me at the moment, courtesy of the bout of stress I'm suffering. I'm hoping that as soon as we get our things moved in, I can finally let go of my stress and relax into country life.

The place reminds me so much of a smaller version of Kate Winslet's cottage from *The Holiday* (only with a far superior garden), and while I'd always thought of myself as more of a Cameron Diaz type, I feel like this is the place for me.

I step out of the car and take a photo on my phone. I want to remember my first glimpse of our new home for the rest of my life. I don't just feel like I've arrived – *I've arrived*. I'm here, outside this perfect house, in a gorgeous small coastal town, about to start my dream job with my healthy, intelligent son by my side. Maybe it is possible to have it all . . . at least, that's what *How to Have It All*, another of my hastily bought self-help books, has been trying to tell me. Packing up and starting your life again is a big deal, so I wanted to do some reading, make sure I was prepared for anything and everything. This job is so important to me, but Frankie is even more important. I just want to be a good mum – preferably one of those you see on Instagram with an adorable baby in one arm, and a wooden spoon in the other, standing in their immaculate kitchen (bigger than all the rooms in my London flat added together), posing in a way that makes them look like a Victoria's Secret model.

My proportions are more Victoria sponge cake, than Victoria's

Secret model. Sure, we're a society who celebrates the 'dad bod' (Leonardo DiCaprio is like a fine wine, only growing more devastatingly gorgeous by the moment) but they won't be putting my 'mum bod' on any catwalks in barely there underwear anytime soon. But each stretchmark and varicose vein maps the journey I went on to come back with my son, and I'd take that over a Victoria's Secret model body any day – even if it would significantly increase my chances with the aforementioned Mr DiCaprio.

I chase my son, who is currently part-boy, part-aeroplane, in the back garden.

'Wow.' My jaw drops.

It is suddenly apparent where Apple Blossom Cottage gets its name from: the army of apple trees surrounding the garden. I don't know much about apple trees, but I'm guessing September is when these beauties are at their best, because there are apples everywhere. Oh boy, when the leaves start falling this cute little cottage is going to be practically buried in them. I don't love the idea of keeping on top of the garden maintenance, but I can't wait to see the colourful leaves taking over the green space.

Frankie runs over to me with an apple in each hand.

'Can we eat them?' he asks.

'We have to wash them first, but yes,' I reply, delighted that my chicken nugget–craving son is suddenly thrilled at the thought of an endless supply of apples. 'We could even bake an apple pie, would you like that?'

Frankie nods.

'Better than the ones at McDonald's,' I tell him, instantly regretting mentioning the 'M' word, but it doesn't seem to bother him. Baking is not something that I'm good at, but I'm sure it still counts if we buy ready-made pastry and simply assemble the pie, right?

I stroll over to the large pond at the end of the garden and lean over, looking at my reflection in the water. Maybe I can earn strong, single-woman, pie-baking, yummy-mummy status here – wouldn't that be nice?

'Can I unlock the door?' Frankie asks excitedly.

'Carefully,' I tell him, handing him the keys from my bag. 'I'll be right behind you.'

Inside my bag, in the hidden pocket usually reserved for 'women's things' and the rape alarm I always felt an uneasy need to keep on me at all times in central London, the corner of a postcard pokes out. I quickly push it back inside and zip it up. I'll worry about that later.

Frankie flies off towards the front door excitedly as I try to keep up with him in my heels. I'm just walking around the corner when I hear his voice.

'Er . . . Mum,' he shouts, and I don't like the sound of it at all.

Chapter 2

When my bosses showed me photos of Apple Blossom Cottage, I was so in awe of its beautiful exterior and ready for my fresh start that it didn't even occur to me to ask for photos of the inside. Now that I think about it, I can't imagine my bosses saw photos of the interior either, because I feel like I've just walked into a nightmare, and there's no way my bosses would knowingly send me to *this*.

'Where's all the stuff?' Frankie asks.

'I was just wondering that,' I reply, strolling around, taking in my surroundings.

An overly minimalist kitchen (what you'd call it if you were being kind) sits at the back of an open-plan living/dining area.

The kitchen boasts a worktop, a small fridge freezer and what I'd guess is a gas cooker and oven. There's a dining table with exactly three chairs, all of which have seen better days, and a living area that consists of a truly Eighties-style grey plush three-seater sofa with a wood-and-brass trim, sitting across from a retro-looking wooden TV cabinet (TV not included).

To the left are three doors, which I'm guessing are the two bedrooms and the bathroom – please, God, let one of the rooms be a bathroom. I don't think I noticed an outhouse in the garden, but I don't think I'd be at all surprised to learn the place didn't have any plumbing. Thankfully, there is one.

A quick scout of all rooms confirms they are as minimal as the rest of the place but, worst of all, everything is so dusty. If this were an Airbnb rental, they would surely be getting an overly generous one-star rating from me – probably from Frankie too, who is currently coming down from his garden high as he tries to wrap his head around the indoor TV aerial. He extends the silver rods one at a time before quickly and carefully putting it down, just in case it's something scary.

I cast my mind back to what Eric, one of my bosses, told me about the cottage. He said it was an ex holiday home, and that it was furnished. I suppose it is furnished, technically, but I didn't expect something so retro.

Wow, did I just get catfished by *a house*? Now that I think about it, despite the cute, rural look of the outside of the cottage, perhaps the ivy might be the only thing holding the place together. This is a new low for me. I *can't wait* to write about this in my new diary.

'This place sucks,' Frankie says frankly.

Any other day, I would have been inclined to agree with him, but my fresh-start enthusiasm is still surging through my veins. 'It's all easily fixable, kiddo. We'll fill it with our own things, we'll clean the place up, we'll buy the things we don't have. It's going to be great. This way, we get to put even more of our own spin on the place and really make it our own.'

Our moving van won't be here until tomorrow, so for now we only have the essentials with us. But once we have all our own things, I'm sure we can make this place feel just like home.

Frankie pulls a face. I don't think he's buying it. I believe what I'm saying though. I'll bring our stuff in, we can go out for some food, I'll buy some cleaning products and everything will be great. I just need to keep telling myself that. Everything will be great.

Chapter 3

I knew that Marram Bay was small, but it's only now that I'm here, in it, that I can feel just how small it is.

I felt that, given my little scene earlier, it was best we stay away from, well, whatever it was that was going down on the seafront. But, it turns out the main street is on the seafront, so we're not having much luck finding somewhere to get dinner further inland. As you travel into Marram Bay, first you pass the farms, then you enter the residential area. It seems like the kind of place that will look beautiful no matter what time of year it is, come rain or shine, but somehow I think the colours of autumn are going to suit it best. I can already see them emerging, teasing what's to come.

If you keep going towards the coast you'll wind up in the touristy bit, where everything is, but trying to find somewhere to eat that isn't in the heart of the town is proving difficult.

It seemed like Clara's, a little café sitting between a row of cottages and a small park in the residential area, might be our saviour, but despite their opening hours including Sunday afternoons, the door is locked and there's no sign of life inside.

'I'm hungry, Mum,' Frankie says, tugging on the bottom of my jacket as I peer through the glass door, my face pressed as close to the glass as I can get it.

'Can I help you?' a man's voice asks from behind us.

I turn around quickly to see a couple, maybe in their sixties, standing at the gate, at the bottom of the café's little front garden. We're on the main road into town but I didn't hear them coming, which means they must have walked here – something that becomes more apparent when I realise the man is struggling to catch his breath. The man is wearing some kind of soldier outfit, just like I saw many people at the seafront wearing, and the woman is wearing a red dress teamed with red pumps, a white cardigan and a fox fur scarf that I so hope isn't real. As they walk up the path I get a better look at the fox, which still has its face, its tail – even its claws. It's not just an eerie sight, seeing its little face upsets me and makes me uncomfortable. The smiling faces of the couple make me feel more at ease.

'I'm sorry,' I say, finally finding the words. 'We just moved here and we were looking for somewhere to eat.'

'We're closed today,' the man informs us. 'Been down at the Forties Weekend.'

'Oh, the Forties Weekend,' I echo. 'We wondered what was going on, didn't we, kiddo?'

Frankie clings to my leg, silently.

'Yeah, once a year we all get dressed up in our Forties best and we have a big celebration. We remember the war, raise money for charity – and, well, everyone goes so no point opening up today.'

'Oh, I see,' I reply. 'Well, it was lovely to meet you.'

I usher Frankie along the path a little, only for the lady to gently place her hand on my forearm. I turn to face her, making eye contact with her fox for a moment, before shifting my glance to her eyes.

'Don't worry, my love, it's not real. I got it from a fancy dress shop,' she explains with a warm smile. 'Come in, we can open up for Marram Bay's newest family.'

'Oh, no, please,' I insist.

'Mum,' Frankie whispers. 'I'm hungry.'

The lady smiles at me and there's this warmth in her eyes . . . before I have a chance to think too much about it, I accept their generous offer.

Inside, Clara's is exactly as you'd expect a country café to be. It's cosy and kitsch, with no two pieces of crockery, cutlery, furniture of soft furnishings the same – even the windows have different curtains around them.

As the man ushers us towards one of the wooden tables, the woman fetches some menus and places them down in front of us.

'I'm Clara,' she says. 'This is my husband, Henry.'

Henry gives us a nod as he takes a seat at the table next to us. He extends one leg out straight, which reminds me that I noticed he had a limp.

'I'm Lily,' I say. 'And this is my son, Frankie. It's so nice to meet you both.'

I glance over the menu.

'So what can I get you?' Clara asks as she removes her fox and fastens her apron.

'What's your poison, lad?' Henry asks Frankie, lightly bumping his shoulder with a fist.

Frankie stares at me.

'He's asking what you want to drink,' I assure him with a smile. 'Juice?'

He nods. I reach across the table and brush his wild, curly brown hair away from his eyes. I am quite pale, with natural golden-blonde hair – not that you can tell, because I have peroxide-blonde highlights – and green eyes, but Frankie takes after his dad. Brown hair, brown eyes and a slight natural tan. He's so cute, with his little button nose and his cheeky little dimples. I still can't believe I made him.

'And to eat?' Clara asks.

'I only like McNuggets,' Frankie informs them.

'Is that right?' Henry replies. 'What if I told you that Clara makes chicken nuggets even better than McDonald's, would you try them?'

'Oh, no, please, we'll just have sandwiches, don't start cooking,' I insist, but Clara is having none of it.

'Nonsense,' she replies with a bat of her hand. 'Chicken nuggets for the boy, what about for Mum?'

'Scrambled eggs on toast would be great, please,' I reply, ordering from their all-day brunch menu.

'Coming right up,' she replies as she trots off to the kitchen in her kitten heels. 'Talk amongst yourself, I'll be able to chat from the kitchen.'

Clara disappears through a multicoloured strip curtain before remerging behind a serving hatch.

'Londoners?' Henry asks.

'Guilty,' I reply with an awkward smile.

'And you say you've just moved here?' Clara quizzes.

'Yes,' I say. I feel like I'm being grilled, but I have nothing to hide. 'We're renting Apple Blossom Cottage.'

'Oh, lovely place,' she replies. 'Just stunning.'

'Yes,' I reply, but my little white lie prickles my throat. I cough to clear it.

'You not like it?' Henry asks.

'It's so beautiful from the outside – Frankie has never seen anything like it . . . The inside is just a little sparse and it needs a good spring clean,' I explain. 'And there's not really too much in it.'

'It was the Nicholsons' holiday home – they had it for years, but since, it's just been sat empty. I suspect they took all their mod cons with them.'

'It seems that way,' I reply.

Henry picks up a newspaper and begins to flick through the pages. The *East Coast Chronicle* looks like an interesting read. The front cover is an appeal for help to find Rufus the chocolate Labrador, who never came home after taking himself for his usual walk to the seafront. I'm guessing this is the dog we heard all about on the radio and it warms my heart to know that he's back home safe. It also amuses me to see that this is front-page news here, rather than yet another story about gangs or tube strikes – further proof, if it were needed, that moving here was a great decision.

'Well, I'm sure we can survive without a TV tonight.' I look at Frankie, who swallows hard. I don't think he's convinced, but I'm sure he can go a night without playing Nintendo. 'We definitely need to clean though, it's far too dusty to sleep in. Is there a Co-op or a Tesco Express or something nearby?'

Henry scoffs.

'We have a local shop but they'll be closed,' he replies.

'Oh,' I say, wondering if I can get the job done with hand sanitiser and toilet roll.

'I can give you some cleaning products,' Clara says as she places my food down in front of me. 'Just a few more minutes for yours, my love.'

Frankie smiles politely. I'm proud of him for being a sweet kid with such great manners, but he's got that unfiltered honesty that all kids have, and I'm worried about how he's going to react to the not-McChicken nuggets that Clara is making him. The last time I tried to make him some – promising him they would be just as good – he told me they tasted like poison.

'You've been so kind to us already,' I insist, taken aback by the kindness these complete strangers are showing us. 'I don't know what to say.'

'We're neighbours now, think nothing of this,' Clara says as she places Frankie's dinner in front of him. 'There you go, my love. My famous chicken nuggets.'

Frankie glances down at the plate of chicken nuggets, proper, thick-cut chips, peas and a large dollop of ketchup. Frankie loves ketchup, but – like most kids – he hates peas.

I raise my eyebrows at him, silently communicating for him to say thank you.

'Thank you,' he chimes politely.

'You're welcome,' she replies, ruffling his hair. 'I'll go get you some drinks.'

With Clara in the kitchen and Henry distracted by his paper, I lean over to my son and whisper into his ear: 'If you try it – or at least pretend you're eating it – I'll buy you a TV for your room.'

I think every good mum has bribed her child at some point. I know that I probably shouldn't, but Clara and Henry have been so good to us, I don't want to offend them.

Frankie nods, sighs and picks up his cutlery.

I finally tuck into my own food which is not only much needed after a long day, but absolutely delicious.

Clara places two glasses of apple juice down in front of us.

'They're from local trees,' she tells us. 'But let me know if you want anything else, or a nice cup of tea.'

'Again – thank you so much,' I say, starting to sound like a broken record, but I really can't thank them enough.

I watch Frankie theatrically pretend to eat his food – it's kind of cute – until he accidentally drops his knife, which makes a loud noise on the floor.

'Not to worry,' Henry says, pulling himself to his feet. He grabs a clean knife from another table, hobbles over to Frankie and begins to cut his food (which up until now had only been pushed around his plate) for him.

'Try this,' he says, stabbing a piece of chicken with the fork, offering it to Frankie.

Frankie looks over at me. I purse my lips and plead at him with my eyes once more.

I watch as my son takes the chicken, chews it and swallows with a much more convincing enthusiasm than before.

'Try it with the peas, it tastes much better,' Henry insists, stabbing another piece, this time making sure to get some peas with it.

Frankie looks back over at me, but he knows what he needs

to do. With Nintendo on his mind, he takes the food down in one bite.

'Good lad,' Henry says, handing Frankie the cutlery back. As he does so, I notice Frankie staring at Henry's hand. Upon closer inspection, I realise that he's quite badly scarred from something.

Henry notices Frankie staring.

'I got blown up,' he tells him, before turning to me. 'Falklands.'

As Henry hobbles past me he places a hand on my shoulder and whispers into my ear: 'I have kids who didn't used to eat their greens either.'

'Thank you,' I reply.

'No bother,' he says. 'Just heading to the little boys' room.'

Clara, still wearing her Forties outfit under her apron, places a bag of cleaning supplies down next to me before taking a seat at the table next to us. She cradles her cup of tea in her hand as she chats.

'Just the two of you moved here?' she asks. She sounds friendly enough, but you'd be amazed at the variety of easy-to-read physical reactions you get from people when they find out you're a 31-year-old single mum.

First there's the unabashed judgemental response. You can practically see the mental mathematics going on behind their eyes, as they try and work out that if a 31-year-old has an 8-year-old, how old was she when she got pregnant. For some it's done with the ease of Will Hunting, whereas you can see others itching to use their fingers. Twenty-two – that's not so bad, is it? I see them wonder. These people will almost always decide that, yes, it probably is bad. Some people just think that kids should be born into loving, conventional family units and there's nothing you can say that will change their minds.

Next up are the people who feel sorry for me, who think about how awful it must have been for me to find myself pregnant and alone, just 22 years old with my entire life ahead of me. You see the pity in turn of their mouth and the weight of their eyelids, and while it comes from a good place, it never makes me feel good.

Worst of all though, of the varying reactions to my 'situation' I've endured over the years, it's the ones I receive from single men that bother me the most, because they don't judge me, nor do they feel sorry for me. Instead they look at things from an entirely selfish point of view, quickly writing me off, because while I'm sure there are men out there who have taken on, or would be happy to take on another man's child, none of them have been any of the (four) men I have been on dates with since Frankie was born.

'Yep, just us,' I reply. 'Always has been.'

I look over at my son fondly, only to see him wolfing down his food.

'Frankie,' I squeak. 'Are you enjoying that?'

'Yes,' he says almost reluctantly, looking at his plate as he responds. He's always maintained that he would never find a chicken nugget to rival his beloved McDonald's, but he has insisted even harder that he would never enjoy a vegetable of any description – obviously, excluding chips and the occasional roast potato. I've tried covering his broccoli in cheese, hiding carrots in his pasta sauce, and even roasting parsnips and trying to convince him they were chips, but my tricks have always failed me. And yet here he is, consciously and contently eating peas.

'He doesn't usually like vegetables,' I tell Clara, unable to hide my happiness.

'I cook them with bacon and a bit of honey,' she explains. 'I haven't met a person yet who doesn't love my peas.'

'Well, you've definitely got yourself some new, regular customers,' I laugh.

'You're not customers today,' she says. 'Consider this our "welcome to the neighbourhood" gift to you.'

'Clara, you've done so much for us!'

'You're our neighbour now,' she points out. 'Think nothing of it.'

I pick up my apple juice and take a sip – it's delicious. I can't wait to get to see what I can do with the ones in my garden . . . not that I'm an especially good cook. I'm just excited to try. Things maybe have got off to a bumpy start but I really do feel like we're going to be happy here.

'So, what brings you here then?' Clara asks. 'Just a fresh start?'

'Yes,' I reply, although that's not strictly true.

Nervously, I take a long drink from my glass and, thankfully, by the time I come out of hiding from behind my apple juice, Clara has shifted her attention to Frankie, asking him questions about his hobbies.

Now isn't the time to tell a woman I've just met about what I'm hiding from.

Chapter 4

I run a hand over the perfectly clean kitchen worktop, marvelling at my own handiwork. I've never really been a *Good Housekeeping* kind of woman. My cooking skills are pretty basic, my cleaning abilities are adequate and as for all the helpful extras, like being able to sew – well, I've never really had time for that.

This kitchen though, it's spotless. From the floor, to the surfaces, to the windows (which, truth be told, I don't even remember cleaning), everything looks great.

What really catches my attention though, is the man in the back garden. I didn't know this place had a gardener, but I suppose it makes sense, with all the beautiful plants, the neatly trimmed lawns and the pond to take care of.

The shirtless gardener is reaching up and plucking apples from the tree. I can't help but stare at his bulging biceps, watching them flex as he extends his arm to grab an apple, before tossing it into the basket on the ground.

Before I know what I'm doing, I've stepped outside the backdoor and called out to him.

'Good morning,' I say brightly.

The man turns around and if he wasn't picking apples in my back garden, in the arse-end of nowhere, I would swear it was

Daniel Craig, with his chiselled good looks, his blond hair and his buff Bond-worthy body.

The man doesn't reply. He reaches up, plucks a bright red apple from the tree and tosses it over to me, which I catch with an unusual ease. I'm not usually this coordinated . . . or confident, for that matter.

I raise the apple to my mouth to take a bite, stopping just before it touches my lips. Bizarrely, it doesn't smell like I was expecting it to; in fact, it smells like lemons. I take another big whiff, only to wake up suddenly, in my new bed, with my Marigold-clad hands wrapped around a can of lemon Pledge. So not only did I fall asleep cleaning, but I dreamt the whole sexy gardener thing! I suppose it all makes sense now. I don't approach men or have a perfectly tidy kitchen, and, now that I think about it, Daniel Craig trimming my bushes in his iconic blue swimming trunks doesn't sound all that realistic.

Disappointed, I place the Pledge and the gloves down on my (half-polished) bedside table and stretch out my back before unplugging my phone. I'm just about to mindlessly scroll my social networks for a few minutes, like I do every morning, when I see the time. Shit! I've overslept! And not only am I going to be late for my first day on the job, but Frankie is going to be late for his first day of school.

I dash to the kitchen and, although it is clean, it's not as sparkling as it was in my dream and stupidly I can't help but feel a little disheartened. I grab a glass from the cupboard and fill it with milk from the fridge before charging into Frankie's room. He's sleeping so peacefully, I almost don't want to wake him up. I hope it's because the bed is comfortable and not because I blitzed his room with too many cleaning products before I put him to bed last night.

'Wake up, kiddo, we're late,' I babble as I place the milk down next to him. 'Drink milk, brush teeth, put clothes on and meet me in the kitchen.'

'What?' Frankie asks, rubbing his eyes.

'We're going to be late,' I tell him. 'Quick, quick.'

'Fine,' he says, sounding a little too much like a moody teenager for my liking.

I dash back into the kitchen, grab his lunchbox and quickly fill it with a ham and cheese bagel, a packet of salt and vinegar crisps and one of those little Freddo chocolate bars – his favourite three things, to make him feel as comfortable as possible on his first day. Frankie has never been through anything like this before and I can tell he's nervous because he's been asking me a lot of questions about his new school since he found out he was going there.

Next, I dash into my bedroom, hurry off yesterday's clothes and quickly wipe off as much of yesterday's make-up as I need to, before carefully applying copious amounts of all the things that make me look awake and alive. Then I hop into the white shirt and the black pencil skirt that I'm so glad I set out ready for myself last night, step into a pair of heels and hurry on some accessories before heading back to the kitchen, where a sleepy-looking Frankie is waiting.

'Aw, look at you,' I can't help but pause to say. 'But where's your tie?'

'I don't wanna wear it, Mum,' he replies. 'I didn't have to wear a tie at my old school.'

'Kiddo, they didn't care if you wore trousers at your last school – remember that day Sam turned up in his Minion swimming shorts?'

'Yeah,' Frankie says, cracking up. 'That was funny.'

'Bring me your tie, I'll fasten it for you,' I tell him.

My son reluctantly does as he is told.

'OK, so we just wrap this bit around a couple of times, pull it through and . . . there we go. My God, you look cute.'

'I look stupid,' he corrects me.

'Stand by the fireplace, I want to take your picture,' I insist.

'Mum,' he whines.

'Please?'

Oh God, I'm *that* mum.

Frankie, knowing that sometimes it's better to just do as I ask than to fight it, slowly walks over to the fireplace and stands, sort of slumped, with a glum look on his face.

'Smile.'

Frankie forces a big, dumb smile.

'When you turn 21 I'm going to put this picture on your birthday cake, and you'll regret pulling that face,' I laugh as I look at it on my phone.

I dash back to the kitchen and grab my handbag, Frankie's lunchbox and a variety-pack-sized box of Frosties before hurrying for the door. I hand Frankie the lunchbox and the Frosties.

'Go wait by the car, I'll just lock the door,' I instruct.

I pause for a split second before I lock up. I'm pretty sure everything is turned off that should be turned off, and everything that should be locked is locked. Back home, I had my morning routine down. In fact, I just did most stuff on autopilot, like locking doors and turning appliances off, but here everything is strange and new. Still, we weren't up long enough to turn things on, so I'm sure everything is fine.

I fasten Frankie into the back of the car, climb into the front seat and set the destination on my phone. Acorn School isn't too far away but I don't know the area yet, so better to be sure of where we're going than to explore and hope we find it.

Marram Bay is a strange combination of coastal town and countryside. The seafront is the touristy part, with the pretty views and the cute little shops. Then, as you travel further inland, you approach the homes where the locals live. Finally, you reach the part of Marram Bay that is mostly farmland and fields, with the occasional cottage or school dotted in the middle of nowhere.

At the end of the road where our cottage sits is a huge, contemporary house. I glance at the sign outside which reads 'Westwood

Farm', though it doesn't look much like any farm I've ever seen.

'Whoa,' Frankie says. 'That's a cool house.'

'It is,' I reply, a pinch of salt in my words, given our current living situation. Obviously the closest thing we've got to a next-door neighbour lives in a house that was most likely on *Grand Designs*. 'We can't stop and stare though, kiddo, we're late. Make sure you eat your breakfast.'

'Yes, crisps,' he chirps.

'Oi, no, eat your cereal, not your lunch,' I say with a laugh. 'Did you brush your teeth?'

'Oops,' Frankie says. I can't really blame him today, we were running so late. Running my tongue across my own teeth reminds me that brushing my teeth was something I forgot to do too.

I stop the car and glance around, looking for something that isn't a field.

'Oh, there we go,' I say, pointing ahead.

Acorn School is an old Victorian stone building with a slate roof and sash windows. It even has a little tower – I'll bet this was some house back in the day. But while it has the grandeur and proportions of an amazing Victorian-era house, as far as schools go it's positively tiny. Acorn School is the only school for kids Frankie's age for miles, but it didn't bother me too much when I enrolled him because the school has a glowing track record and rave reviews. I suppose, because it's so small, there are fewer students and therefore each kid can get much more attention and support.

I hurry Frankie out of the car, through the heavy metal gate and up the stone steps into the playground.

'This way,' I instruct, pointing towards the main door.

We must be extremely late, because there's no sign of any kids – or even any parents on their way out.

There is no way I could have known the large wooden door led straight into their (little) main hall, and that assembly would be well underway. No more than forty kids are sitting on the floor, singing along to 'All Things Bright and Beautiful', which is being played on a piano at the front of the room by a person who is far too short for me to see over the top of the instrument. Leading the assembly is a woman, maybe in her fifties, conducting the children with her hands. She's quite tall, and on the broad side, which makes her appear intimidatingly large next to the little kids, although I imagine if I were to stand alongside her in my four-inch heels, she probably wouldn't seem like such a giant. She's kind of old-fashioned, and a little on the drab side, wearing navy blue trousers, a white shirt and a navy Aran cardigan. She has a pair of glasses hanging around her neck on a chain – something I didn't realise people did in real life, I assumed this was a look reserved for librarians in movies. She has an especially short auburn bob, just skimming her ears, which only adds to her stern, harsh appearance.

As she glances over at us, it confirms one thing, that no matter how old I get, I will always recognise one look: the look from a teacher that lets you know you're in trouble.

As we wait for the song to end, I place an arm around Frankie protectively – or maybe I'm just hoping she'll go easier on me if I use my child as a shield. What is it about teachers and the slightly terrifying air of authority they give off? I can feel it from across the room.

'Well, children, first of all Ms Berry is going to talk to you about all the wonderful things we have in store for you this term. I need to go and welcome our new – slightly late – pupil,' the teacher says, gesturing towards us.

Everyone turns around to look at us so I give an awkward wave.

'Miss Holmes, I presume,' she says as she approaches us.

'Hello, yes, I'm so sorry we're late,' I babble as she ushers us into a classroom. 'We only arrived yesterday and we had a late night sorting the cottage out, didn't we?'

I hear a weird crunching sound, which I quickly realise is coming from my son, who is finally eating his Frosties. I die inside.

'Hello, Frankie,' the teacher says, crouching down next in front of him. 'My name is Mrs Snowball, I'm the headteacher here at Acorn School. I'm also going to be your teacher.'

Mrs Snowball? Really? I couldn't think of a more cutesy name for a teacher if I tried.

Frankie nods in acknowledgement as he crunches his dry cereal.

'Is that your breakfast?' she asks him, returning to my level without waiting for an answer. 'Is that his breakfast?'

'Yes, we were in such a hurry this morning,' I explain. 'He did have the milk before we left.'

Mrs Snowball scrunches up her face.

'I'll get you some nice fruit once Mum has gone,' she tells Frankie.

Good luck with that, darling.

'I can't apologise enough for being late,' I say again, not that I think it's doing me much good.

'Well, I was hoping to show you both around, but I'm not sure there's time now,' Mrs Snowball says. 'How about I go get Frankie a real breakfast and show him the ropes. And then, when you come to collect him after school, I'll show you around.'

'OK, sure,' I reply. 'That OK, kiddo?'

'Come on now, Mum, he's not a baby. You're fine, aren't you, Frankie? What's Frankie short for?' she asks me.

'Probably because he's only 8,' I quip, laughing at my own joke, but I'm getting nothing from my audience. Mrs Snowball clearly has a different sense of humour to me, I must remember that when I do what I always do and fill awkward encounters with terrible gags.

'I meant his name,' she says, not at all amused by me.

'Sorry, just a joke. Frankie is his name.'

'Exotic,' she replies.

'Well, be a good boy,' I say, because I feel like that's a parent-y thing to say. 'And you know that if you need me, Mrs Snowball has my number.'

'He's not going to need you,' she laughs, ushering Frankie away from me. 'We'll see you at three.'

Back in my car, I look at myself in the rear-view mirror. *Why did you have to be late today, Lily? Why?* Of all the days, it just had to be Frankie's first day of school and my first day of work.

Speaking of which, I am now twenty minutes late to meet the site manager at the deli.

My first job, after I had Frankie, was working behind the counter in a YumYum deli. Back then there were only three branches, all in London, but now they're popping up all over England as the business rapidly expands.

No one grows up with big dreams of working in the deli business, do they? I can't say it had ever crossed my mind. I only (reluctantly) took the job because I was a single mum and it was close to home, but it turned out to be a perfect fit for me in many ways.

I've always had a passion for food and working in the deli, I got to share this passion with the customers, giving them recommendations on what to buy and making suggestions for their lunch. I loved the work, I loved the customers and most importantly I loved all the delicious food.

While I was working there I got to know the bosses, Eric and Amanda, a married couple who had no idea that, when they opened their first deli, they would one day be sitting in a swanky central London office, with a thriving deli chain. I think the fact that they didn't expect their success is why they're probably still so humble and generous. Eric and Amanda saw my passion for the products we sold and promoted me, giving me a job in their head office, where I would source new products to stock and make decisions about what we sold in each branch. Sure, I missed the customer-facing work, but I loved looking for new and exciting foods to sell.

I often fantasise about running my own deli one day, but know I'd never be able to afford it. So when, out of the blue, Eric and

Amanda said they were opening a new branch in a tourist town up north, and needed someone who knew the business well to go and oversee the important opening and then run the branch, I jumped at the chance. Not only is this my chance to get as close to running my own deli as possible, the fresh start couldn't have come at a better time.

I pull up outside a little stone building and it's just perfect. Exactly what I had in my head when I conjured up my dream deli. It's a standalone building that looks like it perhaps used to be a cottage. I'm guessing the stone walls have been sandblasted, because it looks almost like new, and unlike weather-beaten Apple Blossom Cottage, you can see all the different-coloured stones that were used when it was built. There is a small, paved section out front, perfect for a few tables and chairs to be put out when we're ready to open, and the walls are adorned with large, absolutely gorgeous hanging baskets. The only thing missing is the sign, which reminds me that it is my job to find a name for this place. The owners don't want their delis to seem like chains, even though they technically are, because each deli is unique and deserves a unique name.

I quickly search my bag for some chewing gum. It's weird how, when you forget to brush your teeth, you feel fine up until the point you realise you haven't brushed your teeth, and suddenly they feel alien in your mouth. I spot a packet with a couple of pieces in that, truthfully, I don't remember buying, but it's not like I plan on swallowing it, is it?

Once again, I see the corner of the postcard poking out of my bag, the postcard I'm trying so hard to keep out of my mind.

As I chew the stale chewing gum, I glance over at the deli again. I'm just thinking about how perfect it is when I notice something propped up outside – it looks like a cardboard sign.

I step out of the car – which I always forget is lime green when I'm in it – and walk cautiously towards the sign.

It reads: 'You're making a misteak' in large red letters. The spelling mistake stands out a mile in bright red letters but that isn't enough to take away from the intimidating message. Is this meant for me? It can't be . . .

I pick the sign up and look at the other side.

'Burger off!'

This can't be good . . .

Chapter 5

When my bosses offered me this job they were keen to mention that it needed someone with both business and shop floor experience. They said that Marram Bay was a hugely popular coastal town, overflowing with tourists who would lap up a YumYum deli, and that autumn would be the perfect time to open one with all our seasonal specialities. I don't think they would have sent me here if they didn't think I was up to the job, but they did neglect to mention one small detail . . .

'What do you mean no one wants us here?' I ask Mike, the site manager.

'No one wants us here,' he repeats himself, just in case saying the exact same thing twice provides a little more clarity.

I blink.

'The locals,' he says in a strong cockney accent that makes me feel both comforted and homesick.

At YumYum we have an in-house team of fitters responsible for decking out the delis with everything they need. Mike is their manager and today he's supposed to be showing me around, except there's just this one little problem.

'I saw the sign outside,' I tell him. 'Are you telling me one of the locals left that there?'

'No, no. They left it in here, I just put it out there, ready to go in the skip. They had a protest, everyone had their little signs. That one was the butcher's.'

That explains the terrible pun.

'Why were they protesting?' I ask.

Mike takes a battered-looking iPhone from the pocket of his paint-splattered jeans and taps the screen a few times before handing it to me. I notice that he's calling Eric, one of the big bosses, so I hold the phone to my ear.

'All right Mike, what's the problem now?' he asks, and it sounds like there's been a lot of problems so far.

'Eric, hello, it's Lily,' I say as brightly as I can manage.

'Lily,' he says, sounding a little sheepish. 'You made it there OK then? You all settled in?'

'Erm, it's not exactly what I had in mind,' I say, choosing my words carefully. I decide that now is not the time to mention the state of the cottage – I'm dealing with it anyway – so instead I get straight to the point about the deli. 'Mike says no one wants us here?'

'No,' he replies.

'No?' I echo, staring to feel like a parrot.

Eric sighs deeply.

'OK, so the locals have a bit of a problem with a chain opening, they want to preserve the town, not make it a clone of every other high street out there . . . so they put in a lot of objections with the council,' he explains.

'But, all the delis have different names and identities, so it's not going to look like a clone. And the foods we sell, they're from all over, and it's not like we're opening a butcher's to compete with the existing one.'

'I know, that's why the council gave us the go-ahead to open,' he assures me.

'But?'

'But the locals still aren't happy. They think the deli is going to destroy the independent shops that define the community and that we're going to damage local businesses. They say we're targeting transient custom, people without roots in the community who don't care about whether or not they enrich local economy over us, who they see as "the man"', he says with a bit of a chuckle. They might be a chain, but they're not exactly ruthless business people.

'So, what now?' I ask.

'So now it's your job to convince them that a YumYum deli belongs in Marram Bay,' he tells me. 'I didn't tell you because I didn't want you to worry about it, to have this hanging over your head. If anyone can make this place a success, it's you. You're a hard-working single mum, not some ruthless businesswoman. Let people get to know the real you, tell them about how we operate, change their minds.'

'And if I don't succeed?' I ask.

'Well, at the moment they're trying to prevent us getting our liquor licence,' he tells me. 'But don't worry about it, OK? Just do your best. Amanda and I have faith in you.'

I feel my face crumple with stress.

'OK, sure,' I reply.

'That's our girl,' Eric replies. 'Call me anytime if you need me.'

'OK, I will. Thank you,' I say, hanging up and handing Mike his phone back.

'Not great, right?' Mike says.

'No,' I reply.

'Anyway . . . show you around?'

'Sure,' I reply.

So far my dream life in a new place has turned out to be anything but what I expected. I can't believe the locals don't want us here, YumYum delis are such amazing places, with a great choice of international food – why would they not want us?

What I'm not going to do is panic or, worse, get upset, because Eric is right. I've got this. This is my chance to show the people of Marram Bay exactly what YumYum delis are all about, and to show the world exactly what Lily Holmes can do. I want to prove to my bosses that I can do it and, even more importantly, I want to prove to myself that I can do this. Well, it would have been boring if it were easy, right?

Chapter 6

After a long day of hurdle after hurdle at the deli, I pull up outside the school to find that, yet again, there's no one to be seen. I know there aren't many kids who go here, but shouldn't there be parents around?

I hurry up the steps as carefully as I can in my heels, only to see Frankie standing in the playground on his own.

'Hey, kiddo, where is everyone?'

'They went home at three,' he says, not sounding his usual self.

'Oh shit, I'm so sorry,' I blurt, realising it was his previous school where he finished at 3.20 p.m.

'Swears,' he ticks me off.

'*Sugar*, sorry,' I apologise, forgetting that, in this family, we substitute our swear words with similar sounding, inoffensive words. I'd say it was our compromise, but it's actually just the only realistic way for me not to swear in front of my kid. Frankie is always telling me off for swearing, but it doesn't seem like his heart is in it today.

'You OK? You don't seem yourself.'

'Yeah, I just wanna go home,' he replies.

'OK, sure,' I say, ushering him towards the car. I suppose I've missed my tour slot, being late again.

As we make the short journey home, I look at him the rear-view mirror. He's looking down at his feet with a glum expression on his face.

'How was your first day then?' I ask.

'OK,' Frankie replies, but he doesn't sound all that convincing.

'Are you sure?' I persist.

'Yes.'

I'm not sure I believe him, but I don't want to push him. Maybe once we get home he'll open up a little.

I unlock the door and watch Frankie walk inside, excited for his reaction when he realises he can play video games, but he doesn't seem bothered.

'I set everything up for you,' I point out, not that he couldn't have noticed. 'Do you want to play some games and just let me know when you want dinner?'

'Can we have it now please?' he asks.

'Erm, yeah, sure. You hungry now?'

He nods.

'OK, go play, I'll make us some food. What do you fancy?'

Frankie shrugs.

'Beans on toast?' I suggest, knowing that one of his favourite dishes is bound to put a smile on his face.

He nods.

I pull a face as I head towards the kitchen and, while I prepare dinner, I watch him like a hawk. He's far too young to be starting the moody teenager act. I wonder what's wrong with him.

It's off, for Frankie to be so quiet at home. Sure, he can be shy around new people, but when it's just us, he's usually anything but quiet.

'So there was a bit of a hitch with the deli,' I tell him, not that he's going to be all that interested. I don't have anyone else to tell about my day though. I didn't have any proper friends in London, not really. My uni friends were all out living young people's lives, while I was at home with my baby, and all the people I met through work, well, they already had full lives, with partners and friends. Maybe I isolate myself sometimes – I'm not sure if it's because I always put Frankie first or because of my trust issues. Maybe it's both.

I chat out loud about the deli, unconcerned with whether he is listening – I imagine having a husband is a little bit like this, if what you see on TV is anything to go by. I wouldn't know because I've never really had a man around.

When I found out I was pregnant with Frankie, I knew that I was going to have to raise him alone but I knew that I was up to the job, that if I gave it my everything I could do it alone, just like my mum did. I don't know who had it worse, me or my mum, because I might have done the whole thing without a man while my mum had my dad for the first year of my life, but he died when his bike was hit by a car. My mum had to cope with a baby *and* a bereavement, when she was a little over twenty, so I just knew that if my mum was made of such strong stuff, then I was too.

As I carry two plates of beans on toast over to the table, I notice that my son has his head in his hands.

'Hey, what's wrong?' I ask him.

'It's been a bad day,' he says as he skulks over to the table.

'You're eight,' I remind him. 'You're too young to have bad days.'

Frankie sits at the table and begins wolfing down his food.

'Steady on, kid,' I say, worried he might choke if he doesn't slow down. 'You gonna tell me what's wrong?'

'No one likes me,' he solemnly.

'It's your first day,' I assure him. 'No one knows you yet.'

'They do,' he says. 'They know who you are too. They said you're evil.'

'What?' I squeak, laughing nervously. '*I'm* evil?'

'Because of the shop,' he tells me. 'It's gonna close all the other shops.'

'Sweetheart.' I grab his hand. 'It isn't, I promise you. And their parents will realise that. They're kids, they don't know what they're talking about. They've just heard their mums and dads saying things. Did Mrs Snowball not help you make friends?'

'She doesn't like me either,' he says, eating a quarter slice of toast practically in one bite.

'Of course she does,' I insist. 'She's the headteacher, she likes all the kids.'

'She wouldn't let me eat my lunch,' he tells me.

'She what?' I ask angrily.

'She wouldn't let me eat my lunchbox.'

'Why the *truck* not?' I ask, remembering to edit my outburst this time.

Frankie shrugs.

'Is this why you're so hungry?'

He nods.

Oh, my poor little baby, why on earth wouldn't she let him eat his lunch?

'Everything is going to be better tomorrow,' I promise him.

After we finish up our food Frankie gets back to his game. I retrieve his lunchbox from the floor by the front door, and look inside, just to make sure. Sure enough, there's his lunch, untouched.

I grab the chocolate and toss it to him.

'Here you go, kiddo,' I say.

'Thanks,' he replies, without the usual enthusiasm you expect from kids on the receiving end of chocolate.

I make myself a cup of tea, grab my laptop and take a seat on the sofa. I connect my laptop to my phone, because there's no Wi-Fi here yet, and begin researching the area, trying to work out some kind of plan to get the locals on board. I can't get Mrs Snowball out of my mind. Why did she think it would be OK to tell my son that he couldn't eat his lunch? And the fact that the kids wouldn't talk to him today, because of me . . .

I grab my phone and set an alarm for the morning, to make sure that I arrive at school early enough to have a word with Mrs Snowball. No one messes with my kid.

Chapter 7

Sitting outside the headteacher's office is not something I ever thought I'd be doing again, not with Frankie being such a little angel.

Back in my school days, my mum would often find herself sitting outside the headteacher's office with me, waiting to find out *what I'd done now*. I wasn't a bad kid, I was just a bit of a rebel.

Looking at me today, you wouldn't believe what I used to look like. I'm five foot eight, which I've always known was tall for a woman, but I only recently learned that my height puts me four inches above the national average, and four inches is a lot – in this context at least. I'm a good shape, I think. Things could be smoother or tighter, but I think everyone thinks that and, anyway, I think my curves complement the girly-girl look I have these days. I like to look good, with my highlighted hair, manicured nails and nice outfits.

Back when I was a teenager my natural dirty-blonde locks were dyed a multitude of colours, sometimes all at once, and my face was a mess of too much eyeliner and plum lipstick, finished off with a nose ring – fake, of course, because for some reason my young, hip, liberal mum wouldn't let me make holes in my face, and for that I'm extremely thankful now.

I was a young rebel, an activist, a bit of a hippy . . . I thought I was going to change the world, one small protest at a time. Of course, I was never going to change the world by fighting to make the school kitchen use free-range eggs, or switch the floodlit school sign off at night to save electricity, but it felt important for me to make a difference, so I tried. Anytime I was in trouble and my mum was called in, it wasn't because I was a bad kid, it was usually just because I'd kicked up a fuss about them cutting down a tree in the car park, or because I'd used a black glitter gel pen to draw the anarchy symbol on the back of my hand. Of course, there was that one time 15-year-old me called our geography teacher, Mr Adler, a bastard because he brought a real ivory pen in to show the class – a story which I mistakenly told Frankie, because now he jokes that, so long as he never does anything worse than that, he can never really be in trouble with me.

Sitting here before school starts, waiting for Mrs Snowball to see us, gives me major flashbacks, except this time I'm not in trouble, she is. I still can't believe she didn't let my son eat his lunch and the longer I sit out here waiting to speak to Mrs Snowball, the angrier I get.

'Good morning, Holmes family,' she says brightly as she opens her office door.

'Good morning,' I say politely. 'I was hoping to have a word about yesterday.'

'Not a problem,' Mrs Snowball replies, before turning to her secretary. 'Tilly, why don't you take Frankie and get him some breakfast.'

I bite my tongue. Perhaps it would be better to have this conversation without Frankie around.

'Miss Holmes, step into my office, take a seat,' Mrs Snowball instructs. 'It is Miss, isn't it?'

'Call me Lily,' I insist.

'Lily,' she says softly, taking a seat behind her desk. 'What can I do for you?'

I glance around Mrs Snowball's office as I take a seat opposite her. Her office isn't what I expected, with not a single scrap of paperwork anywhere – everything must be neatly filed. Instead, the desk, cabinets and shelves are all covered with tiny ornamental cottages, each one unique, and with such intricate detail.

Mrs Snowball catches me staring.

'Do you like my Lilliput Lane collection?' she asks. 'Each cottage is a replica of real cottages and scenery in England and Wales. I've been collecting them since the Eighties – they stopped making them in 2016, you know, so they mean even more to me now. They bring me such joy.'

I contemplate for a moment exactly how these tiny cottages bring Mrs Snowball so much joy, and I wonder if maybe sometimes she lays them all out on the floor and walks around, pretending to be a giant. I watch as she lightly brushes with her fingertip the rooftop of the snow-covered cottage that sits on her desk. I'm not sure if she's dusting it or petting it, but it knocks any thoughts of Mrs Snowball playing *Gulliver's Travels* out of my head.

'I wanted to see you, just to see if you could shed any light on what happened yesterday,' I start. 'Frankie was starving when he got home from school and, it turns out he hadn't had any lunch. I asked him why not and, well, he said you wouldn't let him. I figured it must be a misunderstanding but—'

'No, that is correct. I confiscated his lunchbox,' she says firmly.

I can't help but cock my head.

'You—'

'I confiscated his lunch,' she says again, a little slower this time.

'Why?' I ask, absolutely bewildered.

'He had a bagel.'

I snort with laughter, until I realise she's being serious.

'Yeah . . . so . . . sorry, I'm so confused. It's a bagel, not a bomb.'

'A bagel is the equivalent of three slices of bread, Lily,' she replies seriously.

'So is a glass of wine, but he knocks them back, no problem.'

Mrs Snowball scowls at my joke. Jokes are how I deal with confrontation, awkwardness and disagreements, and this situation is all three.

'And there was chocolate, and *crisps*.'

'Oh my gosh, crisps!' I mock. 'Not crisps.'

'Lily, with respect, his lunch was unhealthy and I couldn't sit by and watch him eat it. I have a moral and legal obligation—'

'To stop kids eating bagels?' I interrupt. 'Look, it was his first day, he was nervous, I just wanted to pack him something nice to cheer him up at lunchtime. Something familiar that would make him happy.'

'He's a big boy, Lily. He doesn't need coddling.'

'No, he needs feeding,' I tell her. 'You really thought it would be better for him not to have anything?'

'Of course not,' she replies. 'I got him a bowl of vegetable soup.'

'Eight-year-olds don't eat soup,' I point out.

'No, they eat the equivalent of three slices of bread, a few grams of saturated fats and a bar of chocolate, shaped like a frog.'

'What's wrong with Freddo?' I ask, defensively. Freddo is iconic – he was a part of my childhood too. I won't have a word said against him.

'They give junk food pretty packages and cute characters to appeal to children and it's not right,' she rants. 'Do you really think this chocolate would appeal to him as much, were it not in the shape of a frog?'

I don't point out to her that, last Christmas, someone bought him a poop-emoji-shaped chocolate, which we both gleefully ate as we watched *Home Alone* and *Home Alone 2* back to back in our pyjamas.

'It was his first day,' I point out. 'He also mentioned that none of the other kids would play with him, he said they knew who he was . . .'

'Ah, yes.' Mrs Snowball removes her glasses from her nose,

allowing them to hang on their chain, around her neck. 'It would seem that the locals are familiar with your agenda in our town, and no one is happy. Children's brains are like sponges, if they hear their parents talking about the new family that's moved in to threaten jobs, well, they're going to pick up on that.'

'Mrs Snowball, that is not what is going to happen,' I insist. 'He said the kids are saying I'm evil. Don't you think that's extreme?'

'Simon Dawson's dad is our local butcher,' she points out. 'Ella Carr's dad is the baker.'

'Whose dad makes the candlesticks?' I quip. Gosh, I really need to quit cracking these jokes.

'Bart and Bernadette's parents are responsible for all of our milk, cheese and yogurt.'

Wow, they sound like cool parents. Not.

'I appreciate what you're saying, I really do, but I haven't come here to take over from these people. I run a deli. We don't sell four pints of milk, we sell speciality products, make sandwiches with them . . .'

'There's a lovely old lady called Clara who runs a café – how do you think she'll feel about you selling sandwiches?'

The thought of upsetting Clara, after she was so lovely to me, breaks my heart a little.

'We're living in a tourist town,' I point out. 'There's more than enough room for all of us.'

'Well.' Mrs Snowball claps her hand as she stands up. 'I'm just the messenger. And I'll try to help Frankie to make some friends today.'

'Thank you,' I reply. 'And, if you could let him eat his lunch . . .'

'Is there a bagel in there?'

No, just a couple of lines of coke and a Stanley knife for playtime.

'No bagel today,' I reply. 'Just two slices of bread.'

'Well, OK then. Work today, is it?' she asks, ushering me towards the door.

'Yes,' I reply, glancing at my watch. 'Actually, I'd better get a move on, or I'm going to be late.'

'Oh yes,' she laughs. 'Punctuality doesn't seem to be your strong suit, does it?'

Nope. Making awkward jokes and killing my child with carbs are my thing.

I smile and say goodbye, before I'm tempted to play Godzilla with her little village.

I walk out of the school gates, passing a few mums on my way. I pass a gaggle of four of them, only to feel their eyes burning holes into my back. I turn around and smile, only to see them hurry inside the building. I'm guessing they've heard of me.

Oh, I so hope Frankie makes some friends today. It seems so unfair, that just because of my job, no one is being nice to him.

Life in Marram Bay is proving to be much harder than I thought it would be. Still, we're better off here than we were in London. Safer too, given recent events.

Chapter 8

I pull the sleeve of my cosy black jumper dress down over my hand before placing it over my nose. I've never been great with strong smells, least of all the smell currently coming from the deli bathroom.

'It's the drains,' Mike insists. 'Someone flushed the lav today, not knowing about the drain problems we've been having.'

'So when is it getting fixed?' I ask from behind my hand.

'Well, that's the problem, darling. No one wants to fix it.'

'What do you mean?' I ask.

Mike, clearly unfazed by the smell, grabs a doughnut from a box on the side and chomps down on it as we chat.

Mike, who is in his forties, has got that rough and ready workman look and charm, only made even friendlier by his jolly apples-and-pears accent. His dimples give him this cheeky glimmer that makes you instantly warm to him, even when he's giving you news you don't want to hear.

'We're having a bit of bother with local tradesmen,' he explains. 'None of them want to help us out.'

'I mean . . . they know they'll get paid, right?'

"Course,' Mike replies. 'Even tried offering them extra.'

'So they're turning work down because they protest the deli?'

He nods.

Well, isn't that just a special kind of stupid? These people are so worried that the deli will harm local businesses, they're actively turning down business – which is harming local businesses. Talk about a self-fulfilling prophecy.

'The gaffer thought it might help sweeten up the locals, to hire some of them for work, but they ain't having it,' Mike says, reaching for a second doughnut. I suppose doing a job like his burns a lot of calories – maybe that's where I'm going wrong. Still, I'm not about to go and dabble in the drains.

'OK, well, I guess you'll have to hire the tradesmen you need from outside the town,' I say plainly.

'Do you think they'll like that?' he chuckles.

'Probably not, but we don't have much choice. Perhaps it will show them that we're serious about staying here. And at least it will keep work ticking along until I think of a real way to get everyone on board.'

'You're the boss,' he says with a cheeky smile. 'I'll get on it.'

Left alone at the counter I glance at the plans laid out in front of me. It really is a shame the locals are set against this place, it is going to be so amazing, and I'm not just saying that because I feel like it's my baby.

I can see the doughnuts out of the corner of my eye, but my usual inclination to eat one just isn't there. It's this horrible sewage smell, filling the room, that's proving to be an excellent appetite suppressor. I'm sure we could make a lot of money with it, were this the location of a SkinnyKwick Club meeting, but we're a deli and we want people to buy food.

'Lily,' I hear Mike calling as he heads back in. 'I'm on with a plumber, he says he can do it, but he wants his travel expenses covered. He's coming pretty far.'

'OK, sure,' I say reluctantly. Well, it's not exactly my own money I'm throwing around, is it? My bosses have given me an impossible job to do, and I'm doing the best I can. 'The sooner he can come, the better.'

'He says he'll be right over,' Mike replies.

'Great,' I reply, semi-sarcastically. Well, it's not great that we have to fork out for plumbers from afar, but it will be a lot easier to get some work done here once the smell is gone.

'I'm going to go outside and scope out the area,' I say.

'OK, sure. You get some fresh air,' Mike laughs. I think he's onto me, but I can't think straight around this smell.

I step out of the main door and onto the paved area out front where I finally take in the view for the first time. We might not be on the seafront, but we're right at the top of the main street that leads down to it, which means that, for the customers who sit outside the deli to eat their lunch, they'll be able to see the sea. It's still quite sunny, even if the warm summer weather is nothing but a distant memory now, so I take my oversized sunglasses from my bag and put them on to get a better view.

Before moving here, I knew that there was an island just off the coast but I had no idea just how close it was, or how big. It's a bizarre and beautiful sight that makes the islands we're used to seeing on the Thames pale in comparison. I really should take Frankie sometime, maybe at the weekend to celebrate his first week at school.

I set off down the cobbled main street, extra carefully in my heels. While I may be blonde, I'm not ditzy . . . that said, I'm not sure why it never crossed my mind to swap out my stylish heels for some more sensible ones. I supposed I assumed the north was paved.

The main street is not only cobbled, it's steep too. If I were to fall, which is something I'm prone to doing from time to time, it would not be one of my more graceful tumbles. Not on this hill, in these shoes, wearing this dress that doesn't quite reach my knee.

My most graceful fall to date happened two years ago while Frankie and I were ice-skating at the Natural History Museum outdoor ice rink. Frankie was having a blast, zipping around on the ice whereas I carefully clung to the edge and moved just a few inches at a time.

'Come on, Mum, it's easy,' he assured me. He was only six at the time and I figured, if a six-year-old can do it, then so can I. I was wrong. Holding Frankie's hand, I left the comfort of the outside edge and skated into the middle of the rink, to get a closer look at the big Christmas tree that sits in the centre.

'You did it, you did it,' he chirped, bursting with pride, sort of like I did when he took his first steps.

The only problem was, Frankie figured I'd be fine after that, so he skated off on his own again. That's when the fear kicked in. I think half my problem with ice-skating was a confidence thing, and without Frankie to hold on to, I was too scared to move. Kids and adults were zipping past me with ease so, after psyching myself up for a few minutes, I made my move, skating out, taking it a few inches at a time, and I was doing it, I was really doing it . . . and then I got too confident, I forgot to be careful, and I lost control. It felt like I was flailing around, completely out of control for a long time, but I don't suppose it was more than a few seconds. By some miracle I managed to not only stay upright, but glide into the arms of a tall, blond, handsome man, and for someone who struggled to meet men – let alone introduce herself – this was almost too good to be true.

'Hi,' I blurted.

'Hey,' he replied.

'Do women always fall at your feet or am I the first?' I joked awkwardly, like I do.

'Erm, just my wife,' he replied, nodding to the leggy brunette to his left.

The flirting might not have been great, but the fall and the recovery were excellent.

My least graceful fall to date was six months ago, in Tesco, where I literally slipped on a banana skin and ploughed into a display of toilet rolls. The landing was soft, at least.

The main street has a real mixture of shops, from quirky little gift shops to a shop, hilariously called Fruitopia, that appears to sell nothing but jam.

There's a shop that sells women's clothing, but if the mannequins in the window are anything to go by, it's probably not to my taste. The next shop along, though, is a cool gallery and bookshop that looks like it might have some interesting stuff inside.

I step inside the large white room to the murmur of a classical music tune that I recognise but couldn't name. It feels lovely in here, with the warm air blowing down on me as I browse the photographs and paintings on the walls. It seems like most of them were taken or painted locally, which is cute. The books all seem to be similar in theme too – perhaps I could pick up something to give me an insight into the local area.

'Hello,' I say brightly to the man sitting behind a desk in the centre of the room.

'Hello,' he replies, taking off his glasses. 'Can I help you?'

'I was after a book about the local area.'

'We have lots of them,' he replies straight-faced.

'Yeah.' I laugh awkwardly. 'I was hoping you could maybe recommend a specific one. Whichever is your favourite.'

'Oh, sure,' he replies.

He casts an eye over a table of books before picking one up and handing it to me.

'This one should do it. It's all about the history of the area, places for tourists to visit, local customs, etcetera.'

'Brilliant,' I reply. 'I'll take it.'

The man, an awkward thirty-something, scans the book.

'Can I interest you in some postcards featuring stunning local scenes for the folks back home?' he asks, loosening up a little, as he points to a rack of cards to his left.

I glance at them.

'No thanks,' I reply, my smile dropping.

I can't help but think about the postcard in my bag, the one from someone back home, and if there's one thing I don't wish, it's that *he* were here.

Chapter 9

Standing in the playground, waiting for Frankie to finish school, I fantasise about taking my shoes off, and maybe soaking them in the bath for a couple of hours before dinner. It's been a long day at the deli, making sure that everything is going to be ready in time, but at least the plumber turned up and fixed whatever problem was causing the smell. I damn near gave him one of my kidneys and he left, pound signs rolling in his eyes as he counted his money (which included his travel bonus). This only reminds me that I would never, ever, in a million years be able to afford to open my own deli, because even if I could gather some money together, you never know when you're going to have to pay a big plumbing bill – if this really were my place, I probably would have had to give him a kidney. It's all good though, because tomorrow when I turn up for work, it's going to smell glorious, like fresh wooden counters, and it's going to remind me that, even though we're running into problems, I'm solving them.

I notice the gaggle of women from this morning, staring at me once again. They're probably just curious, wondering who I am. If it were up to me I'd stay here, at the opposite side of the playground, hiding behind my sunglasses, but I know that I have a lot of work to do here, and it would probably be good for the business if I go over and introduce myself, show them that I'm a normal mum, just like them, and not at all 'evil'.

By the time I walk over, there are just three women left, all standing in a line, facing me, anticipating my introduction.

'Hello, ladies,' I say, wearing the biggest smile my face can accommodate. 'My name is Lily Holmes, I'm Frankie's mum. We've just moved into Apple Blossom Cottage and, erm, I'll be running the new deli on Main Street.'

I continue to smile as I wait for their reply.

'We know who you are,' the woman in the middle says. It's funny she should say that, she looks familiar to me too. 'We knew you were coming, we just didn't know who you were. Now we can put a face to the person who is trying to ruin this town.'

And, here we go. It's so funny, the way she describes my arrival, like it's some prophecy you hear at the start of a horror film before the monster turns up.

'Listen, I know there's a lot of animosity towards the deli—' and me, apparently '—but I'm not here to make trouble. There's nothing even close to a YumYum deli in town, and there are lots of hungry tourists. There's room for all of us. I promise, I am no threat to your or your families' livelihoods.'

I feel my face fall into a more relaxed smile, happy with my response.

'Do you know who I am?' the woman in the middle asks.

If she's asking, I must know her from somewhere.

To her left is a short woman with a mess of black curls on her head. She's wearing a beautiful pair of tortoiseshell Gregory Peck–style glasses that I would love if I didn't wear contact lenses most of the time. I'd ask her where she got them from, although I suspect a compliment right now would seem insincere.

The mum to the other side is tall and slim, with her mousey brown hair in two plaits that go down almost all the way to her waist. With her make-up-free face and her plaid shirt and jeans combo, she looks fresh off the farm.

And then, in the middle, there's the ringleader of the three angry stooges. I stare at her for a moment when it hits me – I *have* seen her before. She looks a little different, without her Forties dress and her victory rolls, but it's her all right. The woman from the seafront, who was staring at us the day we arrived. Oh, and these two must have been the women standing either side of her that day. Wow, I wonder if they always have to stand in the right order, like Ant and Dec do.

I'm just about to tell her where I recognise her from when she speaks again.

'This is Jessica,' she says, nodding to her short friend. 'Jessica Dawson, as in Dawson's Butchers, that she and her husband own.'

'Oh, "burger me",' I blurt giddily. 'I found one of your husband's signs outside the deli. He's a very pun-ny man.'

'This is Mary-Ann,' she continues, unamused, nodding towards her tall friend. 'She and her husband run the dairy farm.'

I nod in acknowledgement. She looks like the kind of woman who would name her kids Bernadette and Bart.

'Is your husband the baker by any chance?' I ask. What is it with the women in this town? Other than the women working in the school, it's like they're all defined by their husbands' jobs.

'No, I'm Avril Newman, wife of Bradley Newman – the local plumber.'

Oh *carp*.

'I passed the deli today,' she tells me, as though I don't know how this one is going to end. 'There was a plumber's van parked outside. A plumber from a town *thirty* miles away.'

'We did call your husband,' I tell her. 'He didn't want the job.'

'Well, of course he didn't,' she replies. 'We don't want to be seen supporting a business that the locals don't want here. But you giving the work to another plumber, from out of town, well, that's taking food off our table, out of our little Jacques's mouth.'

I laugh inside my head at her paradoxical argument. She's upset at me for giving a job to someone other than her husband after her husband said no. So, I should be giving them my business, but they don't want it, so . . . I'm not really sure what she wants from me.

'Avril, I wanted to give your husband the job. I don't want to take food from Jack's mouth – in fact, it would be so nice if Frankie and Jack could be friends. I think he's having a bit of trouble settling in,' I confess.

'*Jacques*,' she corrects me.

'Sorry, what did I say?'

'Jack.'

'Right.'

'It's *Jacques*,' she says again.

Of course it is.

'Maybe your family just isn't supposed to be here, Lily. We're a tight-knit community and you only need to look over the Marram Bay Facebook group page to see that you're just not wanted.'

'Can I join this group?' I ask, undefeated.

'Well, it's for locals only,' she says quickly.

'I'm local now,' I point out with a smile.

Avril thinks for a moment.

'I'll have to ask the group. Apple Blossom Cottage sits just outside the main town, and the group is for the main town only. I'm sure you understand.'

'Oh, I understand,' I reply.

'Perhaps it's best to bow out now, before more upset is caused. You said it yourself, your son isn't fitting in. And, well, our children are smart. They can tell we're upset and if they know you're to blame, your poor son is going to be collateral damage. Perhaps you need to put your son first – we always put our children first, it's so important.'

I purse my lips, lest a 'go *duck* yourself' escapes from between them.

Right on cue, the school bell goes and all the Little Acorns come charging out of the door.

'See you around, ladies,' I say, before walking off to meet Frankie.

After the horde of kids, my own finally appears, all alone, without the gleeful smile or the urgency the others showed. Oh no, it must have been a bad day again.

'Hey, kiddo,' I say brightly. 'She try to starve you to death today or did my threats work?'

Frankie laughs, just a little.

'Good day?'

He shrugs.

I usher him towards the car and strap him in.

'I know we're off to a bit of a rocky start, and that it feels like we're not fitting in, but we've only been here two days,' I assure him. 'Things will get better.'

'No one likes us,' he says, sounding dejected.

'No one knows us,' I remind him. 'Let's just give it a bit longer, OK? I will if you will.'

Frankie nods. He really is an amazing little man, which is probably why this is making me so mad. He should be so happy here and it's not fair that the Mumsnet brigade are making him 'collateral damage' – well, I won't have it. We will be happy here, and they will accept us. I'll make sure of it.

Out of nowhere a quad bike flies past us at a junction. I stop my car and breathe for a second. First the locals ask us to leave, now it's like they're literally trying to drive us out of town. Well, they're going to have to try harder than that.

Chapter 10

I'm the first person to hold my hands up and say that I'm clumsy. I make awkward jokes at inappropriate times. I know some words that sailors don't, but I'm working on all of the above. I can identify my shortcomings, and I think that's something we all should be able to do.

Similarly, I know my strengths, and one of those strengths is coming up with plans to try and achieve the things I need to do. So last night I sat down – I was going to write in my as yet untouched diary, but I'd rather wait and start it when I have much nicer things to say – grabbed my laptop and figured out a plan of attack, to get the locals on board with the deli. I made a list of ideas, all of which I think could make a real difference, and then went to bed happy, ready to start the following day with a plan of action that would bring me results.

Yep, today was going to be a great day, until thirty seconds ago when I pulled up outside the deli to meet Mike.

'Oh sh—'

'Exactly,' he laughs. 'Cow, I'd guess.'

'But . . . how?'

We stand together at the front of the deli, staring at what used to be a beautifully clean stone wall. Today, however, it's covered in cow dung.

'And you thought the drains smelled bad,' Mike laughs.

'Mike, it isn't funny,' I insist. 'You know someone has done this on purpose, right?'

'No?' he replies. 'Surely not . . .'

'Well, unless a herd of cows just happened to pass by last night – cows who have perfected their aim, and the art of synchronised sh . . . *sitting*.'

I'm quick to correct myself. Just because Frankie isn't here, doesn't mean I shouldn't try.

'I was thinking maybe it was just because of a malfunctioned tractor or something – that's pretty effed up,' Mike replies, rubbing his stubbly chin. I can't help but notice he edited himself there, which means he's obviously picking up on my efforts. 'The locals really don't want this deli to open, do they?'

'They don't. You know they've got some little town Facebook group where they talk about us, right?'

'Is that so?' he asks. 'I'll have to tell the lads they're famous. Might make them slow down though, if it goes to their heads.'

I like having Mike around, with his positive attitude and his cheeky chappy cockney accent. I don't know what I'll do when the fitting is finished and the lads pack up and go home.

'You come up with a name for it yet?' he asks.

'Not yet,' I reply. 'I was thinking Main Street Deli, but I don't think that's going to cut it now. They'll probably begrudge us using their street name.'

'What about Cow Crap Deli?' Mike suggests. 'Given the latest addition to the walls.'

'Or No-One-Is-Going-To-Come-Here-So-We-Might-As-Well-Give-Up Deli,' I suggest.

Mike thinks for a moment.

'Nah, that's a bit long,' he says with a laugh.

I can't even think about giving the place a name right now, not when it seems so pointless.

I hear the hum of an engine coming from behind us. Curious, I turn around and see a man sitting on a quad bike. He's wearing a helmet, so I can't see his face, but I recognise his bike as the one that sped past me yesterday. It's bright red, with a 'Westwood Farm' logo on the front.

'You,' I yell. 'You did this.'

As fast as he appeared, the man on the bike speeds off.

'How do you know he's our man?' Mike asks.

'I saw him yesterday. I was driving along and he drove past me, kind of dangerously. Also, he's a farmer. Who else do you know with an unlimited supply of crap?'

'Good point,' he replies. 'So, what are you going to do?'

I exhale deeply.

'I suppose I'll give Eric a call, fill him in on everything that's going on. Then, I don't know, I'll see what he says and try to figure it out from there.'

'Sure thing, boss,' Mike says as he heads back inside. He hovers in the doorway for a second. 'I suppose you want me to get rid of the mess . . .'

'Please. If you don't mind,' I reply. 'I don't know where to begin.'

Chapter 11

I have never, in my entire adult working life, been so delighted and relieved to make it to Saturday before. Sure, I've had long weeks, difficult weeks, tiring weeks – but nothing like this week.

Hurdle after hurdle have popped up at the deli and I don't even feel like I'm clearing them, I'm just carelessly running through them and hoping I don't get disqualified. And then there's the situation at school. Poor Frankie still doesn't have any friends, and after playgroup bully mum Avril let me have it, she and her little clique have left me alone, other than the occasional dirty look. I actually believe Avril thought if she laid it all out on the line for me, that I would just bow out. Like I could, even if I wanted to because, as they keep pointing out, we're a chain. Even if they do drive me out of town, my bosses will just replace me. For a group so intent on sabotage, I don't feel like they've really thought it through. I'm not sure how much they've thought *any* of it through, to be honest. I really can't wrap my head around their outrage. Sure, if we were opening a competing business, or a supermarket that was going to put all the little guys out of business, but we're a deli, and Marram Bay doesn't have a deli. A café, a local shop, things like butchers, bakers and greengrocers – the only things they have in multiple is restaurants (and even they all seem to be vastly different to one another) and bed and breakfasts.

I understand that it is a small town with very few businesses, and that the locals want to keep it unique and beautiful, but I really don't feel like a little deli will threaten that. In fact, I'd go as far as to say that a place as fantastic as a YumYum deli will only add to the appeal of the place.

I had a glorious lie-in this morning. Then I got up and had breakfast with Frankie before he went to play in the garden and I made myself comfortable on the sofa. I have my notebook, ready to try and get some of my thoughts down, a large pot of tea and a box of something special my bosses sent me from one of their delis. If they think a box of treats will go even a little bit of the way to making me feel better, well, they would be right. The bright green box (that arrived all beautifully tied up with straw) is full of cannoli – a Sicilian dessert that is basically deep-fried pastry tubes filled with sweet ricotta and chocolate chips. Each end of the tube overflows with the filling, just a little, and is garnished with a piece of candied orange peel. They are absolutely delicious, and something that we frequently sell out of in all branches of the delis – so popular, in fact, that we had signs made apologising for being sold out.

I lift the lid, practically drooling with excitement as I reach to lift one out, only to be disturbed by a knock on the door. How typical that the second I relax, someone interrupts me.

I close the lid and head over to the door, adjusting the pink tracksuit I wear for lounging about the house just before I open it, because the trackies always seem to ride up a little too high when I sit around in them. I'm also wearing my glasses – something I don't like to do outside the house because I feel like they make me look dorky. I'm aware that sometimes my eyes need a break from the contact lenses, so I do that when I know I'm not going anywhere or expecting company.

'Hello,' I say to the stranger.

'Hi,' the man replies.

He's tall – well over six feet. In fact when I opened the door, I tried to make eye contact with his chest. I'd guess he's in his mid- to late thirties because he's got that kind of 'young but starting to look a little older' look that looks oh-so sexy on men. When we women notice it on ourselves, we start googling 'botox', but on men, we think it's amazing, which is a bizarre double standard – what a time to be alive, eh? Our predecessors fought for our right to vote, and we can't even make a case for growing old gracefully. His dark brown hair is long on top and, as he lowers his gaze to look down at me, it falls forward a little – something he quickly fixes by running a hand through his hair. Backlit by the sun, I can't help but notice the curve of his bicep, something that reminds me how long it's been since I had a man. I mentally tick myself off for checking out the random man at my door, even if he does look like Josh Hartnett, with his smouldering brown eyes and his thick eyebrows. I remember watching *Pearl Harbor* when it came out and being obsessed with Josh Hartnett for a while – I even had posters of him on my bedroom walls. I might not have had Daniel Craig trimming my bushes, but a dead ringer for my teenage crush knocking on my door is a great consolation prize.

'I think I have something of yours,' he says, his North Yorkshire accent much weaker than anyone else's that I've encountered here so far.

'Of mine?' I ask, my mind racing. What on earth could he have of mine?!

The giant man steps to one side, to reveal my tiny son hiding behind him.

'Frankie!' I squeak, grabbing him and hugging him. I feel the backpack on his back and go cold.

'I found him on my farm, up the road,' the man explains. 'Told me he was running away from home. I reckon he would've got further if he'd ever seen an alpaca before, lad was mesmerised.'

The farmer laughs, and I'm sure it was a funny sight, but my child tried to run away from home and I was too busy stuffing my face on the sofa to notice.

'Thank you so much,' I tell him, until I notice something behind him that changes my tone immediately. 'Frankie, I'm so sorry you felt like you had to do this. Go wait in your room, I'll just thank the nice man and I'll come see you and we'll figure this out, OK?'

'OK, Mum,' he says with a sigh so deep it breaks my heart. He looks like he feels awful and I'm not sure if he's embarrassed about trying to run away, or disappointed that someone stopped him.

'He's a good lad,' the man says as Frankie shuffles off.

'And you're an idiot,' I reply.

The man looks immediately taken aback.

'Erm . . .' he starts, before laughing awkwardly.

'I know who you are,' I inform him, pointing at his Range Rover, parked outside the cottage. On the door there's a Westwood Farm logo, just like the one I saw on the quad bike of my stalker. 'You're the man who drives a quad bike.'

'And you're the woman who drives around in a Brussels sprout – what's the problem?' he laughs.

'You tried to run me off the road a couple of days ago, and yesterday, you were outside the deli, admiring your handiwork,' I say accusingly. 'The cow dung . . .'

'I was in a hurry, so I might have sped past you a little fast – I apologise, but I wasn't trying to run you off the road,' he explains. 'And I'm not your manure guy.'

'You're a farmer, aren't you?'

'Not really,' he replies with a laugh.

'So why were you there yesterday?'

'Well, officer,' he mocks, 'I was on my way home from Fruitopia, if you must know.'

'You just desperately needed some jam?' I ask, not buying his story.

'No,' he replies. 'I make it. I make it and Fruitopia sells it.'

'Oh,' I blurt.

The man brushes his hair from his face again.

'Can I come in?' he asks. 'I want to talk about your kid, I'm not going to burn your house down.'

I think for a moment.

'OK, yeah,' I reply, not sounding like I mean it. 'I'm Lily, by the way. I just made some tea, would you like a cup?'

'Oh, I've never said no to a brew,' he replies, rubbing his hands together. 'I'm Alfie. Alfie Barton, from the farm up the road. I suppose we're next-door neighbours.'

'I suppose we are,' I reply.

'I found Frankie in one of my fields, having a staring competition with an alpaca. Soon as I heard his accent I figured he'd never seen one before.'

'And if he hadn't got distracted, God knows where he would've ended up,' I say quietly.

'London was his goal,' he tells me. 'We had a quick chat on the way back here, he said he was going to stay with someone called Viv?'

'My mum,' I reply. 'His gran – long story.'

I feel the need to clarify their relationship, given that he calls his grandma by her first name.

'I know who you are,' Alfie confesses, not that it comes as a surprise. 'I'd meant to come round sooner, actually.'

'Wonderful,' I reply sarcastically. 'To threaten me? Kill me? Put an alpaca's head in my bed? Would you like a cannoli?'

Alfie is taken aback by my shift in tone once again. He laughs, confused.

I open the box and offer the contents to Alfie.

'They look nice,' he says, taking one. 'Thank you.'

'They're from the evil deli, just to warn you. I don't know if that's going to stop you eating it. Oh, so are the Assam teabags.'

Alfie raises his eyebrows and I realise I'm ranting.

'Sorry,' I say softly, taking a cannoli from the box and putting it in my mouth before I can say anything else.

Alfie finishes his in seconds, washing it down with his tea.

'I'm not sure what I'm eating or drinking, but I'm really enjoying it.'

'Tell your friends,' I joke.

Alfie sits back on the sofa, making himself more comfortable.

'I've been meaning to come and see you, because I've been you,' he explains. 'I grew up here, on Westwood Farm, with my dad. He was a dairy farmer, and he made it pretty clear he wanted me to follow in his footsteps, even though I made it just as clear that I didn't want to. I left home when I went to uni and I'd been living in Manchester until five years ago, when my dad died and left me the farm.'

'So you came back?' I ask curiously, pulling my legs up on to the sofa.

'I'm not saying that all dairy farms are cruel places – in fact, I'd say my dad cared more about his cows than he did me. His ladies, that's what he used to call them. When I was a kid, I was a bit like your son, just in awe of the animals, thinking they were all my pets. So when my dad died, and I inherited the farm I decided to move back, but to change the way we did business. I sold off all the dairy equipment and decided I'd make a living off our apple trees instead.'

'That sounds like a lovely thing to do,' I reply.

'Ah, well, what I actually started doing was making and selling fruit-infused alcohol, which the locals were *not* happy about at all. Sure, some of them remembered me from when I was a kid, but I hadn't lived here for ten years and then I just came back and closed down the local dairy farm. To sell alcohol,' he points out again.

'Ah,' I reply. I can see why they'd have a problem with that. 'So, how did you change their minds? Get them all drunk on cider?'

He laughs.

'A bit of time and a lot of hard work,' he replies. 'I showed them that my big idea would pay off and eventually they embraced it. These are old-fashioned folk – even the younger ones. They're creatures of habit and they don't just dislike change, they actively protest it.'

'I realised this when I learned they had a literal protest outside the deli.' I laugh. 'So why do you have alpacas?'

'Have you ever seen one? They're cute,' he says with a big smile. 'I have alpacas, loads of ducks – I have a pygmy goat called Phillip, who is just this little angry-looking ball of fluff.'

I smile. There's something so attractive about a man who loves animals. Just listening to him talk about them with such passion and love, with a big, dumb grin on his face, is melting my heart.

'The point is that no one wanted me here either, or my business, and now you can buy my booze all over town. I've even recently started making alcoholic jams, which you'll be able to buy in Fruitopia,' he says with a wink.

I think about his words for a moment. If they didn't want him here and he managed to turn things around then maybe I can too. Perhaps the locals are just stubbornly set in their ways and reluctant to change. The locals are a force I just don't understand. Even after I learned they were against the deli, I didn't expect them to be so open about it, and right to my face. They must care a lot about their town and, if Alfie could make them come around to him then I'll do the same. 'Thanks for this,' I tell him sincerely. 'For bringing Frankie back, for the pep talk . . . and for being nice to me.'

'Thanks for the food,' he replies. 'You'll bring people around to your way of thinking a lot quicker if they taste these.'

'We'll see,' I laugh.

'We will. Well, I should get back to work,' Alfie says, pulling himself to his feet. 'I do know what you're going through, and I know that it's crap, so if you need an ally, you know where I am, OK?'

'OK,' I say, all smiles. He might know what I'm going through, but he has no idea what his kind words mean to me.

'You don't seem convinced . . .'

'You underestimate how horrible people are being to us,' I tell him.

'Why don't you and Frankie come over tomorrow? I'll show you around the farm, he can meet all the animals properly.'

'That . . . that would be amazing, thank you.'

'What are neighbours for,' he says with a smile. 'Plus, it might distract him from running away for another twenty-four hours.'

As soon as Alfie has gone I go to speak to Frankie, after a quick detour to my bedroom to grab something.

'Hey, Dick Whittington,' I tease as I walk into his room. Frankie is sitting on his bed, doodling in his sketchbook. For as long as I can remember, Frankie has loved doodling, and he's pretty good now – and, no, I'm not just saying that because I'm his mum. I had plenty of rubbish, shall we say abstract, pieces of art on my fridge before we got to the ones that were objectively impressive for an 8-year-old.

'I'm so sorry you felt like you had to run away,' I tell him. 'Alfie said you were heading back to Viv's?'

'I hate it here,' he tells me quietly. 'I just want to go home.'

'I know that things kind of suck here at the minute . . . but you know that running away was the wrong thing to do, don't you?'

Frankie nods.

'I am working on trying to make things better. I know things have been difficult and a bit boring . . . I have a few things that might cheer you up, though. First of all, I want you to have my old iPhone.'

Frankie's eyes widen with surprise and delight.

'Don't get too excited,' I tell him. I'm not crazy, I'm not about to give an 8-year-old an expensive phone to keep in his pocket. 'It will only work on Wi-Fi, so it lives at home, OK? But you can use it whenever you want to FaceTime your friends. I'll have a word with their mums, I have their numbers, so you can talk to your friends and you can see them when you're feeling lonely. How does that sound?'

'Awesome.' Frankie beams.

It's just a gesture really, and a way for him to see his friends. Plus, if he feels like he has a phone, even if it doesn't really have a connection unless I connect it, he might feel less isolated here.

'And, Alfie, the nice farmer who just brought you home, says we can go over tomorrow and meet all of his animals. How do you feel about that?'

'Yes!' he replies, finally excited about something for the first time since we arrived. 'I think I like him.'

'Yeah,' I agree. 'I think I might too.'

Chapter 12

'I can be there by tonight,' my mum insists.

'Viv, really, it's fine.'

My mum, finally back from her cruise, has just called to check in on me, and I've made the mistake of telling her everything.

'It's not fine,' she replies. 'You're struggling and you need your mum.'

I laugh to myself because I'm 31 years old, with a child of my own. Still, I suppose you're never too old to need your mum, are you?

'Things just came to a head yesterday, that's all,' I insist. 'But I've made a friend and we're going to see him today. He has a farm with cute animals, Frankie is so excited.'

'He doesn't sound like the only one,' she replies, with an unmistakable tone.

'He just a friend, Viv,' I insist, licking my fingertip before removing a smudge of mascara from under my eye in the bedroom mirror.

'Frankie needs a man in his life,' she tells me – she's always telling me.

'Hey, I never had a man in my life, and I turned out just fine,' I remind her.

'No, you turned out thinking you're just fine, but you need a man too.'

I laugh.

'Honestly, we're fine. I've given Frankie my old phone to use – it doesn't really work but I can connect it to Wi-Fi so he can video-call you, if that's OK? Maybe after we visit the farm?'

'Of course, baby,' she replies. 'I have yoga for an hour at seven, but no plans otherwise. Unless the new male instructor, Fabian, takes me home and ravishes me.'

'Oh, God, Mum, please,' I babble, careful to call her Mum instead of Viv, to remind her that I'm her daughter and that, no matter how young and vibrant she may be, I don't want to think about her having sex with her yoga teacher – or anyone, for that matter.

'Promise me you'll call me if you need me,' she says seriously. 'You know I've got nothing going on, other than my hectic social life. I can be there.'

'Thank you,' I tell her sincerely.

'So, are you dressed up to meet this new friend?'

'No,' I lie.

Maybe I am, just a little. I figured after yesterday, when Alfie caught me in my tracksuit and glasses, with my hair piled on top of my head, it might be nice for him to see me looking smart and clean. I washed and straightened my hair, layered on the make-up and slipped into a black-and-white dress and my trusty leather jacket. Hopefully, despite having tried really hard, I don't look like I've tried too hard.

'Have fun, baby,' she says. 'Call me tonight.'

I hang up, feeling a little brighter for speaking to my mum, and excited to be going over to Alfie's. Frankie is even more excited than I am, to be going to the big house we drive past on the way to school every day.

'You ready, kiddo?' I shout.

'Yep,' Frankie replies, appearing almost out of nowhere. Wow, he really must be excited to go.

With Alfie's farm not being too far up the hill, we decide to walk up there, to properly take in the scenery around us.

Apple Blossom Cottage is protected by walls of trees, encasing it in leaves, hiding it from the outside world. But as you walk up the road towards Westwood Farm, no matter whether you look to the left or the right, all you can see is fields. At first, I thought this was beautiful, so much untouched green earth, free from big, ugly fossil-fuel-consuming buildings full of stressed out, vaping corporate sheep. Now that we've been here a week, I feel differently. I feel claustrophobic, which I realise makes little sense given that I'm looking at such wide, open spaces, but I feel so isolated out here – yet another reason I'm so pleased that we've made friends with Alfie. I might not have enjoyed having four neighbours in the London flat (one either side, one above and one below) but there's something unnerving about the nearest house being so far away.

Once we're outside Alfie's gate, I press the buzzer and, after a few seconds, the gates open and we begin walking up the driveway.

From the outside, Alfie's spectacular, contemporary house is all white walls and glass. If the back has as many floor-to-ceiling windows as the front, he'll have a panoramic view of the countryside that would make anyone jealous. It's such a new, modern-looking house that he must've had it built since his dad died. It certainly isn't an old-fashioned dairy farm. When he said he'd sold the dairy part of the business to another farm, I imagine that's when – oh, what were they called, the ones who gave their kids weird names? Anyway, I imagine that's when they took over selling dairy to the town. Well, God forbid Marram Bay would have two sources of one thing.

'It's like something from a movie,' Frankie marvels as we approach the front door.

'It is,' I reply. Like something a Hollywood hunk or an evil supervillain would live in.

Never, ever, ever, in my wildest dreams would I be able to afford to live in a place like this – to be honest, I never even thought I'd get invited in to one. I guess dairy farms sell for a lot of money, or he makes a lot selling fancy alcohol to the locals – maybe it's both. Although, you'd think if they were all hitting the bottle, they'd be a lot happier.

'Hello,' Alfie says warmly as he opens the door, but his welcome pales in comparison to the one we get from the chubby little pug who charges past him and jumps up at us, begging for attention. Frankie instinctively drops to his knees, offering his face to the pug who kisses him excitedly.

'This is Pugsley,' Alfie laughs. 'And this is how we greet people in this house.'

'Has he learned that from you?' I joke, instantly regretting it.

'I'm a little fussier,' he laughs. 'Come in, please. Pugsley, down boy.'

Pugsley dutifully obeys his owner, but he can't take his cute little bug eyes off Frankie as his tail wags wildly. Well, I say that, but in true pug style Pugsley's tail is curled up at the bottom of his back, so when he does try and wag it, it looks more like he's twerking – oh God, my heart!

The only thing more captivating than the adorable dog is Alfie's enormous, open-plan living space, so incredible I am suddenly very self-conscious of my own.

'Your house is bigger than my school,' Frankie blurts.

Alfie laughs.

'Yeah, it's all right. Just me and Pugsley living indoors though.'

Hmm, so there's no Mrs Barton, then. Interesting.

'Take a seat on the sofa,' Alfie instructs. 'I'll bring some drinks over.'

We sit down on the sofa, both on our very best behaviour, keeping our limbs glued to our bodies just in case we knock anything over.

'Relax,' Alfie insists as he carries a tray of drinks over, placing it down on the glass coffee table in front of us.

If he hadn't made it obvious that he lived alone, I probably could've worked out as much from his decor. This place is the very definition of a bachelor pad, with its clean white walls, black leather furniture and hi-tech gadgets everywhere you look – some of which I can't identify. The only thing he doesn't seem to have is a television, bizarrely.

Right on cue, Alfie's robot vacuum cleaner whizzes past us, closely followed by Pugsley.

'I know, it's a bit of a madhouse,' he laughs. 'Here, have a drink. One of Westwood Farm's finest blackberry ciders for you to try, and a teetotal version for Frankie.'

I take the glass and examine the contents.

'Sorry, I should've asked if you liked cider, I just thought you might like to try what we make,' he quickly adds.

'I love cider,' I assure him. 'It was all I drank when I was young – when I was old enough to drink, of course.'

'Oh, of course,' he laughs.

I take a sip, expecting a fruity cider, but this is so much more than that.

'Wow, this is gorgeous,' I admit. 'It's so fresh and fruity.'

'Thank you,' he says, smiling humbly. 'How's yours, Frankie?'

I watch as my son carefully places his empty glass back down on the table with both hands.

'I think that answers that question,' I laugh.

'That's all the review I need,' he replies. 'So, I thought we could take Pugsley for a walk, and I can show you around the farm – you can meet all the animals.'

'Now?' Frankie replies.

Perhaps he didn't really enjoy his drink as much as we thought – maybe he's just so looking forward to meeting the animals.

'Do you want some different boots to wear? What size are you?' Alfie asks me.

I look down at my own boots with their impractical wedge

heel. That might be a good idea.

'What is this, a bowling alley?' I laugh.

'No,' Alfie chuckles. 'But the vet left hers here, I'm sure she wouldn't mind you borrowing them.'

'I'm a seven,' I say, after a moment of hesitation. He might as well learn about my giantess feet now, just in case it's a deal breaker. I told you, I'm five foot eight, I'm not going to have cute little girly feet, am I?

Alfie thinks for a moment – probably about my flippers.

'Hmm,' he replies. 'Wait right there.'

Alfie dashes off, closely followed by Pugsley, but only until he reaches the stairs. Once he has safely escorted his master, Pugsley bounds back over to us, jumping up on the sofa and wedging himself between us.

While we wait for Alfie, I give Pugsley's ears a quick scratch, but whenever I stop, he places a paw on my leg, to remind me that he's still there, still wanting attention.

'Well, aren't you just a typical man,' I say to him, in that voice adult humans reserve for animals and babies.

When Alfie finally appears with a pair of wellies and some balled-up socks, Pugsley takes this as a sure-fire sign that he's going for a walk, transforming him from a chilled-out pup who just wants his ears scratched to a little furry Catherine wheel, going crazy on the floor.

'I figured you'd be more comfortable in a pair of mine,' he says. 'We just need to pad them out with a few pairs of thick socks.'

I'm not sure if he's not mentioning sizes because my feet are almost man-sized, or because his are on the small side. Either way, it doesn't really matter.

I layer up on socks, slip my feet into the wellies and we're ready to go for our tour of the farm.

First Alfie shows us the apple trees, which put our few to shame, then he briefly shows us the facilities where the drinks and jams are made, although we don't go inside. Alfie says it's no place for kids – mostly because it's boring, apparently.

Alfie has so much wide, open space here, all his own, except, of course, for where his animals live.

Pugsley charges off ahead of us, like he knows where he's going.

'So, down here we have Leonardo, Donatello, Michelangelo and Raphael,' Alfie says. 'Pugsley loves them, as you can see. Leonardo has a bad leg at the moment and Pugsley is really upset he can't play with him.'

As we approach the gate, four alpacas come hurrying over to greet us. They're such bizarre animals, with their curly fur and their long necks. If you crossed a giraffe with a sheep – with a little bit of poodle thrown in for good measure – you'd get an alpaca.

'Hi,' Frankie says, cautiously approaching his new friends.

The alpacas line up at the gate, ready to get some attention.

'Is that the noise they make?' I ask Alfie, referring to the weird gentle humming noise coming from them.

'Yeah, that's the sound. But it's the same sound they use to show a whole bunch of emotions, so you have to learn to read them. They can make a piercing yelp if they want to, but it's rare that they do. Male alpacas actually have a song that they sing, for impressing the ladies. They're such intelligent animals. They have great memories too.'

'Wow,' I reply sincerely. 'You really know your stuff.'

'Thanks,' he replies. 'And if you'll follow me this way, you can meet Phillip.'

'Who is Phillip?' Frankie asks as he follows. As we walk across the muddy field, I feel my feet sinking into the ground and I realise why Alfie suggested I change my shoes.

'This is Phillip,' he says, leading us into another field. 'He's a pygmy goat, they're much smaller than your average goat.'

'Hello, Phillip,' Frankie greets him.

'I adopted him from France,' Alfie explains. 'So he only knows French commands.'

Phillip is very small indeed, with long fluffy hair that's grey and white, with occasional flecks of black. He is tiny but chunky and impossibly cute.

'Pygmy goats are generally quite friendly animals but, er, Phillip has some issues,' he tells us.

'Oh?'

Information from the back of my mind suddenly comes to the forefront: that goats are closely associated with the devil, but why is that? Of the very few dates I've been on since Frankie was born, I remember one far more vividly than the rest. The guy invited me to the cinema, which even I know is a terrible idea for a first date, and I made the mistake of letting him choose the movie. I've never really been a big fan of horror movies – too much of a big baby – but I've always been a fan of love, so if he wanted to see a horror movie, I was willing to take one for the team, because who knew if this was the man I was going to spend the rest of my life with? We went to see this movie called *The Witch*, about a Puritan family who come up against evil forces in the woods where they live. There was a goat in that, and it is truly one of the most terrifying things I have ever experienced in my life – and I gave birth to my son on the tube. Seriously, credit to the filmmakers, because that film left me unable to sleep for days after, and it was all thanks to the goat, which, now that I think about it, was called Phillip too.

He seems harmless enough but he's staring right at me so I take a step away from him, only for my oversized boot to get stuck in the mud and pull straight off my foot. The boot stays upright in the ground but I fall backwards, and not even putting my bootless foot down on the ground can save me. Next thing I know I'm flat on my back in the mud, with Pugsley licking my face. Usually, when I take a tumble, I jump straight back up and pretend that I'm fine, hoping no one noticed, but today I'm just so mortified that I lie still for a moment, because in this gloopy mud I feel like there's a genuine chance the ground could swallow me up.

'Phillip, *viens ici*.'

Why won't the mud just take me away?!

'Lily.' I hear Alfie's voice before I feel him yank me to my feet with an ease that could convince me that I didn't eat two cannoli yesterday. 'Are you hurt?'

'Just my ego,' I reply.

'She does this *all* the time,' I hear my embarrassed son explain.

Finally on my feet, I examine the damage. My bootless foot is covered in mud, as is the entire back of my body, and the boot that came off has fallen on to its side, sinking deeper into the mud. We're far enough from the house that I'm not sure how I'm going to get back – with only one boot on, I suppose.

'OK, hop on,' Alfie insists.

'What?' I laugh awkwardly.

'On my back,' he insists, turning around.

I cackle.

'Don't be crazy, I'll break your back,' I insist.

'I work on a farm, I'm used to carrying heavy things,' he reasons, before quickly adding: 'I didn't mean it like that.'

Without a real excuse, I do as he suggests and hop onto his back.

'Let's go back to the house and get your mum cleaned up,' Alfie says to Frankie, who charges back towards the house with Pugsley.

With my arms locked tightly around Alfie's neck, and my head resting on his shoulder, I speak softly into his ear. 'Thanks for this.'

'It's nothing,' he replies. 'Stay for dinner?'

'Are you sure?' I ask, blown away by his kindness and his hospitality.

'I'm sure,' he replies. 'It's nice having some company.'

I couldn't agree more.

Chapter 13

The good news is that dinner at Alfie's was amazing. The bad news is that, by comparison, Apple Blossom Cottage sucks – to borrow a word from my son's vocabulary.

As soon as we got back to the house Alfie explained to Frankie that *Zootropolis* is Pugsley's current favourite movie and asked if he would like to watch it with him.

Frankie happily obliged and then the mystery of where Alfie's TV lived was promptly solved. He opened up a drawer containing countless remote controls, grabbing four before pointing them at different parts of the room, each doing something different. One closed the blinds, another turned on the projector on the ceiling that I hadn't noticed, and another lowered the 140-inch screen that had been hiding at the top of one of the large white walls. Alfie hit play on the movie, plonked Pugsley down on the sofa next to Frankie and then escorted me upstairs. He showed me where his bathroom was – and it was, of course, bigger than my bedroom at Apple Blossom Cottage – before returning with some of his clothes for me to change into.

He quickly ran me through the shower controls before heading for the door, lingering in the doorway for a second.

'Are you wanting me to ask you in?' I joked, instantly regretting it.

Alfie just laughed.

'I'll go make a start on dinner,' he said.

I stepped into the massive shower cubicle, cursing myself for yet another in a long line of awkward jokes, but I was soon distracted from my thoughts by the most impressive shower I have ever seen in my life. It boasted not one, but two shower heads, as well as a seat. It wasn't like being in a shower at all, it felt like standing in gentle, warm summer rainfall. Simply amazing, and a million times better than the bath I've been using at the cottage.

After I got dressed and slipped on a pair of Alfie's trackies and a T-shirt, I headed downstairs.

'Did you use the body dryer?' he asked me when I found him chopping up carrots in the kitchen.

'The . . . towel?' I asked.

Alfie laughed and explained to me that there was something in the corner of the bathroom that dried you after you take a shower – I was in awe.

'I don't know if the movie is rubbish or they're just tired from the walk,' Alfie said, nodding towards Frankie and Pugsley, who were fast asleep, cuddled up on the sofa.

'They look so comfortable,' I said, with a big involuntary sigh.

'You guys will settle in here,' he assured me.

'I really hope so,' I replied.

'If they can embrace me and my booze, they can embrace you and your tubes.'

'My tubes?' I laughed. I knew what he meant.

'Your *pastry* tube things. What else do you guys sell?'

I told him all about our stock, and how most of it comes from abroad, or is made in the style of international cuisine – mainly European. We haven't forced ourselves into a corner as far as what we sell goes, so long as it's all a little bit different or interesting. Basically, somewhere you can go for lunch, or to pick up a treat for after dinner, where you can hope for more than a cheese and pickle sandwich and a slice of carrot cake.

'I'll have to give you some samples, you can tell me what you think the people of Marram Bay will like,' I suggested.

'That would be great,' he replied enthusiastically, before his tone shifted quickly from upbeat to slightly nervous. 'I was thinking of going for a drink in the local tomorrow night, if you fancy it.'

'Me?' I squeaked.

'No, Frankie . . . yes, you,' he laughed.

'OK, sure,' I replied, grinning wildly. Until I remembered my situation. 'Actually, I can't. What about Frankie?'

'Unless you want to bring him for a pint . . . there's a babysitter I can vouch for. Clara, at Clara's café. She's a lovely lady, she looks after Pugsley for me.'

I laughed.

'Not that I think your kid is like a dog, I just mean she's happy to help me out,' he added quickly.

'It's OK, I knew what you meant. We've actually met Clara and Henry, they seem lovely. Although I don't think they knew I was the enemy when they met us . . .'

'I'll have a word,' he assured me. 'Even if they've gone off you, they still love me.'

Dinner was amazing. Alfie, who it turns out is pretty good in the kitchen, made sausages, mashed potatoes, carrots, peas and Yorkshire puddings. Not only does he already know Clara's trick for the peas, but he loaded a bit of everything into Frankie's Yorkshire puddings, and he happily ate them. That's right, my son ate three vegetables. For dessert he made us an apple pie – with his apples – that was just so delicious. The three of us chatted as we ate. It was nice, to see Frankie out of his shell, asking Alfie lots of questions about the farm. Alfie has promised he'll teach him all about the animals and how to look after them, which made Frankie confidently announce that he wants to be a farmer when he grows up.

After dinner I offered to help Alfie tidy up, so we loaded the dishwasher before he said he'd walk us home. Before I knew what

I was doing, I'd invited Alfie in – I immediately kicked myself, because why would I invite him in, after we'd already spent all day together? But he said yes and we ended up sitting up late chatting, long after Frankie went to bed.

I thought things were finally starting to look up . . .

It's Monday morning now and my date with Alfie tonight is on my mind – I say 'date' for want of a better term, it's not a date-date, obviously. I was buzzing last night which meant that I couldn't get to sleep, which meant I overslept, which means I'm currently driving Frankie to school in my pyjamas. I can go home and get ready after I drop him off, but there's no sense in both of us being late.

The sooner this day is over, the sooner I get to see Alfie again, and that's what is motivating me today.

Let's forget that he looks like my type for a second. Alfie is sweet and caring, he's funny, he's great with Frankie, he's kind to animals – he's everything I look for in a man. Oh, and he's treating me like a human when everyone else is treating me like trash.

'Promise you won't get out of the car like that,' Frankie pleads.

'Oh God, am I an embarrassing mum?' I laugh. 'I remember Viv coming to pick me up from school with her rollers in one day and I was mortified. But don't worry, I'm going to drive you right to the gate, watch you in from the car, and then I'm going to go home and get dressed.'

I remember the day my mum picked me up in her rollers like it was yesterday. She was just standing there with her hair all rolled up, secured in a pink silk headscarf, like it was the most natural thing in the world. I was only twelve, and I was mortified – of course a few of the kids brought it up for a couple of days after, like kids do. I try, every day, to make sure that I don't ever embarrass Frankie, because I know how it feels.

Driving down the quiet country road towards the school, the chances of seeing anyone feel slim. The only house we pass is Alfie's, and it seems like all the other mums come from further into town. Throw into the mix the fact that we're running late, and it seems even less likely I'll be caught in my PJs.

We're about halfway to school when the car starts juddering, and this time it's not because I can't get used to the gears. The engine splutters and then all of a sudden it just cuts out, and we slowly grind to a halt.

'*Fudge, fudge, fudge,*' I say, hitting my hand on the steering wheel. I grab my phone from my bag, only to learn we're in a signal dead zone. Being late is bad enough, but being stuck here in my pyjamas – my pink Disney Princess pyjamas – is even worse. I don't know what would be more frustrating – if someone passes or if someone doesn't.

'Ergh, why is everything going wrong at the moment?' I ask, not expecting an answer from my 8-year-old. I'm trying to remember if my life was this disastrous back in London, but other than my healthy dollop of clumsiness and my non-existent love life, things were fine. It's almost like the north just knows we don't belong here and it's trying to reject us, like a body refusing to accept a transplanted organ.

If anything, we're a little closer to the school than we are to home, but what am I going to do, walk him to school in my pyjamas and then call for a taxi? So much for promising I wouldn't embarrass him.

'Are we going to be late?' I hear Frankie ask from the back of the car. 'Mrs Snowball is *so* angry when I'm late.'

'I'm sure she isn't,' I insist. Not with Frankie, at least.

For the last few days I have made a special effort to avoid Mrs Snowball, lest she tell me off for something – anything. I just don't think I'm her kind of mum, if you know what I mean. I think she likes her cute little housewives with their priorities straight, not disorganised whirlwinds of chaos like me, trying to juggle her son *and* her job *and* her home. And now her broken down Brussels sprout.

'Mum, Mum, someone's coming,' Frankie says, relief in his voice.

I look up, hoping that it might be someone who can help us out. My face falls when I recognise Alfie's Range Rover.

'Oh, no, anyone but him,' I whine, looking down at my pyjamas.

Spotting my car – because how could he miss it? – Alfie stops in front of us, gets out of the car and heads over.

'Are you guys OK?' he asks, approaching my window. I notice his concern and his warm and welcoming smile turn into amusement as he glances down at my pyjamas. The slogan emblazoned across my chest – 'My favourite Disney Princess is me' – has never felt more obvious.

'We've broken down,' I say simply, with a straight face.

'On the way to where? Bed?'

I hear Frankie laughing in the backseat.

'Hey, it's not funny,' I insist, even if it is a little funny. 'I need to get kiddo to school, head back home to get ready and then get to work, all without a car.'

'Come on then,' he says, his northern accent sounding stronger than it usually does. 'I'll ferry you around. I'll drop you at work and then get your car taken care of.'

I blink at him for a second. Why is he so nice to me?

'Aren't you busy today?'

'Nah, not really,' he replies.

'It's a company car,' I point out. 'Work will take care of it.'

'They'll tell you to take it to a garage and then foot the bill,' he explains. 'Come on.'

See, this is what I expected when I thought of Yorkshire folk. Friendly, salt of the earth, would give you the shirt off their back types. Movies and TV shows have misled me my entire life, teaching me that northerners are all friendly, no questions asked. Thinking about it, movies and TV shows have taught me a lot of things that I'm now realising haven't come to pass.

'Thank you so much,' I blurt, stepping out of the car, severely self-conscious of my outfit – even more so when I realise I'm wearing the unicorn slippers Frankie bought me for Christmas.

I transfer the contents of my car from mine to Alfie's as quickly as possible and we're moving again. Thankfully we still have enough time to make it without being late.

'Here we go,' Alfie says, pulling up outside. 'Shall I take you in, Frankenstein?'

I expect my son to say something about this nickname because, having a name like Frankie, he's heard them *all*. The remarks usually come from older people, making reference to things he has no idea about. Why, no, my 8-year-old hasn't read Mary Shelley's *Frankenstein*. Your suggestions that he 'relax' or 'goes to Hollywood' fall on deaf ears too. And then of course there's people asking if he remembers them, a reference to a song by Sister Sledge that came out in 1985, that even I had to google.

'Yeah,' Frankie says enthusiastically.

Oh, apparently it's fine when Alfie does it. And apparently he'd much rather Alfie walk him into school than his pyjama-clad mum. Normally I'd take offence, but I don't want anyone else to see me in these either.

'I guess I'll just wait here,' I say.

'Yeah, have a nap,' Alfie teases as he closes the door.

I watch as Alfie and Frankie walk up the stone steps and disappear into the building. I didn't realise he was going to actually take him all the way inside.

I never really stop to think about it, but I guess Frankie doesn't spend much time at all around men.

Before I know it, Alfie is back.

'I don't think anyone was expecting that,' he laughs as he fastens his seatbelt.

'What do you mean?' I ask.

'Well, Mrs Snowball asked if I was Frankie's dad, before she looked up and realised it was me. She was a little taken aback.'

'Probably because you're fraternising with the enemy,' I point out.

'Is Frankie's dad not on the scene?' he asks curiously. 'We don't have to talk about it if you don't want to.'

'No, it's fine,' I insist, pausing to carefully consider my words before I say them. 'No dad on the scene, never has been. I think that might be why he's taken such a shine to you. I mean, you're a really nice man, of course – but he doesn't have many male role models, least of all ones with a zoo of awesome animals and a house full of gadgets.'

Alfie laughs.

'Small family?' he asks. I nod. 'Me too. My mum left my dad when I was a teen – she said he loved the farm more than he loved her, which is a pretty fair assessment, if we're being honest. She moved away and remarried, she's happy and I have a half-brother I see when we all meet up. Otherwise I was an only child, and my dad inherited the farm from my granddad when he died, which is why it was all left to me.'

'I'm an only child too,' I say. 'I always kind of wished I'd had some brothers and sisters – some allies, growing up – but it was just me.'

'It's lonely, isn't it?'

'I was so jealous of my friends who had siblings. My best friend when I was at school had a brother and a sister. She was always complaining about them, how her little brother annoyed her and her older sister fought with her. I remember one day when we were teens, we were just sat watching TV and her sister came in, yelling at her, asking if she'd borrowed her denim skirt. "No, burglars broke in and stole just your skirt," my friend clapped back sarcastically. They were so annoyed at each other, but it made me wish I had someone to bicker with.'

Alfie laughs.

'So just you and your parents?'

'Just me and my mum,' I reply. 'My dad died when I was a baby. I had my grandparents though. My granddad did everything he could to fill the void for me, spoiling me, attending all my school events – he'd always told me he'd give me away if I got married, but that never happened, and he died four years ago. I think Frankie remembers him just enough to miss him. My grandma is in a home, in London, she's not doing so good. My dad's family just sort of faded away after he died, I don't know if it was too painful for them to keep in touch, or they just didn't care, or what.'

'That's awful, I'm so sorry,' Alfie says, using his left hand to squeeze mine.

'It's OK, my mum has always been amazing. She was never very mumsy – I suppose because she was only 20 when she had me. She's 51 now and she'd be devastated if she knew I'd told you that because she likes to pretend we're sisters. Annoyingly, she gets away with it – but hopefully I've inherited her young genes.'

'Well, she sounds err . . . great,' Alfie says.

'She is.'

I smile to myself. Sure, she can be embarrassing at times, but only because she's my mum. Mums aren't supposed to be cool or overtly sexual, but mine thinks we're gal pals, and if she pulls on a night out, she wants to tell me all about it.

'OK, you run in and get ready,' Alfie instructs. 'I'll wait here, take you to work and then I'll get that car towed and fixed up for you.'

'I really can't thank you enough,' I insist.

'It's nothing. Just buy me a drink tonight?'

I feel a little flutter in my stomach.

'OK, deal.'

'OK, go put some adult clothes on,' he laughs.

There's something about the way he teases me that I just love. In fact, I'm yet to find anything wrong with him at all which begs the question, why is he still single? I'll have to try and find out.

Chapter 14

'Don't mess it up this time,' I mentally tell myself as I walk through the door of The Hopeful Ghost, Marram Bay's local pub. I don't know if it's the only one, but Alfie told me it's where all the locals drink.

I always give myself this little pep talk before a work meeting or date. I mean, I didn't necessarily mess it up the last time I had a meeting or went on a date, or the time before that, but if it's something I'm having to do again then I clearly haven't made enough money to retire or married a Prince Charming, so time to try again, and *this time* I'll do better. It's also setting myself a nice low bar, so that anything other than messing up seems like a victory.

Tonight isn't a date, is it? As much as I secretly want it to be, I suppose the pressure is off if it isn't a date – dating is hard. Being in the same relationship through my teens, and then finding myself pregnant at 22, I've never really done much dating, just a few dates here and there. And when I say 'dating' I mean the painstakingly awkward act of going to public places to make small talk with men in an attempt to see if there's anything between you before making your excuses to leave – that's all. Getting it on is not something that goes hand-in-hand with dating for me

– my personality, it turns out, is the best contraceptive I know of. But dating is so much more than sex and, do you know what, it's so hard.

It should be easy: turn up, eat dinner, be awesome, live happily ever after – but that's not how it goes at all, especially these days. Sure, you'll find men who want to date you, but it'll turn out you're just one of a whole bunch of women they're pursuing – especially now so many people of all ages are doing online dating, not that I would dare venture down that avenue.

Maybe I've never given any of my first dates a real shot, but after my poor judgement when I was younger, I just feel like life is too short to waste on people who aren't worth it.

I feel a few eyes on me as I walk up to the bar and order a drink – one of Alfie's ciders, of course – so I take my drink and find one of the few quiet corners to sit down in.

The Hopeful Ghost is quite a big pub, with a large round bar situated right in the centre. I imagine, when it's even busier than it is tonight (it is a Monday after all), that people will wait to be served from all angles. It's a cute place though, very rustic. I'm sitting next to a large fireplace, which really adds to the cosy appeal of the place, and I noticed a man at the bar who has his dog with him, which I like. Glances from locals aside, it feels like a lovely, welcoming place – much nicer than the nearest bar to where I lived in London, which was an Eighties-themed karaoke bar. Sure, it was fun, but you had to be in the mood for it, because when all you want is a quiet drink, the last thing you want is a fifty-something man singing 'Livin' on a Prayer' (badly) at the top of his voice.

An acoustic guitar and a woman's voice fill the air – I've only just realised there's a live duo playing at the other side of the bar. I just sit peacefully, sipping my drink, listening to the music as I wait for Alfie to arrive.

My phone buzzes on the table in front of me. I look at it and see Alfie's name and I immediately think that, if we hadn't swapped numbers earlier when he took my car to get fixed for me, he wouldn't be able to text me and bail on me now.

'I'll be there in 5 mins. Is it OK if my mate Charlie comes for a drink? It's been a bad day,' the message reads.

I punch a message back saying it's fine. It's so like Alfie (if I can say that after knowing him for three days?) to be kind to his friends too. Of course I don't mind, in fact, it might mean that I make another friend, which will make a grand total of: four.

Alfie made plans with Clara and Henry, for them to babysit Frankie, and he promised me they were cool with it. I thought twice about it but when I floated the idea by Frankie he was more than keen to see them again – I think he has a lot of questions for Henry, most of which are about him getting blown up.

I only have to listen to the band for a couple of minutes before Alfie hurries over, taking a seat at the table next to me.

'Sorry I'm late,' he says, even though he's technically on time. I actually showed up early, just to forcibly break my current late streak. 'Good choice with the drink. Charlie is getting ours so I thought I'd come and find you, let you know we were here. How was work?'

'Oh, work was the usual level of rubbish,' I admit. 'We've been running adverts, looking for staff, for weeks now and I found out today that no one is applying. So I guess I'll be running the place single-handedly.'

'I can help with recruitment,' he says. 'And failing that, I can help out behind the counter.'

I'm not sure if he's kidding about the latter.

A petite brunette carries two drinks over. She's your typical girl next door, with her pretty looks and her easy smile. She's maybe five foot two or five foot three – the two pint glasses are enormous in her hands. She's rocking the 'jeans and a nice top' look, teamed with a pair of pastel pink Timberlands. I assume she's the barmaid, as she places the glasses down on the table, but then she sits down next to Alfie . . .

'Hello,' she says in her soft Yorkshire accent. 'I'm Charlie, nice to meet you.'

'Hi, I'm Lily,' I say, shaking her hand. I assumed Charlie was a boy, not a babe.

'Thanks for letting me tag along. I was up at Alfie's, I mentioned I was having a bad day, so he invited me.'

I'm jealous. Why am I jealous? Because she was at his house? Do I think I'm the only one allowed in his house?

'Oh no, what happened?' I ask, curious as to what equates to a bad day in her world. Somehow I don't think it includes getting covered with crap.

'I lost a cat,' she says, before quickly elaborating. 'I'm the local vet. I'd hoped I could save the cute little fella, but it wasn't meant to be.'

'She stopped by to check on Leonardo, to make sure the sore on his leg had healed. I'd totally forgotten she was coming over. But then she started crying and she told me what had happened. I thought a drink and meeting a new friend might cheer her up.'

Oh, she's perfect. Not just perfect on paper, but perfect for Alfie. She's local, gorgeous, cute as a button, and she's got a great job caring for animals. And then there's me, like a young (taller) Barbara Windsor, fresh out of a *Carry On* movie with my comedic clumsiness, my cheeky jokes and my London accent, that feels so out of place up here.

'Oh, I'm so sorry,' I say sincerely. 'You must have to deal with that all the time.'

'It doesn't make it any easier,' she insists – not that I was suggesting it did. 'So you're the deli girl.'

'Guilty,' I reply.

'I'm not objecting to it – it's not going to threaten my livelihood,' she assures me, although I don't exactly feel like she's giving me her blessing.

'Thanks,' I reply, unsure what else to say.

After a few seconds of awkward silence, Alfie takes his vibrating phone from his pocket.

'I've been tagged in the town group,' he says. 'Last time this happened, Phillip had got out and he was frightening someone's cats, apparently.'

He seems so amused by this, but that sounds like classic, terrifying Phillip to me.

'We have this town Facebook group that all the locals have joined,' he explains. 'People use it to sell things, find things, see what's going on in the community, complain about things and just generally gossip.'

'You'll have to invite me,' I suggest. I don't tell him that one of the mums at school already told me about it and told me I lived too far out of town to join, because Alfie lives farther out of town than I do, so Avril was obviously lying.

As Alfie reads something on his phone, Charlie smiles over at me. I feel like she's assessing me, mentally looking me up and down. I know that I shouldn't be so fussy, given how few friends I have here, but I just feel like her face is smiling, but her eyes are showing me something different.

Alfie chuckles to himself.

'This is hilarious, listen to what someone posted in the group,' he says. '"Saw Alfie Barton dropping the Apple Blossom Girl's child off at school this morning" and then they've used the eyes emoji, the ones that look off to the left.'

'They probably think something is going on between you,' Charlie says. 'Like you spent the night together.'

'Just the evening,' Alfie says with a laugh. 'Let them think what they want, right, Apple Blossom Girl?'

'A nickname, just what I need,' I say sarcastically.

'They've been calling you worse,' Charlie insists. I feel my eyebrows shoot up in surprise – at the fact people have been calling me names, and her frankness.

'Just because of the deli,' she adds.

'I've heard people saying things about the deli, but I haven't heard them saying anything about Lily specifically,' Alfie points out. I don't know if that's true or if he's just being kind, but I appreciate it.

I examine the contents of my glass anxiously, not really knowing what to say next. Rather than go into a protective shell, I decide to change the subject.

'So how long have you two known each other?'

'Since we were at school,' Charlie replies.

'Well, so she tells me,' Alfie says with a cheeky smile.

I smile, puzzled.

'Alfie was a few school years above me, but I remember him. He was a good-looking older boy though, I was too intimidated to talk to him.'

'Ha,' Alfie laughs, banging his hand on the table. 'She says this, but it's not true. I was a chubby teenager and I was painfully shy. I don't reckon she had a clue who I was.'

'I did too,' she insists with a playful shove. 'That's why, when you moved back to the farm, I came straight over to say hello, silly.'

Hmm.

'So you say,' he laughs. 'But I remember school, and no one wanted to be my friend. I was shy and I smelled like a farm – or so the meaner kids told me.'

He may be joking around, but my heart breaks for child Alfie.

'After that, we became inseparable,' Charlie says. 'I helped him settle back in, build his house. I remember one night, we stayed up late drinking your sloe gin, and we got so drunk we bought a goat online.'

'Phillip,' Alfie tells me. 'We were worried he'd be put down if no one took him in.'

Why do I feel like I've just walked into a random couple's house and got in their bed?

'Lily, Alfie tells me you have a son,' Charlie says, changing the subject. 'I'll be doing a talk about animals at his school tomorrow, if he's a little acorn.'

'I do. Frankie. He's 8.'

'How old are you?' she asks. 'Just curious.'

Just wanting to do the maths, is more like it.

'I'm 31,' I reply, pausing while she subtracts eight, or nine, if she remembers to account for the nine months I spent pregnant.

'Are you and his dad still together?' she asks.

'All right, Charlie, don't grill her,' Alfie laughs, swigging his drink.

'No, we're not.'

'Divorced?'

'No, we never married.'

'Oh,' she replies. 'Does he still see Frankie?'

'Charlie, seriously,' Alfie says, a little firmer this time.

'Sorry, I was just curious,' she replies.

'No, he doesn't. He never has, it's only ever just been the two of us.'

Charlie's face falls. There's that pitying look I know and hate.

'I'm so sorry,' she says. 'That must have been so hard for you. Going through it all alone, being pregnant, giving birth . . .'

'I was anything but alone during the birth, actually,' I tell her. 'I gave birth on the tube.'

Charlie and Alfie both stop in their tracks. They stop drinking, they have nothing to say – I'm not even sure they're breathing.

'The tube?' Alfie eventually says, sounding surprised.

'Is that normal in London?' Charlie asks.

'Erm, no, it's not actually. Frankie was only the fourth child to be born on the underground. It wasn't rush hour or anything, but there were plenty of people around. People were very helpful and considerate. In London we tend to keep ourselves to ourselves, especially on public transport. It was kind of moving, really, how willing people were to take care of me. Frankie was a little early – and members of the Holmes family are rarely early – so

I figured I was fine out and about on my own. I'd been to visit an old uni friend, just for a catch-up. She worked in central London, so I popped out to meet her on her lunch hour and, I don't know, maybe it was the excitement or the jerky motion of the tube carriage but my waters broke and the next thing I knew I had a baby in my arms. With the exception of a couple of squeamish suits, everyone got involved and helped out, and a few even gave me their contact details so I could keep them posted on how Frankie was doing.'

The story of how my son came into the world might be unconventional, but I wouldn't change it for the world, and I'm always proud to tell it because I think it shows all that is good in the world.

'I think some of my animals give birth in better conditions,' Charlie giggles. 'So you're single then?'

'Yep.'

This is so uncomfortable.

'Well.' I knock back what is left of my drink. 'I'd better go find Frankie and get him to bed.'

'You've only had one drink,' Alfie points out. 'Can't you stay for one more? Tell her, Charlie.'

'Yes, stay,' she sings.

Nope, that wasn't sincere at all.

'I'd really better get going,' I insist.

'Maybe I'll see you tomorrow?' Alfie says.

'Maybe,' I reply. 'Have a great night.'

'See you later, Blossom,' he says cheekily.

Well, that wasn't only absolutely not a date, but a disaster too. Good work, Lily.

Chapter 15

I'm too scared to believe it, but I think I have someone coming in for a job interview today. I only dare to say 'I think' because this could just be a trap – another act of sabotage from an angry local.

I feel like I'm in one of those movies where everyone in town is in on something and I'm just the bemused outsider who turns up and winds up nearly getting murdered.

Other than Alfie, Clara and Henry, no one has been all that friendly yet – even Charlie, who Alfie introduced me to with the intention of helping me make another friend – isn't exactly being all that pleasant. I actually saw her at school this morning, standing outside the school gates talking to the mums – most notably: Jessica, Mary-Ann and Avril.

I know it's going to sound like I'm paranoid, but I saw Charlie look over at me, and she never came to say hello. You'd think she would, right? We hung out last night, it's a small place where we're all oh-so friendly . . . I was early for once, as well, so I had to endure several minutes of standing around outside, watching them all chat together. I tried to encourage Frankie to go and mingle with the other kids but he said he'd rather stand with me – he'd probably have more luck making friends if he pretended he didn't know me. He has made one friend though . . . Henry.

Obviously I'd rather he had friends his own age, but he had so much fun hanging out with Henry and Clara last night. He came home and told me what a great time he'd had, listening to Henry's old war stories and doing jigsaws – *jigsaws*! My son, whose favourite toys all require electric power, doing a jigsaw and enjoying it.

I look at the email enquiry about the position at the deli on my screen. I'm expecting 21-year-old Chantelle Horne. She didn't send a CV, just a cover letter, so I invited her over to the deli and asked her to bring her CV with her.

Chantelle is late – currently only six minutes late, and I know I'm always late, but this is a job interview. My naturally tardy tendencies allow me to give her the benefit of the doubt.

Eight minutes after the time we arranged, I hear a knock on the deli door. Before I open it, I can see a young woman standing on the other side of the glass. She's dressed entirely in black, with pale skin and dark make-up – she kind of reminds me of a young me, if I'm being honest. Her hair is black, but obviously dyed that way because it doesn't match her complexion, and her look is finished off with a septum piercing. My nose tickles just looking at it.

'Hello,' I say cheerily as I open the door. 'I'm Lily.'

'Hi, I'm Channy,' the girl replies, shaking my hand.

'Come in, sit down – excuse the mess, the fitters are still hard at it,' I say, ushering her towards the counter where Mike and I usually have our meetings. 'Did you bring your CV?'

'I didn't,' she replies. 'I don't exactly have one. But I figured we'd be chatting now, so I can tell you what you need to know.'

'Oh, OK,' I reply. 'Well, tell me a bit about yourself then.'

I shuffle on my stool to make myself a bit more comfortable.

'OK, sure. Name's Chantelle – Channy to my mates. I'm 21, lived in Marram Bay my whole life.' At this fact, Channy pulls a displeased face. 'Went to school here, left after my GCSEs.'

'What GCSEs do you have?' I ask. We're supposed to seek out

candidates with English, Maths and Science, not that I've ever really understood why. Supposedly it shows a well-rounded individual, if they've got good GCSEs. It shows that they've worked for something, I guess.

'C in Science, D in Maths. I got a B in my English Lang, but I got a U in my English Lit. I'm not dumb or anything, I just muddled my days up and slept right through it. Duh!' Channy adds with a laugh.

'Oh, OK,' I reply, not really sure what else to say. 'So, why do you want to work here?'

'I want a job so I can save up enough money to move away – somewhere more fun, y'know? Like, it's real pretty here and whatever, tourists seem to like it, they visit and have a great time but then they go back to their lives in real places. I want to live somewhere exciting, where there are nightclubs and more than eleven people on Matcher, y'know?'

I really don't, but I appreciate her honesty.

'Do you have any experience in customer service?' I ask.

'No.'

'Any work experience at all?'

'No.'

'Do you have a keen interest in international cuisine?'

'No,' she says again, shaking her head for emphasis this time.

'Are you interested in food at all?' I ask.

'Well, I eat it, if that's what you mean.'

That wasn't what I meant.

'Channy, I'm going to be frank with you, because I appreciate your honestly. Why should I give you this job?'

She smiles.

'Because A, I can give you the low-down on all things Marram Bay – everything you could possibly need to know about everyone, and B, because I'll bet I'm the only person who has applied.'

I think for a moment. Well, she's right. She really is the only person who has applied, so she has that going for her, and I suppose if she can educate me on the town, maybe that would help. Plus, she's clearly smart enough to realise I need her, so maybe she's more intelligent than she seems.

'OK, you're hired,' I say happily, and not just because she's the only person, or because she knows the locals, but because I see myself in her. Once upon a time I was a twenty-something misfit, with my unapproachable outfits and my dreams of getting out of my hometown. If I can help her achieve her dreams, then great.

'Awesome,' she replies. 'When do I start?'

'I'll keep you posted,' I tell her. 'We're just waiting to see when the work is done, and when we get our liquor licence, and we'll need another couple of staff members . . . I will need some help in the run-up to opening though.'

'Great,' she says.

'If you want stick around for a bit, I'll make you a drink, and there's always some cakes or some doughnuts somewhere. You can start filling me in on the town.'

'Yeah, all right,' she replies. 'Nowt else to do.'

I make two cups of tea before rifling through the large box of biscuits Eric and Amanda sent for the workmen to have during their breaks. See, that's what I mean about them, they're such great bosses and it's so amazing to work for them.

I spy a box of French madeleines – delicate, mini sponge cakes flavoured with lemon and dusted with sugar – before spotting a few bags of Mulino Bianco biscuits. Mulino Bianco are an Italian brand I hadn't encountered until I started working at the deli. We have always been encouraged to take products home with us, just as a treat or to review them – Eric and Amanda like us to have proper knowledge of all products on offer. I couldn't think of a more amazing job perk if I tried. One day, not long after I started working for YumYum, the very first thing I took home to try was a bag of Mulino Bianco Pan Di Stelle biscuits. They are delicious chocolate and hazelnut pastry biscuits, topped with white stars and sugar. They're so crunchy, and delicious without being overly sweet – they soon became my favourite biscuit, kicking the reigning champ, the humble bourbon, off my top spot.

'Here we go,' I say, setting the drinks down on the counter. 'Where do we start?'

'Well, who have you met?' she asks, tucking straight into the biscuits.

'Mrs Snowball,' I say, to get the ball rolling.

'Ha, she's an old bag, isn't she? She taught me, back when I was a "Little Acorn" and I hated every moment of it. She always used to tell us that "mighty oaks grow from little nuts" which, now that I think about it, is pretty effed up . . .'

I snigger.

'I find it right weird that she's a teacher who doesn't have any kids of her own. She's married, lives with her husband, but they just never had any. She says the school kids are all the kids she needs. You might think she's a prim middle-aged woman but she was a proper goer when she was younger, apparently. I remember not too long ago, a photo did the rounds online, of her getting arrested. She was protesting something, back when she was at uni – she didn't have a bra on.'

Oh, wow.

'Wow,' I blurt. 'Erm, any more interesting characters here?'

'Oh, yeah, for sure. We pretend we're this perfect little place, but we're just as barmy as everywhere else. Who else have you met?'

'Clara and Henry . . .'

'Yeah, they're all right. Clara is an interesting one though – she isn't the original Clara, if stories are to be believed.'

All sorts of thoughts fight for attention in my head . . . Not the original Clara? What does that even mean?

'Her mum had a little girl named Clara when she was a teenager,' she explains. 'We're talking a long time ago, back when it wasn't chill for a teen to get pregnant. Long story short, the postman and his wife couldn't have kids, so her parents gave Clara away to them. Then, when Clara the First's mum got married and had another daughter, she gave her the same name.'

I feel my eyes widen with horror. Clara's gran made her mum give her baby away because she was young? I fell in love with Frankie the second I knew he was growing inside me and there was no way anyone was going to take him away from me – not that anyone suggested they would. I can't even imagine how hard that must have been for her. I know we're talking about a different time, but even so, that's just horrendous.

'Know anything about the mums?' I ask.

'Er, let's think, who has kids . . . Katy and Graham, who have a little kid at Acorn School – Buster, he's a first year, I think. Anyway they made the local news when he proposed to her. There's an abbey over on Hope Island, it's a proper romantic spot, lots of couples go there – and I know what you're thinking, that sounds like a proper banging proposal, but it turns out, because they're proper into their murder mysteries, he arranged for her to be "kidnapped" as a surprise. So she was just going about her day when she was bundled into a van, tied up, blindfolded, gagged! The van drives her to Hope Abbey where Graham is waiting to propose to her. She said yes – probably because she was scared not to, if you ask me. I can't even get a text back and she's got her own boyfriend kidnapping her.'

Channy shakes her head.

'Know anything about Avril?'

'Avril Newman?' she asks. 'Head of the PTA? Nah, doesn't mean there's nothing to know though. People are having affairs, avoiding tax and driving out into the sticks to flash their headlights, just like everywhere else.'

I'm not sure that last one is as typical as she thinks – or maybe I've been living a sheltered life.

'We've even got our own Lothario,' she says excitedly.

'Oh really?' I reply.

'Yep,' Channy says through a mouthful of biscuit. 'Bad-boy farmer, Alfie Barton.'

I choke on my tea.

'Alfie?'

'Yeah, you met him?'

'Erm, yeah, I met him and Charlie in the pub the other night,' I say, embarrassed.

'Ha. Charlie the vet. Everyone knows that as soon as Alfie moved back to town and inherited all his dad's money, she was all over him . . . but bad-boy farmers don't take wives,' she laughs. 'Charlie is playing the long game, waiting for him to change his ways. In the meantime, he's ploughing all over town. Can't blame women for falling for him – rich, charming, gorgeous. I would.'

Alfie has got to be at least fifteen years older than Channy. I can't blame her though, I fell for his charms too.

'So, he's not a good guy?' I ask, sounding a little bit like a kid who's just found out Santa Claus isn't real.

'He's not a bad person,' she insists. 'But he moved back into town, started making alcohol instead of milk, and since then he's just been dating loads of different women, wooing the tourists – I think he likes a challenge.'

And what bigger challenge than a single mum who has lost all faith in men. Then again, look at me go – going over to his house, literally falling into his arms, meeting him for a drink and just palming my son off on a couple I met once . . . I haven't been playing that hard to get, have I?

'How do you know all this?' I ask. Am I refusing to believe her? Why would she make this up?

'Nothing stays a secret in this town,' she tells me. 'I've always been a good listener, well, outside of school. Always listen to my mum gassing on the phone – kids hear everything. And who doesn't love a good gossip?'

'Wow, so much to take in,' I say, pausing to clear my throat. 'I, er, I'd better get back to work.'

'OK, yeah,' she replies, standing up. 'I don't suppose I'm gonna get paid for today?'

I glance at my watch – she's been here forty-five minutes.

'How about you take the biscuits and the cakes?' I suggest.

Channy looks down at the sweet treats on the worktop, shrugs and gathers them up in her arms.

'You've got my number, yeah. Call me when it's time to start.'

'Sure thing,' I call after her. 'Thanks for the gossip.'

'Plenty more where that came from,' she calls back.

Mike and his team are working in the back room today, so I sit here, alone, thinking about everything Channy told me. How could I be so dumb, to be taken in by the first handsome face I meet?

I take my phone from my bag, only to see that I have a message from the devil himself, asking if I have any plans tonight. I quickly reply, a little too bluntly perhaps, saying that I'm busy this evening, before turning my phone off.

If Alfie Barton thinks he can add me to his list of conquests, he can think again.

Chapter 16

Walking up the steps to the school, with yet another bad day under my belt, I realise that it isn't over just yet when I see Mrs Snowball standing in the school doorway with Frankie next to her, her hand placed on his shoulder to keep him in place.

I approach them cautiously, although I'm not sure why – Frankie is usually good as gold and, for once, I don't think I've done anything wrong.

'Lily,' Mrs Snowball greets me. 'A word, if you don't mind?'

It sounds optional, but I don't think it is.

'Sure,' I reply.

The playground has pretty much emptied, so Mrs Snowball directs me to a wooden picnic bench. Well, it is such a lovely day – far too nice to be stuck inside getting a telling-off.

Mrs Snowball removes an iPhone from the pocket of her maroon trousers and places it on the table.

'Do you know what this is?' she asks me.

'Wow, SATs are getting easier,' I joke. 'It's an iPhone.'

'Correct,' Mrs Snowball replies.

I shrug.

'Your son brought it to school.'

I look over at Frankie, who looks down at the table.

'Oh?' I say coyly.

'Oh, indeed,' Mrs Snowball replies. 'I realised something was amiss at lunchtime, when I noticed a crowd of children around him. I went over and, one of the boys, who I shan't name, was trying to search for something I shan't mention.'

Ship! I told Frankie the phone was only for using at home. It's not like anyone could've used it today, it only works when I connect it to my phone or to the Wi-Fi at the cottage. Still, I don't suppose explaining this to Mrs Snowball is going to do anyone any favours.

'I asked him what he was doing. He said he was trying to ring you.'

'Is everything OK, kiddo?' I ask him, but Mrs Snowball isn't having any of it.

'Lily, listen, I don't know how things were in London, but here we don't give our 8-year-olds iPhones to pop in their backpacks.'

'I didn't do that, I assure you,' I tell her.

'And then I tried to call you, but it didn't connect. Anyway, I've confiscated the offending phone.'

Frankie looks up quickly, panicked. I suppose, to him fully functional or not, that phone is his only connection to the outside world.

'You can't do that,' I insist. What is it with this woman and confiscating things? First his lunch, now the phone . . . I suppose the second one is a little different, but these are tough times for my son and me. 'It's my phone.'

'This is your phone?'

'Of course it is,' I reply. 'Eight-year-olds don't have iPhones.'

'And that phone . . .' Mrs Snowball starts, nodding at my actual phone, on the table next to my bag.

'. . . is my business phone,' I say. 'That one is my personal phone. You won't bring my phone to school again, will you, Frankie?'

Frankie shakes his head.

'Well, I can't confiscate your phone from you, I suppose,' Mrs Snowball tells me reluctantly.

'Nope,' I reply. 'Don't worry, I'll have a word with my son.'

'Please do,' she replies. 'If not, we'll have to seriously reconsider his place at this school.'

I take my son's hand and lead him across the playground and down the stone steps. We walk along the road, past my car, until we reach a little beauty spot at the side of the road. I sit down on a bench, patting it to tell Frankie to sit next to me. He does.

I've been a mum for eight years now and I have never seen my son so miserable. When I'm not busy with the deli, I'm stressing out about it. The poor kid is going to a school with a militant headteacher, where he has no friends – I'm not surprised he's so sad.

'I'm sorry,' he says, before I have chance to ask him any questions. 'I kept the phone with me, just in case, and then today I just needed to talk to you.'

'What happened?' I ask, sensing a bigger issue.

'Is my dad a murderer?' he asks.

His question stuns me into silence for a moment. I feel my hands lightly shake as his question continues to sink in. As far as Frankie is concerned, he doesn't have a dad, and seeing as he's only 8, I've never expanded on that. I always knew that, when he grew up and learned a lot more about where babies come from, he would ask questions, but I figured he'd find the truth much easier to understand at that age. I'm sure that, in this day and age, my son probably knows more about sex than I would like (I think every mum wants to keep their child a baby forever, right?) but I don't think he's in a position to understand how a young woman can find herself pregnant and alone, not without each answer resulting in another question.

'Of course not, who told you that?'

'Some of the kids were saying that they'd heard their mums talking about how my dad was in prison for murder!'

It doesn't matter how hot and sunny it is – I go freezing cold from head to toe.

'I promise you that isn't true, Frankie. I promise.'

He nods in agreement. There's a sad, confused look on his face, but I know that he believes me.

'Things aren't getting better, are they?' I say. Frankie shakes his head. 'Well, I can't just leave the deli without someone to run it, but I can have a word with the bosses, tell them it's not working out. In the meantime, what about if I ask Viv to come and stay with us, would you like that?'

'Yeah,' Frankie says enthusiastically. I wouldn't say he sounds excited, it's more relieved.

'Yeah? She can help us out, while we sort things out, and I'll see what the bosses say,' I assure him.

'Do you not like it here either?' he asks.

I could lie to him and hope that, if he thinks I like it, he'll like it too, but the last thing I want is for him to think that there's something wrong with him because, honestly, living here is a nightmare so far.

'Not at the moment,' I tell him honestly yet tactfully. 'It'll be great when Viv is here though, right? We always have fun when Viv is around.'

'Yeah, like when she used to take me to karate every week and then we'd go to McDonald's,' he says. I don't have the heart to tell him it's because she wanted to (and did) sleep with his karate teacher. Frankie absolutely loves Viv, and I don't think he loses out by not having a little old knitting nana, I think he appreciates her even more for being younger and cooler than his friends' grannies.

'Yeah, it'll be great,' I assure him. Plus, it will be nice to have an ally – a real one, that isn't just trying to bed the new girl in town.

'Maybe we could go see Clara and Henry, get some chicken nuggets,' I suggest. Well, it has been over a week since he had them last, so I'm sure Mrs Snowball won't be calling Social Services in too much of a hurry if she gets wind of it.

'Yes!' Frankie cheers. I love that he's so sweet and pure, that the day can be turned around with chicken nuggets.

'Hey look, it's Alfie,' Frankie says excitedly, pointing over at his car.

Alfie has pulled up alongside my Beetle and now he's walking over to us.

'You broken down *again*?' he asks as he approaches us. 'I'll take it back for you, mechanic said he'd fixed the problem . . .'

'No, no, it's fine,' I say quickly. 'We were just having a chat.'

'Oh, OK,' he replies. I think he's picking up on my coldness. 'So you guys have plans tonight?'

'We're going to see Clara and Henry,' Frankie tells him. 'For chicken nuggets.'

'Oh,' Alfie says again, turning to me. 'Is that all your plans are? Because I was planning something for you – and it involved Frankie going to Clara and Henry's for some chicken nuggets.'

Oh, I'll bet it did.

'You should go out with Alfie, Mum,' Frankie tells me. 'I like hanging out at Clara and Henry's, we play games and puzzles and Henry tells me stories.'

'I don't want to leave you again,' I tell him.

'Mum, I'm not a baby,' he insists. 'You can go out with Alfie.'

'I do have a surprise arranged . . .' Alfie adds.

I don't know how to say no, not without an explanation, but I can't exactly tell my son my reservations, and I can't really tell Alfie that I know what a womaniser he is, so could he please stop being nice to me.

'OK, sure,' I say, not sounding all that convincing.

'Great stuff,' Alfie says optimistically. 'I just need to go and make some arrangements, then I'll text you and arrange a time.'

'OK,' I reply, forcing a smile.

'OK,' he echoes, kicking the grass gently with the toe of his boot. 'See you later.'

I watch Alfie walk to his car before turning back to Frankie, who has the cheekiest little smile on his face.

'What?' I ask him, laughing awkwardly.

'What?' he repeats back to me, still smiling.

I narrow my eyes as I smile at him. He thinks there's something going on between Alfie and me, bless him.

'Come on you,' I say, getting up from the bench before holding out a hand to Frankie. 'Let's go call Viv and beg her to come and look after us.'

You really are never too old to need your mum.

Chapter 17

After calling my mum and asking for her help (she jumped at the chance) and getting Frankie changed out of his school uniform, I made a start getting ready for this evening. When Alfie messaged me he told me to dress comfortably which, other than my PJs or my tracksuit, isn't really something I do. I hopped into a pair of black skinny jeans and a black Bardot top, gave my hair a blast with some dry shampoo and reapplied the parts of my make-up that had faded over the course of the day. What? This isn't a date so I'm under no obligation to dress nice or laugh at his jokes.

We dropped an excited Frankie off at Clara and Henry's before driving to the coast in awkward silence for the most part, peppered with occasional small talk.

'So that, over there, is Hope Island. It's a tidal island, so sometimes it's connected to the mainland, other times it's just a little island out there on its own.'

My ears prick up reluctantly. This is actually kind of interesting.

'This road we're driving along – the causeway – isn't always here, sometimes it's completely covered in water.'

'Do people ever get stuck?' I ask – my first sincere attempt at conversation this evening.

'Oh yeah, people get over and don't check the times for the

tide and get stuck at one side or another. Every couple of months we'll have a car get stuck halfway along. The coastguard has to come out and rescue them.'

'How long is the causeway?'

'The road is little over a mile. It's not like the tide comes in out of nowhere, but it's faster than you might think. Some people think they can chance it, but cars can float in just a foot or two of water. At high tide, the water can be six-feet deep, it's not worth the risk, even in a 4x4.'

'Fascinating,' I say in awe. I might not like it here, but I can't deny its unique beauty and intrigue.

'Don't worry, I've checked the times. We'll make it back.'

'Good,' I reply, a little too firmly. 'So, what's the plan?'

I gaze out of the window as we drive along the causeway. It's so strange to be driving, I guess, through the sea. Being able to look out over the water like we're in a boat, except we're in a car. It's kind of scary really, to think that where the car is right now will be deep underwater soon.

'You know how I told you I could sort all your problems out?' he says. I'm not looking at him, but I can practically hear his smile and his optimism.

'Yes . . .'

'It would be fair to say that you're not a fan of Marram Bay – true?'

'I guess,' I reply. 'I feel like it's a circumstantial dislike though.'

'Don't get bogged down in a chicken or egg debate,' he insists. 'A place like Marram Bay, it's not just a town, it's so much more than that. It's alive, in the scenery and the businesses and the locals. So if you want Marram Bay to love you, you're going to need to learn to love Marram Bay – it's a mutual thing. You're going to need to get on board with everything.'

'Listen,' I start. 'I didn't just come here with an open mind, I came here excited to be starting a new life, in a beautiful place, with a real sense of community. But when I get here, all I'm greeted with is hostility, hatred and a knackered old cottage.'

'I am going to make you fall in love with this town, Lily Holmes. And then this town is going to fall in love with you, OK?'

I shrug.

'Will you let me try?' he asks, laughing at my stubbornness.

'Sure,' I say, giving in, although I'm not expecting much. This is probably just a line, to woo me into bed before he never speaks to me again.

'This is Hope Island,' he tells me as we pull off the causeway. 'It's just green grass and beach for the most part, but there's a little village down one end with restaurants, B&Bs and houses.'

'Some people live on the island?' I ask, amazed. Imagine living somewhere you could only leave at certain times of the day.

'Yeah,' he replies. 'People love it over here.'

'I'd hate it,' I admit. I have to admit that the island is beautiful, it's just so small and isolated. I might feel lonely at the cottage, surrounded by green, but here you're surrounded by green and then nothing but sea. 'How big is the island?'

'About a thousand acres,' he tells me.

'I can't believe I never knew this was here,' I admit. 'It's amazing, it really is.'

'Phase one of making you fall in love with the place,' Alfie informs me.

'Buddy, it's going to take a lot more than some cool geography to turn this frown upside down.'

A short drive across the island leads us towards the ruins of an old building. I've seen it before, across the sea from the pub we were in last night.

'This is Hope Abbey,' Alfie says, in full-on tour guide mode. 'Well, what's left of it. It's an eighth-century building, but it's been in ruins since the eighteenth century. People travel from all over the place to see it.'

Alfie parks the car near the abbey, alongside just one other car. We get out and begin our walk towards it. It's starting to get darker now, and a little chillier. I suppose because we're out here on the island, we'll be really feeling the breeze.

'I've not brought you here for a history lesson, not a traditional one anyway,' he explains. 'The Hopeful Ghost pub is named after Hope Island's most popular urban legend. A long, long time ago a young bride and groom tied the knot here, in the grounds of the abbey. It was a beautiful wedding ceremony and a perfect day, until the bride found herself unable to locate her groom.'

'Erm, I'm not one for scary stories,' I insist, as Alfie leads me into the centre of the abbey. My gaze goes from the ground, to the high stone walls, to staring at the sky above us, where the roof used to be.

'You don't want to hear the rest?' Alfie asks.

I think for a moment. Curiosity has got the better of me now.

'OK, keep going, but no jump scares,' I warn him.

'It's just a story,' he laughs. 'So the bride goes off looking for the groom and finds him, tucked away in the corner of one of the old rooms, with her younger sister. The sister tells the groom he should have married her and then they kiss.'

'This is an awful story,' I point out. 'So depressing.'

'It gets worse,' he says dramatically. 'To teach her groom a lesson, the bride decides to hide, to give him a scare, to make him realise that he does in fact love her more than anything. Rumour has it there's a secret tunnel underneath the island, that monks once used to escape the abbey, and the bride found her way into it . . . she never found her way back out though. It's said that, to this day, on a night like this, the bride's ghost emerges from underground, looking to exact her revenge on the first couple she finds.'

I stare at Alfie for a second, blinking occasionally.

'Wow,' I finally say.

'I know,' he replies. 'Scary stuff.'

'And . . . you thought you'd bring a girl here?' I ask in disbelief. 'For that?'

'No,' he laughs, ushering me through a gap in the wall. 'For this.'

As I look out towards the sea, I notice a picnic blanket, all laid out with food and drink. Little lanterns are dotted around, creating a scene fresh out of a romantic movie.

'What's this?' I ask.

'It's a surprise,' he says. 'For you. To cheer you up, show you the sights. Do you like it?'

'I love it,' I reply. 'No one has ever done anything like this for me before . . .'

'I'll get off,' a man's voice says, causing me to jump out of my skin.

'Lily, it's OK, it's my mate Andy. He lives on the island, I set things up and asked him to watch over it while I picked you up. See you later, mate.'

Andy, amused at my pathetic little scream, laughs as he heads for his car.

'Just the two of us now,' Alfie says. 'No mates, no ghosts . . .'

'It's so bizarre,' I say as we both sit down on the blanket. 'It's like the most romantic thing I've ever seen, in the least romantic place I've ever heard of.'

'It's actually a very romantic place really,' Alfie tells me as he pours me a glass of white wine. 'Lots of people get married here, proposals happen here.'

'Yeah, I met a girl yesterday who told me a story about that. She told me a lot of stories about a lot of people.'

'Ah,' Alfie says. 'You heard some stuff about me?'

'Maybe,' I reply casually, picking up a smoked salmon blini and popping it in my mouth.

'Yes then,' he laughs. 'What did you hear?'

I pull a face and shrug, as if to say 'I don't know' when I absolutely do.

'I know the rumours about me, you know,' he says. 'And I can confirm that they're just that. Rumours.'

'I heard that you go on a lot of dates with a lot of women – but never the same one twice,' I say, immediately wishing I hadn't. I don't want to seem like I care.

'It's true, I do go on a lot of dates, but that goes with the bachelor territory. People try to set me up with their friends or, I meet someone, and I'm not ready to give up hope just yet that I might find someone who is right for me. So, sure, I'll go on first dates, but I don't get far past them because I haven't met the right girl.'

'You don't have to explain yourself to me,' I tell him.

'Yes, I do,' he replies. 'Do you think I've brought every girl in town out here?'

'Kind of,' I reply, sheepishly.

'I've never done this before,' he tells me, taking me by the hand. 'I really do want to help you fit in here, and I do know how you can do it, and if I like spending time with you – is that so bad?'

I shake my head.

Alfie massages his temples for a second before knocking back his drink.

'I suppose that was my one glass of wine, given that I need to drive us home later,' he says with an awkward laugh. 'I didn't think I'd be getting into this today but, here we go. Trusting people is not something that comes easily to me.'

It's my turn to take Alfie by the hand.

'You owe me no explanation,' I insist. 'Your life is your life.'

'It's OK,' he replies with a smile. 'I didn't have the best childhood. It was just me, my mum and my dad – and they didn't exactly like each other. My dad was preoccupied with the farm, my mum struggled with depression – probably thanks to my dad – and that left me kind of lonely. My dad didn't really approve of me. He wanted me to be a good farmer's lad, to drink real ale and watch sport and be a real manly man. I wasn't like that though, I liked science fiction, video games, comic books. I was a chubby kid who hated sport – both playing and watching. When the football was on, my dad would try and make me watch it with him, even though I'd be much happier reading a book. I wasn't exactly popular at school either. Is there any crime greater – in the eyes of your peers – than being chubby at school? As time went on I got chubbier, shyer, and I became isolated from everyone else. When my mum eventually moved out, things got worse between me and my dad.'

Alfie pauses for a second. He swallows his saliva, hard, as he searches for the right words.

'He started drinking more and more and, er, well, he started hitting me. He said he wanted to toughen me up, that I'd never be able to run the farm, being such a soft lad.'

'That's horrible,' I say, squeezing his hand. 'Did you tell anyone?'

He shakes his head.

'It seems messed up to me now, but I believed him. Running off crying to tell someone felt like a "soft lad" thing to do. So I took it and then I left home the second I could, and I didn't come back until I knew he was gone.'

'I'm so, so sorry you had to go through that,' I tell him.

'It's OK,' he replies. 'It was a long time ago. And then I moved back and suddenly, all the people who didn't want to talk to me before, were interested in me. I didn't trust them and, to be honest, if you can't trust your own dad – your flesh and blood, the person responsible for you being alive . . . well, who can you trust?'

I nod thoughtfully.

'I see a little of myself – well, young me – in Frankie,' Alfie says. 'He seems a little lonely here. When I saw him for the first time, on the farm, it was weird, it was like looking at myself at that age. It scared me for a second, I thought I was imagining things.'

'Well, the good news is that my mum is going to come and stay with us, while I figure out what I'm supposed to do. Neither of us is happy here though, that's for sure.'

Alfie picks up a mini quiche and examines it thoughtfully.

'I'm doing my best to fix that,' he says.

'Thank you,' I reply sincerely.

We sit for a while, chatting, eating and drinking. It's so

beautiful, watching the sun disappear as the little lanterns seem to grow brighter. As it starts to feel a little colder, Alfie takes a second blanket and wraps it around my shoulders.

The conversation takes a cheerier turn – Alfie tells me about his happy childhood memories, and how he too used to spend a lot of time hanging out with Henry. Clara and Henry just seem like such genuine, lovely people, happy to do anything for anyone.

'So when are you expecting your mum?' Alfie asks.

'Viv should be here tomorrow evening,' I tell him. 'We must remember to call her Viv, she doesn't like anyone knowing she's a mum – or worse, a gran – she thinks it hurts her chances with men.'

'Do you think that's true?' he asks. 'That having kids puts men off?'

'Oh, I have eight years of anecdotal evidence that it does,' I laugh. 'Guys don't want the baggage, I guess.'

'I don't know, I'd imagine each situation is different. It's just you and Frankie, and he's a great kid, it's not like you've got a psychotic ex on the scene. Last night, after you left, Charlie pondered why Frankie's dad might not be on the scene and wondered if he might be in prison.' He laughs at how absurd this sounds to him. 'I told her that her imagination runs away with her.'

I feel my face fall. So that's where the rumour came from – Charlie.

'Sorry,' he says. 'I was just trying to say that your situation shouldn't put men off. Frankie is a bonus, if anything.'

'Thank you,' I reply. I have another profiterole to distract myself from the increasingly negative thoughts I'm having about Charlie.

'So you think things will be better once Viv is here?'

'I hope so,' I tell him. 'Even if it's only until I can get on to my bosses about getting someone else to take over.'

'Take over from you?' he asks, sounding surprised.

'If things don't change, I would be crazy to stay here,' I tell him honestly. 'The locals won't have won, they'll just send someone else to run the deli. But at least me and my son will be happy.'

'No one wins if you leave,' Alfie starts. 'Least of all me.'

I turn to face him, cocking my head with curiosity.

Before I have a chance to ask any questions, Alfie places a hand softly on my face and gazes into my eyes. The idea of him being a Lothario pops back into my head. Is this what he does? Gets women out here and tells them stories about ghosts to get their guard down, before hitting them with a double whammy of a romantic picnic and a childhood sob story?

Looking back into his eyes, I don't know. I can see the sadness behind them. I can feel the warmth coming from his hand. If he is manipulating me, it is working because . . .

He leans forward and places his lips on mine softly, hardly moving, just holding position for a few seconds. I can feel his breath, warm against my lips, and it smells like the apple juice he was drinking moments ago. A bad guy wouldn't stick to glasses of apple juice to stay sober enough to drive me home, a bad guy would be getting wasted and trying to trap me here, so we've no choice but to check in to a B&B. Everything about Alfie is screaming Mr Perfect – everything but the rumours. I suppose, there are rumours about me too now, and none of them are true. Perhaps he really is the amazing man he seems to be.

It only takes one movement, one split second of Alfie taking my bottom lip between his, before something inside me comes alive. It's passion, passion I didn't realise I had, and it's all for him. Now we're kissing – really kissing. I lie back on the blanket, pulling Alfie down with me with my lips. It's been so, so long since I had a great kiss, I'd almost forgotten how amazing they can feel.

I wrap my arms around his neck, only for us both to be suddenly brought to our senses by Alfie's phone ringing.

I furrow my brow, as he goes to take the call.

'It's my alarm,' he says. 'We need to set off now if we're going to make it home before the tide comes in.'

We both hurry, to pack everything up, to make sure we don't

leave any rubbish behind. We bundle everything into Alfie's car and then set straight off, hitting the causeway while it's still open, with plenty of time to get home without getting stuck in the middle.

I feel breathless, but it's not from rushing, it's from that kiss. I puff air out of my cheeks.

'Are you OK?' Alfie asks.

'I am, I . . . I just haven't had a kiss like that for a while.'

'I haven't had a kiss quite like that, ever,' he replies with a smile.

The butterflies in my stomach are flapping their wings harder than ever, so much so I can't help but place a hand on my tummy.

'So I, er,' Alfie starts, but as we pull up outside Clara and Henry's, we spot Henry and Frankie outside.

I hurry out of the car.

'Is everything OK?' I ask.

'Fine. It's fine,' Henry says. 'We saw a hedgehog so we brought some food out.'

'He reminds me of Richie,' Frankie says excitedly, not looking up from his new friend to say hello.

'Richie was, erm, the rat that once got trapped in the hall of his old school,' I say, wincing at how awful that sounds.

'Better he makes friends with a hedgehog,' Henry laughs. 'Well, Frankie, run in and get your things so your mum can get you to bed.'

Frankie does as he is told.

'You two have a good night?' Henry asks, his eyebrows rising curiously. There's a little glimmer in his eyes that doesn't go unnoticed by either of us.

'Yeah, great,' Alfie replies. 'We went to find the Hopeful Ghost. The actual ghost, not the pub.'

'Young love,' Henry laughs, just as Frankie reappears.

'Right, well, say thank you to Henry for having you,' I instruct.

'Thank you,' Frankie sings, running over to give him a cuddle. 'Can I come again soon?'

'Sure thing, lad,' Henry replies. 'Goodnight all.'

He waves as he heads back into his house.

'OK, in the car then,' I say.

We all get in Alfie's car and begin the short journey home. Neither I nor Alfie says a word – I don't think either of us knows what to say, not in front of Frankie anyway.

'Well,' I start as we pull up outside. 'Thank you for a lovely evening.'

'You're welcome,' he replies.

I turn around and look at Frankie in the back of the car. He's grinning like a Cheshire cat.

'Out, cheeky chops,' I laugh.

'Lunch tomorrow?' Alfie says as I climb out of his car.

'OK,' I reply, all smiles. 'Goodnight.'

'Sweet dreams, Blossom,' he replies.

Chapter 18

Three . . . two . . . one . . . I've been counting down the seconds to lunchtime and it's finally here. This morning I made sure I was up early so that I could wash my hair, do my make-up and slip into something nice.

'Look at you,' Mike said when I walked into the deli this morning. 'Give us a twirl.'

I obliged and he and his workmates woo'd in appreciation – probably just being polite though.

Today I'm wearing a fitted white shirt – with maybe one less button fastened than I should have – along with a tight black skirt, combined with my red patent-leather heels and a bright red lipstick to match.

'How's it coming along?' I ask Mike, making conversation as I linger by the door, waiting for Alfie to pick me up.

The place finally looks like a real deli now. The counters are all in place, the fridges are installed and the plumbing no longer turns my stomach. As soon as we get some tables and chairs in here all we'll need is food and we're good to open – providing we have some customers, of course.

'Good,' he says. 'We'll be done in a day or so.'

My heart jumps into my mouth.

'So soon?'

'Yeah, well, we were at it for a while before you arrived. It's nearly ready.'

Mike is my ally from the south, I don't want him to leave.

'I'll miss you,' I tell him honestly.

'You'll be fine,' he laughs. 'You've got someone looking out for you.'

Mike nods towards the Range Rover outside the deli. He knows all about our lunch date today – without a girlfriend to talk to, poor Mike has become my confidant.

Alfie steps out wearing a pair of jeans, a muscle-fit white T-shirt and a pair of aviator sunglasses. Damn, he looks cool.

'Don't wait up,' I joke to Mike as I head for the door. 'Really though, I'll be back in an hour or so.'

'OK,' he laughs. 'Have fun. Tell him he's got me to answer to if he messes you around.'

'Hello,' I say brightly as I walk outside.

'Wow, Blossom, look at you,' he says, lowering his sunglasses to get a better look. I love that he's started calling me Blossom. Well, I suppose it's snappier than what everyone else refers to me as – Apple Blossom Girl. I don't like that at all, it makes me sound like a kid.

'What's the plan?' I ask.

'Hop in,' he instructs. 'We'll figure out where to go.'

Just like he said he would, Alfie starts sounding off ideas about where we can eat. All I can think about is kissing him again.

'Do you want to go to the cottage?' I ask, interrupting him.

'Your cottage?' he replies, sounding a little surprised.

'Yeah. Well, I've got loads of food in, and some more bits and pieces from the deli that I'm sure you'd like to try.'

'OK, yeah,' he replies. 'I'd love to.'

'Let's go,' I say excitedly.

It's only a short drive and, by the time I pluck up the courage to say something, we're outside the cottage.

'Last night was great,' I say as we walk up the path.

'It was,' he replies. 'It's a shame it was cut short.'

'It was a shame . . . what do you think would've happened if it hadn't been cut short?'

'I don't know,' he replies. 'I didn't want to stop though.'

As I unlock the cottage door, I can feel my body tensing up with nerves. I can't feel Alfie standing close behind me, but I can sense him. All I can think about is feeling his hands on me again.

'Back in a sec,' I say, hurrying off to the bathroom. I close the door behind me and look at myself in the mirror. What am I doing? Why have I brought him here? More importantly, why does he think I've brought him here? To put the moves on him? God, I want to put the moves on him. What moves though? I don't think I know any moves any more.

'Just be cool,' I whisper to myself, quiet enough so that Alfie can't hear, but loud enough to hopefully make me pay attention. 'Now get back out there.'

With my pep talk having zero effect, I find Alfie in the kitchen and lean on the worktop next to him.

'What do you fancy?' I ask. 'We've got a bunch of stuff for sandwiches – the company I work for keep sending me new samples . . .'

The air feels thick with sexual tension, which makes it hard to breathe. I bite my lip in an attempt to disguise my shallow breathing.

'I fancy you,' he says.

'For lunch?' I joke awkwardly. Ah, me and my jokes. It's no wonder I'm single.

Alfie takes a step closer to me slowly. Then another one. My breathing quickens as I hang in suspense. It's like we're playing chicken, trying to decide who makes the second move first.

Deciding to just go for it and see what happens, I reach forward and pull him close to me, and that's all it takes for us to resume our passionate kissing from last night only this time, it's kicked up a gear.

Alfie grabs me by the hips and sits me down on the kitchen worktop – the worktop that I'm so glad I took the time to clean last night. I'd been thinking about inviting Alfie for lunch, so I did it just in case. God knows what I'd be sitting on right now if I hadn't.

I am very conscious of the fact that, other than a couple of awkward encounters over the years that never went anywhere, the only person I have ever had regular sex with is my ex – Frankie's dad – and that was nine years ago. Sex hasn't changed, right? People are still doing the same stuff . . . I see it in the movies and, other than the things you see in *Fifty Shades*, it doesn't seem like it's changed much. It occurs to me to grab a spatula from the drying rack next to the sink, just in case he's that way inclined. I giggle to myself through our kisses.

Probably best I just pretend I know what I'm doing and see what happens.

I wrap my arms around his neck and my legs around his waist as we continue to kiss. This is so unlike me, being ravished by a sexy farmer on my kitchen worktop – mostly, I suppose, because I've never met a sexy farmer or had clean worktops. This just feels right though – so right.

A loud knock on the window behind me destroys our passion once again. I'm too frustrated to even think about who it might be.

'There's a man in your garden,' Alfie says breathlessly. My mind darts back to my Daniel Craig dream – but only for a second. Now I'm mostly just mortified someone was watching me, erm, in a . . . romantic clinch – that's what we'll call it.

I glance over my shoulder to see who is lurking in the back garden, for whatever strange reason. It's probably not Daniel Craig, is it? It's a miracle I've got one man interested, there's not about to be another one.

'Oh God,' I say softly, staring at the man on the other side of the glass.

'Lily, are you OK?' Alfie asks me. 'You look like you've seen a ghost. Who is that?'

I swallow hard.

'It's . . . it's Frankie's dad.'

Chapter 19

Nathan was my childhood sweetheart. We met the week we started secondary school and became almost immediately inseparable. Before I met Nathan, I was a good, simple girl. I loved pop music, trashy movies and make-up; I just wanted to grow up and marry a member of a boy band and live a happy life. Nathan wasn't like the kind of guy you'd find in a boy band though. He didn't care about being cool or dressing like the other kids, he cared about the environment and whether my lip gloss had been tested on animals. He made me care about things that your average teenage girl didn't care about, and I felt like it made me a better person. I adapted to his vegan lifestyle, which, if truth be told, I probably wasn't very good at. My mum didn't understand it, so I was responsible for my own food consumption, and without all the trash your average teenager eats, I quickly lost weight.

'You look like a starved and abused animal from an RSPCA poster,' I remember my mum telling me one day, when I came home with a patch of my long hair shaved off at one side.

Nathan's middle-class parents didn't approve of his rebellion either, so when he was 16 he finished school, got a job and started renting a flat. Sixteen-year-old me though she was so cool, with her boyfriend who had his own home. Most 16-year-olds spent their time sneaking around, trying to grab private moments with their boyfriend, but not me. We would hang out on an evening, like an old married couple, watching documentaries and cooking healthy vegan meals (he did most of the hard work, if I'm being completely honest, but he let me help). It was just the two of us against the world, until I finished my A levels. I got a place at Middlesex University – my mum was so proud of me, she said I'd be the first person in our family to go to uni – but Nathan didn't want me to go. We'd never really talked about what the plan was, but I thought I was going to go to uni and hopefully start some kind of career after, and he thought I was going to move in, get a job and start contributing towards the bills. We fought about it for days before eventually breaking up. I tried my best to think of a compromise – I was only going to be living in student accommodation a couple of hours away, and the plan was to come home at weekends – but Nathan wasn't interested in any of them.

By the time I was halfway through my second year, I'd changed – a lot. While my hippy style remained (it just felt like a big part of my personality) I found myself with less free time for all the causes Nathan and I would spend our days fighting for. I also found myself dropping my vegan diet which was down to a combination of opting for quick and easy foods, and trying to put a little weight on because I was self-conscious of how skinny I was. It worked though, and soon enough I was just your average student, living in a flat that I shared with my friend/course mate Jasmine. Until one night that changed everything.

'I really don't think that's the answer to your problems,' my friend Jasmine said, looking at my laptop over my shoulder as she leaned forward to grab another slice of pizza. A piece of pepperoni fell off, landing on the living room floor; my friend simply shrugged.

'Online dating or eating chocolate?' I asked.

'Both.'

'I'm just seeing who's out there,' I replied. I took a break from staring at my laptop screen to grab a handful of chocolate buttons. As I attempted to remove a few, I struggled to free my hand from the bag. I sighed.

'Are the bags getting smaller or are my hands getting bigger?' I ask my friend.

'It might be a bit of both,' she laughed. 'And you'll have an even harder time bagging a date with fat hands.'

Having been single since Nathan and I broke up, I began browsing dating websites that evening, and this was before they were an everyday thing like they are today.

'I'm just looking because I'm bored,' I admitted, shutting my laptop before placing it on the beanbag next to the sofa.

'You should take my advice,' she replied.

'And why is that?'

'Because I have a date tomorrow and you don't,' she reminded me.

'Is this the same guy as last week, or a new one?'

'A new one,' she replied casually. 'Haven't heard from that guy from last week since I slept with him. I've sent him a few texts and he hasn't replied so, that's it, I'm not gonna text him any more.'

'Oh, wow, that'll show him,' I teased. 'You want to try withholding sex instead of text messages.'

Jasmine grabbed a cushion from the sofa and launched it at me. 'Hilarious.'

I remember walking over to the freezer to check for ice cream, but we didn't have any. We had plastic ice cubes, microwave meals that no one wanted to eat and a bag of peas that had been defrosted more times than I've probably ever eaten peas, because we only used it for icing injuries – I'm sure, by now, you appreciate just how often I experience those.

'Ergh, we ate all the ice cream,' I moaned.

'You're only eating because you're bored anyway,' Jas said,

pouring the remaining chocolate buttons into her mouth as she hit play on another episode of *Scrubs*.

'I'm bulking for the winter.'

'We're nearly into February,' she reminded me. 'You should be working on your summer body.'

'Yeah, that's why I was looking for ice cream,' I replied, stretching out my arm to grab my laptop again.

There were two tatty old sofas, so naturally we'd always take one each. Jasmine lay back before lifting up her T-shirt and patting her belly, which was bloated from all the carbs we'd consumed that evening.

'Ahh, if only the men of London could see us now,' she joked.

My phone buzzed with a text message – something it didn't often do, which made me eyeball my phone suspiciously.

'Someone loves you,' Jasmine said. She would say this every time anyone got a text.

I picked up my phone and I couldn't believe my eyes. It was a message from Nathan – after over a year of no contact. He was just texting to see how I was doing, but we ended up swapping messages back and forth for a couple of hours before chatting on the phone until 5 a.m.! It was weird, like we'd never been apart, and it made me realise just how much I missed him. A couple of months later, when I went home for Easter, we ended up meeting up and then one thing led to another – and by 'one thing led to another' I don't mean that we had sex that night. Well, we did, but what I actually mean is we realised we still wanted to be together and the only way that seemed possible was for me to drop out of uni after my second year and move back home to be with him.

I know what you're thinking, and you're right, that was an insanely stupid thing to do for a boy, but I thought I was in love, and I was so much happier with him around. It wasn't that I wasn't enjoying uni, because I loved student life, but I knew that was only ever going to be a temporary arrangement and my relationship with Nathan was for the rest of my life – or so I thought.

Jas thought I was stupid, quitting for a boy (I told myself she just didn't know – or love – him like I did), and while I'd guess my mum thought the same, she told me that she'd always support me, so long as I was sure of what I was doing.

Of course, I was terrified that he'd hate me if he knew I was a dairy-consuming, meat-loving 'murderer' now, so I never owned up to that fact, snapping back to vegan life for the man I loved. Sure, cheese seemed like an insignificant thing to give up when you compared it to something like *my education*, but I thought I was in love.

So I moved in with him, I got a job, and we started saving up for our future together, which we decided we'd spend travelling the world, helping people in need. All we needed was enough money to get our tickets and to live on until we got settled, and we'd be good to go. This happened much quicker than we expected and, by the time I was 22, I was getting ready to travel the world with the love of my life. Just eight weeks before we were due to leave, I found out I was pregnant.

'What do I do?' I ask Alfie, my legs still locked around his waist. I'm not sure why I'm asking him, it's not like he has the backstory needed to offer any kind of advice.

'Talk to him,' he suggests.

There's a knock on the front door.

Still in shock, I hop down from the worktop and answer it.

'Surprise,' my mum says, holding out her arms for a hug, a bunch of flowers in one hand and a bottle of Prosecco in the other.

'Viv, you're early,' I say, grabbing her and giving her a hug.

'And your blouse is all the way open,' she says with a laugh, nodding towards my bra. I guess Alfie must've undone it while we were kissing – God, he's good.

I quickly wrap it closed, holding it with my arms.

'I thought it might be a nice surprise if I got here early,' she says. 'I didn't think you'd be busy, I . . .' My mum breaks eye contact as her voice trails off.

'Well, hello,' she says, as I realise Alfie is standing next to me in the doorway. I see that glimmer in her eyes, the one she gets when she sees a handsome young man. My mum is such a cougar.

'Hello,' he says politely. My mum passes me the flowers and the Prosecco, which I struggle to hold on top of pulling my shirt closed. She offers Alfie a hand to shake, but as his hand touches hers, she pulls him close for a hug.

'Mum, Nathan is here,' I whisper weakly. Seconds later, he appears. I notice my mum's expression change as she suddenly realises.

'We thought we'd surprise you,' she says.

'Well, you did that,' I say, annoyed.

'Hey, Lil,' Nathan says, finally breaking his silence. I ignore him.

'This is a terrible surprise, Mum,' I tell her. 'He has no right to be here.'

My mum, embarrassed, changes the subject. 'So, is this your neighbour?' she asks.

'Er, yeah,' Alfie replies awkwardly, running a hand through his hair.

'I have every right to be here,' Nathan insists. 'I'm here for my son.'

I laugh wildly.

'Are you joking?' I reply. 'Would you even know him if you saw him?'

'Viv showed me photos. He looks just like me.'

'He looks *nothing* like you,' I insist. 'You have no right to just turn up and think you can be his dad – he has no idea who you are.'

'Oh, because you're such a great mum?' he replies. 'Banging the neighbours on your lunch break.'

I feel the rage bubble up inside me.

'I should go,' Alfie says.

'Tell you what,' my mum starts, taking Alfie by the arm. 'Why don't you give me directions to the school, and maybe a nice local café, I can get a cup of tea in me while I wait for Frankie to finish. We can leave these two to talk.'

'I'll give you a lift,' Alfie suggests.

'I have nothing to say to him,' I insist, annoyed that he's turned up like this and driven Alfie away.

'Just hear him out, darling,' my mum suggests.

I sigh. 'Alfie, I'll call you later, OK?'

He gives me a half smile. 'See you, Blossom.'

'Blossom,' Nathan sniggers once they're gone.

'I suppose you should come in,' I say reluctantly.

Chapter 20

I step aside to let Nathan in. I wait for him to walk past me before placing down the gifts from my mum and finally – and hurriedly – buttoning up my shirt.

It's so strange seeing him after nearly a decade. In my head he hadn't aged a day and yet here he is now, not only looking older than I expected but older than his years. Travelling has aged him but otherwise, he doesn't look all that different. He's still dressing the same (in fact, he absolutely had that T-shirt when we were together) but his hair is much longer now. The last time I saw him he had just decided that he wanted to grow his brown hair into a ponytail – which he has, a long one, so at least he's stuck to that.

'You look good,' he says. 'And surprised to see me.'

'I am,' I eventually reply.

'Didn't you and Frank get my postcards?'

Oh, I got his postcards all right, but I never showed them to Frankie. Well, when you receive a 'happy birthday' postcard from Nepal two months after your son's sixth birthday, from the dad he didn't know he had, what are you supposed to do? And then, of course, there was the postcard he sent me just before I accepted the job here, saying that he was coming home to see his 'family'. I'd be lying if I said that this job didn't appeal partially because it meant I could get away from him. I thought we'd be hidden away from him up here. I didn't count on him going to my mum, or her bringing him here! It's not that I don't want Frankie to have a dad, but Nathan made his decision a long time ago. He can't just show up and pick up where he left off, nine years later.

'I destroyed them,' I lie.

'So, what, my son doesn't know I exist?'

I can't believe he's annoyed at me.

'No,' I reply firmly. 'Par for the course when you abandoned his mum the second you found out she was pregnant.'

Nathan rolls his eyes.

'Lil, we had plans, people were expecting us. We had jobs lined up—'

'I had your son growing inside me,' I interrupt him.

'I wasn't ready to be a dad, I hold my hands up,' he admits. 'I wanted to travel, to make a difference in the world – you did too. You might have been prepared to give it up, but I wasn't. Not after we worked so hard for it. We could've had more kids eventually.'

'Frankie is the best thing that ever happened to me, he is amazing,' I tell him, sick at the thought of a life without him. 'And talking about giving things up . . . I gave up everything for you. I dropped out of uni for you.'

'Lil, you've got to let the past go,' he insists. 'You're obviously doing OK, despite not finishing university, so why not just let it go, hmm?'

'I'm doing OK because my wonderful employers gave me the time and the resources to finish my degree,' I tell him. Eric and Amanda not only gave me a job, but they helped me to finish my degree while I was working for them, and then they promoted me so I could put my new qualification to good use in their head office. Without their kindness, I don't know where or what I'd be. YumYum really is such an amazing company, from taking care of their employees to doing their bit for the environment to donating chunks of their profits to charitable causes. They've always appealed to the hippy that still lurks deep down inside me somewhere.

'Lil, I'm here now. We can be a family now – it sounds like you need me.'

'I definitely do not need you. They need you somewhere building wells – we don't need you here.'

'You can't even button up your shirt,' he laughs. 'I'm supposed to trust you with my son?'

I think he's kidding – my God, I hope he's kidding.

'I'm not actually needed anywhere right now,' he says. 'Work dried up and I had a few accommodation problems in Port Douglas, so I worked a few temp jobs to get enough money together for a plane ticket home – and I bought a rad VW campervan to drive around in, and, y'know, live in until I figured out what the new plan was. I wanted to come here with Viv but I didn't have anywhere to leave the van, so we convoyed all the way here. It was fun.'

'Wait, Port Douglas? The postcard you sent me was from Ghana . . . Isn't Port Douglas in Australia?'

'Well, yeah,' he says, scratching at his unwashed-looking hair. 'I'd been in Australia for a little while. I was working on a farm but there was a . . . misunderstanding with the farmer's wife.'

'There weren't any other women in Australia?'

'Not there,' he says truthfully.

I pull a disgusted face.

'After that I headed to Noosa Heads, but couldn't find any permanent work. One night I had to sleep on the beach – it was beautiful though. Sunshine Beach is something else, I'd love to take you and Frank on holiday one day.'

From where I'm sitting next to him on the sofa, I only need to lean over a little to sniff the air around him.

'Are you high?' I ask.

'Not right now . . .'

'We're not going on holiday with you. And stop calling him Frank – his name is Frank*ie*.'

'Isn't that a girl's name?'

I sigh, and for a moment we just sit in silence.

'I just want to be a part of my son's life,' he says softly. 'I'm not trying to make you angry, I'm just upset you never gave him my postcards.'

'Because I wanted him to grow up feeling loved, and me giving a 5-year-old a pile of postcards from the dad who abandoned him, saying what an awesome time he was having on his never-ending holiday, would've made him feel unwanted and unloved – and what's to say you'll stick around now?'

'Please, Lil, just give me a chance? I've changed. Sure, I was the live-to-travel-type before, but I want to settle down, and this seems like a great place to do so.'

I rub my temples as I think for a moment. I have no idea what I'm supposed to do. All I wanted was for Frankie to have a relationship with his dad, before he waltzed off travelling. Now I'm worried it will do more harm than good, but who am I to stop him meeting his dad? And anyway, if I say no, he could just take legal action to see him, and that would be so much worse. Better we do it now, on my terms.

'OK,' I eventually say. 'You can meet him.'

'You won't regret this, Lil,' he says, grabbing me hard, pulling me close for a hug.

It's crazy to me right now, to think that I was ever attracted to this man. He looks grubby and he smells like damp – although I suppose that could just be circumstantial. It's so strange how someone I felt so much for – someone I was willing to give up on my education to be with – I suddenly view so differently. I used to think he was the sexiest, smartest man I had ever met. I was forever dragging him to the bedroom. The only place I want to drag him now is the hell out of here or, failing that, to the bathroom for a good scrub. Did he always look this unclean?

Did *I*? It's funny, thinking of who I was back then, because that girl doesn't even feel like me. I remember when I was at high school, I had these short, fine, barely visible blonde hairs on my legs and all I wanted to do was to shave them off. Thinking back, I don't suppose they were at all unsightly, I think I just wanted to feel like a grown-up. Skip forwards a few years to when I decided I was a strong, independent feminist, so sure of her own mind, and the only person who had the right to judge her own body, I did a complete U-turn, refusing to shave my legs 'for a patriarchal society'. My mum, who had been so adamant that I didn't shave my legs when I was younger, was suddenly buying razors and waxing strips for me, to try and encourage me to fit in, but I wouldn't have it. It's funny because, these days, I take an almost excessive pride in my appearance. I'm just like any girly-girl who loves to get her nails and her hair done. That said, I've been known to skip a shave or two in the winter months – well, it's not like anyone is going to see, is it? Plus, it acts as an extra layer of insulation.

'Can you make yourself scarce for a bit?' I ask. 'I need to talk to Frankie when he gets in, to explain everything to him carefully, before you just jump out and ask him if he wants to play Nintendo.'

'Oh, I'd never play video games with him,' he insists firmly. 'They're terrible for children. It cuts into their exercise time, encourages idleness – not to mention the fact that it makes them more aggressive. And then what have we got? A bunch of fat, violent kids.'

'Dad of the year,' I say sarcastically.

'Sorry,' he laughs. 'I'm just nervous.'

I notice a softer side to Nathan lurking under the surface. Perhaps he really does just want to make things right.

'Dinner this evening then?' I suggest.

'OK,' he replies, clapping his hands excitedly. 'I'll go wait in the van.'

I don't really know where else to tell him to go – I can't imagine the locals embracing him, especially if he drops into conversation that he knows me. Anyway, he did say that it was a campervan, I'm sure he'll be fine for a few hours.

I see him to the door and watch as he climbs into the back of the tired, old van. It's bright orange (or at least it was bright orange, once upon a time) with a white roof. Parked alongside my green Beetle, they bring out the worst in each other visually. It looks like I'm holding some kind of ugly German car convention.

With Nathan out of the way I search for my phone and call Alfie. It rings and rings but he doesn't answer – you can't really blame him, can you?

Don't ever make the mistake of thinking that things can't get any worse, because that's exactly when life proves you wrong. I've always been one for thinking that it's always darkest before the dawn, that the only way is up, that things can only get better . . . but the truth is, things can and do get worse sometimes. I'm never going to be younger than I am right now. Every day I find myself with more responsibilities, more obstacles to overcome. But now that I've acknowledged that things can – and do – get more difficult, I can concentrate on making things better, rather than hoping they will.

The first thing I need to do is introduce Frankie to the dad he never knew he had . . . but God knows how I'll do that.

Chapter 21

With my mum by my side, I sit Frankie down on the sofa and try to explain to him that he does have a dad and that he's here if he wants to meet him.

Frankie just stares at me for a moment. I can practically see the cogs in his brain turning.

'Would you like to meet him?' I ask.

Frankie continues to think it over. I look over at Viv for support.

'Your dad is a very important person,' she tells him. 'He's being doing work all around the world, I'm sure he'll have a lot of stories to tell you.'

'OK,' Frankie says. He looks terrified, the poor little thing.

'How about, I finish cooking dinner and you, your mum and your dad sit down at the table and just have a chat, see what happens.'

'OK,' he says again. It's hard to read him, to figure out if he doesn't want to meet Nathan or if he does, but he's just nervous.

'You sure, kiddo?' I say, squeezing his hand.

He nods.

I lead him over to the table and sit him down before heading outside to get Nathan. I feel my heart sink as I watch a cloud of smoke escape from the window of the campervan.

'Nathan,' I call out. He pokes a head out of the window curiously, a small rolled-up cigarette hanging from his mouth as he looks to see who might be calling his name.

I widen my eyes at him, which causes him to quickly stick his head back in, closing the window behind him. In a few seconds he's out of the van, hurrying over to the front door.

'You didn't think a change of clothes might be nice?' I say.

'None with me,' he says. 'If you fancied washing me some maybe?'

He makes a move for the front door, but I stop him.

'Nathan, listen to me. Frankie is the most important thing in the world to me. If you hurt him . . .'

'You'll what, kill me?' he laughs.

'I'm serious,' I insist. 'You're getting a second chance that you absolutely don't deserve.'

'Take a chill pill, Lil,' he says. I'm not a violent person, but I could change my mind for Nathan.

'OK,' I say softly. I want to believe that this is the right thing to do, but for some reason it feels like I'm jumping out of a plane without a parachute, just hoping and praying I find a soft landing.

Frankie looks dumbstruck as Nathan walks over to him.

'Oh wow, look at you,' Nathan says. 'My little boy, all grown up. The man of the house.'

I don't point out that he never actually saw Frankie when he was a baby, or that he's only the man of the house because Nathan left.

'Should I hug him?' he asks me.

'Maybe just give him some space,' I suggest quietly, seeing how nervous and confused Frankie looks. 'You're basically a stranger.'

We both take a seat at the table. Frankie is sat at the end and Nathan and I are either side of him, facing each other.

'I'm sure you have a lot of questions for me,' Nathan says.

'Were you in prison?' Frankie asks him. I exhale deeply. I can't believe those are his first words to his dad.

'No, of course not,' he says before turning to me. 'Although there was a little incident with a bag of W-E-E-D when I was in the States that saw me locked up for a night.'

I think that was supposed to impress me.

'Nathan, he's 8 years old. He can spell,' I point out.

'Oh, right, sorry.'

'Didn't you want to be my dad?' Frankie asks him.

Just hearing him say these words hurts me, so I can't even begin to imagine how he must be feeling and, as for Nathan, that must sting.

I watch as Nathan struggles to find a worthy explanation when, the truth is, that he didn't want to be a parent, he wanted to go off travelling and have fun with zero responsibility, so he left me alone and pregnant to figure things out for myself.

'Your dad didn't want to leave you,' I lie. 'He had important work to do abroad, that no one else could do.'

At this stage, I feel like I'm practically being sarcastic. I hate lying to my son, but if it spares his feelings, then it's worth it. Nathan meaningfully nods along with my tale.

'And, the truth is, we didn't know if he'd ever be able to make it back, he was so far away. And he knew that I could look after you all on my own, so he went off to look after kids who didn't have a mummy or a daddy, to make sure they had water and an education.'

Frankie nods. He's such a sweet kid, of course he's trying to understand.

'Dinner is nearly ready,' Viv calls.

'Your dad just wants the chance to get to know you, if you'd like that,' I tell him.

'OK,' Frankie replies.

'OK?' Nathan says. 'Awesome. Come here.'

He leans over and gives Frankie's shoulder a squeeze.

'Well, we can all hang out and just see what happens,' I say.

'This is great,' Nathan says. 'So great. Totally rad.'

I try to remember if 'rad' was in his vocabulary when we were together. I really hope not.

Viv places a large bowl of mashed potatoes and a jug of gravy down on the table before heading back towards the kitchen area. She comes back with a plate of sausages and places them down before taking a seat opposite Frankie.

'Bangers and mash,' she says enthusiastically. 'I'll bet it's been a while since you've had my bangers and mash, ey, Frankie?'

'Whoa, Viv, what are you doing?' Nathan says, horrified.

Viv gives him a puzzled look.

'Meat?'

'Oh, sorry, darling, are you still doing that? I suppose I just assumed you'd grown out of it like Lily did when she was at uni.'

'You gave up being a vegan at university?' he shrieks in my direction. 'Lil, what happened to you? Wait – we were together after that. You never said anything. Oh, so, I'm not the only one who makes mistakes then.'

I roll my eyes. If Frankie weren't here, I'd point out to my darling ex that giving up not eating meat and giving up a child are hardly comparable.

'So Frank eats meat and dairy too?'

'Who?' I ask him.

'Frank,' he replies, before he realises what I'm getting at. '*Frankie*. You eat meat and dairy?'

'Yeah . . . is that bad?' he asks Nathan.

'Only if you're down with the torture and slaughter of helpless animals,' he replies.

'OK, enough,' I interrupt.

'You're in luck,' Viv says. 'I made too many potatoes, so there are a few boiled ones left over.'

She hurries over to the kitchen and grabs them, before setting them down in front of Nathan. Just a plate of boiled potatoes.

'Gravy?' she asks.

'Is there meat in it?' he replies.

'There's Bisto in it,' she laughs.

'Yeah, there's meat in it,' I tell him as I serve Frankie his dinner, before loading up my own plate too.

'What do you eat?' Frankie asks him seriously.

'I enjoy a nutritious diet, rich in whole foods,' he tells him, as though that's going to mean anything to him. 'Fruit, veg, whole grains, nuts and seeds.'

'That sounds rubbish,' Frankie says honestly.

'Well, sausages might taste nice, Frank, but pigs have feelings too, y'know. They want to be happy, living in beautiful places, not raised on crowded factory farms, only to be murdered so you can eat them.'

Frankie's eyes widen with horror.

'Nathan, he's 8 years old,' I insist. 'Stop preaching, just eat your potatoes and be self-righteous and hungry.'

Frankie pushes his food around his plate.

'It's OK, kiddo, don't let him put you off.'

'Can I make you an omelette, Nathan?' Viv suggests. 'No cheese.'

'Viv, omelettes are eggs,' he points out.

'But, hens lay eggs anyway? I don't understand.'

'Let's not get into it now, hmm?' I say.

The number of foods my son is interested in eating is too few as it is. He can't afford to be put off the few things he does enjoy or he'll starve.

'So are you staying locally?' I ask Nathan. 'There are so many B&Bs here.'

'I, er, wondered if I could stay here,' he says hopefully, popping an entire potato into his mouth.

'Here?' I reply, shocked. 'There's no room here, sorry.'

I mean, there really isn't any room here, but even if there were, there's no way I'm going to let him just move in. He feels like a stranger.

'Oh . . . it's just, I don't really have any money at the moment. It was hard enough scraping together enough to get home.'

I feel my brow furrow, because I see what's going on here. The only reason he's come back is because he has finally run out of money and options, and to pretend that it's because he wants to finally connect with his son is despicable.

'You can sleep in your van, right?' I say.

'Erm . . .'

'It's a campervan, right? They're made for living in. You can use the bathroom here.' *Please!* 'But you'll be fine on the drive, won't you?'

If Nathan really does want to be here, he'll be happy to sleep outside, just to be close to his son.

'Yeah, OK,' he says, although he doesn't seem happy with my suggestion. 'Just you watch, Frankie, I'm gonna turn everything around. I'm gonna get a job, I'm gonna show you what a great dad I am – your mum will be begging me to move back in.'

I stab an entire sausage with my fork and raise it to my mouth.

'Don't count on it,' I say, before taking a meaningful bite.

Chapter 22

I am doing something tonight that I haven't done in a long, long time – I am sharing a bed with my mother.

'This is fun,' Viv says. 'Just like old times.'

My nightie-clad mum climbs into the double bed next to me because, it turns out, after promising my mum she could have the bed, I am just that little bit too long to sleep on the sofa. My mum insisted I share with her, that I used to do it all the time when I was younger. Between my ex sleeping in my driveway and my mum sleeping in my bed, I'm not sure I could do more to put Alfie off if I tried – not that I've heard from him.

'It's not awkward at all,' she insists.

'Actually, there is one elephant in the room,' I start. 'Why on earth did you bring Nathan here? Without telling me?'

'I thought it might be a nice surprise,' she says brightly.

'You didn't though, did you? You know I hate surprises.'

My mum's smile drops.

'I guess I just thought that . . . raising a child is hard work as it is, and here you are, struggling, trying to do everything alone. And I'm not saying that you're not doing a great job with Frankie, because you are, but if I have one regret, it's that you never had a dad in your life. So when Nathan showed up at my door, asking for you, it seemed like fate – so I brought him with me.'

'I understand why you did what you did,' I assure her. 'But I'm not sure it was the right thing to do. It sounds to me like he ran out of money and had nowhere to go, so he thought he'd come here and sponge off us.'

'That may be the case,' Viv replies. 'But now that he's met Frankie, how could he not be head over heels in love with him? Even if his intentions were wrong, he might make things right now. Can you imagine, if he steps up, and makes a life for himself here?'

'I can,' I say.

I try and imagine a life where Frankie and I live here, happily, with Nathan just down the road somewhere, always around, always in our business. Suddenly thinking he's a part of our lives and that he can tell me how to raise my son – and all the while scaring off any man who even looks at me.

Having Nathan around really is the last thing I want but I have to put my son first. And maybe my mum is right, maybe this will be just what he needs to step up and be a real dad.

'So, how's the deli going?' my mum asks. 'Ha, look at us, we're like an old married couple, tucked up in bed early, asking each other how our days have been.'

'Early? Viv, it's 10.30 p.m.'

'On a Tuesday,' she points out. 'I have singles salsa on a Tuesday.'

How could I forget that my mum goes to singles salsa? 'Psychological repression' is what they call it, I think.

'The deli isn't going all that well. It's pretty much ready, from a construction point of view, and it's looking amazing. But we're still waiting on the liquor licence – I think the locals kicked up a fuss there, as a means to stop us from opening. And I still need to name the damn thing, not that there's going to be much point if it doesn't open.'

'Do you have any ideas?'

'Run away, change my identity and start my life again,' I suggest. My mum laughs. 'I meant for the name.'

'Oh. No, nothing yet. I wanted something that would honour the town, maybe, not that they'd appreciate it.'

My mum thinks for a moment.

'What about Deli-cious?' she suggests. 'Like delicious, but with emphasis on the deli part.'

'I like the pun, but I don't know if the locals will. Then again, they have a jam shop called Fruitopia.'

My mum snorts.

'That's fantastic,' she says. 'I'll have to visit tomorrow, pick some up for breakfast. Do vegans eat jam?'

'Vegans are no trouble – Nathan is a nightmare. I remember everything he ate would be preceded by a ten-question form, ensuring it was vegan friendly, Fairtrade and whether or not the person who grew the apple was in a good mood when he picked it.'

She laughs.

'I really did think I was doing the right thing, bringing him here. I thought a male influence would do Frankie good. I didn't realise you and Alfie were so close.'

'*Were* being the operative word in that sentence. I haven't heard from him since earlier.'

'I went for a cup of tea with him,' my mum says. She bites her lip theatrically.

'Oh, God, Mum, please don't.'

'I'm teasing, relax,' she laughs. 'It's not that he's too young for me, but you did see him first. We don't want another David Dixon on our hands, do we?'

Oh God, I'm never going to live that one down. David Dixon is one of the few people I dated after Frankie was born and, for once, I actually felt like our first date went well. For our second, however, he offered to cook me dinner at his house. My mum and Frankie dropped me off, only for her car to break down outside. When she texted me to tell me that's why they were still parked outside, I read her message out loud and David insisted I invited them in for some dinner. I was taken aback – not only was he on board with me having a kid, but he wanted to cook him and my mum dinner on our second date. I should have known he was too good to be true then. David spent the entire night flirting with my mum, right in front of my face. For me, that was enough to put me off the guy, but – and you're not going to believe this – he has kept in touch with my mum. I was the one he dated briefly, and yet he kept in touch with her. They still exchange birthday and Christmas presents, which I find entirely weird. My mum assures me nothing romantic happened between them – I don't care if it did, I just don't want to think about it.

'Alfie was supposed to be helping me with the deli, well, changing public opinion of the deli, but I don't suppose he'll want to be around me now, not after what happened today.'

'He seems like a lovely person, don't write him off just yet.'

I smile. We'll see.

'Well, I spoke to my bosses earlier and they said that, in the short term, there's not much I can do, not until they figure the licence issue out, so I've got some free time to spend with you and Frankie.'

'Oh, lovely,' she replies. 'You can show us the sights. Nathan too, I suppose.'

'Yay,' I say sarcastically. 'Like one big, happy family.'

Chapter 23

'There's someone at the door,' I say brightly as I lift a pancake out of the pan and place it on Frankie's plate. Pancakes, strawberries and maple syrup – one of his absolute favourite breakfasts, because he's having a rough time at the moment and Frosties just won't cut it today.

With Frankie sitting at the table, concentrating on one of his drawings, I take the pan off the heat and go to answer it myself.

'It's Nathan,' I say, opening the door. 'In his underpants.'

'Morning,' he says, inviting himself in. 'Am I too late for breakfast?'

'This isn't a hotel,' I point out. 'We're having pancakes so just help yourself to whatever you fancy.'

'Rad,' he replies, hurrying over to the fridge. I didn't realise just how skinny he was yesterday, but seeing him now, I can't help but notice.

There's another knock at the door.

'I'll get it,' I say, as my son eats his breakfast, my ex rifles through the fridge and my mum hogs the bathroom.

'Lil, we need to talk about this fridge,' Nathan calls after me, his head practically inside it. 'It's almost all meat or dairy.'

'I work for a deli,' I remind him. 'They keep sending me things to try.'

'It's not good for our boy,' he shouts.

I can't help but roll my eyes as I open the front door.

'Oh, hello,' I say, greeting a deliveryman.

'Good morning,' he replies. 'I've got a delivery of cheese for Miss Holmes.'

I clap my hands and jog on the spot excitedly for a second.

'Music to my ears,' I reply.

'Whoa, no, absolutely not,' Nathan says, hurrying over.

The deliveryman looks taken aback by the angry, underpants-wearing vegan marching towards him.

'There is absolutely too much cheese in this house already,' he insists.

'Please ignore him,' I say brightly, signing for my cheese. 'Nathan, they're samples. It's my job.'

'When did you sell your soul?' he asks me.

'Probably around the time I became a single mum,' I reply.

I don't have to go into work today, mostly because there's nothing I can actually do at the moment except go through some of the samples Eric has sent me – a day eating food and getting paid for it, how awful.

'Mum, I need the toilet,' Frankie says.

'I'll go hurry Viv,' I reply.

As I head for the bathroom there's another knock at the door.

'It's like a madhouse here today,' I say.

'I'll get it,' Nathan insists. 'If it's more cheese, I'm telling them to take it away.'

'Don't you dare,' I call back as I knock on the bathroom door. 'Hey, Viv, are you going to be long? There's a queue out here.'

'Nearly done,' she calls back.

I dash into my bedroom to grab my phone before heading back into the living room. I glance over at the front door, expecting to see Nathan refusing dairy products. Instead I find him standing face to face with Alfie.

'It's barbaric,' Nathan tells him.

How long was I out of the room?!

'I grew up on a dairy farm,' Alfie starts, but Nathan doesn't let him finish.

'There we go, dude, you're part of the problem,' he insists.

Alfie just rolls his eyes.

'I'm not arguing with a man in his pants,' Alfie says. 'I'm just here to see Lily.'

'Hey,' I say, rushing over. 'How's it going?'

'Yeah, not bad. Everything OK here?' he replies.

'Hmm,' I say with an awkward laugh.

'I wondered if we could talk,' Alfie says.

'Erm, yeah, sure. Let me ask my mum if she'll drop Frankie at school – we can talk now.'

'There's no rush,' he insists.

'No, no. It's fine.'

'*I'll* take him to school,' Nathan says.

'You don't know where it is,' I point out.

'Frankie can tell me.'

'He's 8 and he's only been going there for a week. I don't know if you've noticed, but everything looks the same outside – green.'

Nathan frowns at me.

'You don't trust me?'

'No?' I laugh.

'We can take him together,' Viv says diplomatically, appearing behind us. 'Bathroom is empty, Frankie. Go get ready.'

It suddenly occurs to me that Frankie has just been sat silently witnessing all this as he ate his breakfast.

'OK,' he replies, hopping down from his dining chair.

I hurry over to him.

'Love you, kiddo,' I tell him. 'Sorry things are a bit weird at the moment.'

He gives me a half smile.

'Love you,' he replies quietly.

'Can I get you a drink?' I ask Alfie.

'A gigantic glass of milk,' Nathan suggests.

I shoot him a filthy look.

'You should probably go put some clothes on,' I tell him. 'You turn up at school like that, they'll put you on a list.'

He glances down at his nearly naked body.

'Yeah, OK,' he replies.

'We'll meet you outside,' Viv suggests.

'OK,' he says again. 'You two, remember, we eat in that kitchen.'

'We?' I laugh. 'You haven't even been here twenty-four hours – or eaten for that matter.'

Nathan goes outside, much to Alfie's confusion.

As soon as Frankie is done in the bathroom, he grabs his lunch and heads out with Viv, leaving Alfie and me alone to chat.

'Tea, coffee, the blood of the innocent?' I offer.

'Tea,' he laughs. 'Your man has a real thing about diary, doesn't he? When he opened the door to me, he started banging on about how cheese was evil.'

'He's just upset that I'm not raising his son vegan,' I tell him. 'And he's not my man.'

'He's answering your door in his underwear, but he's not your man? Are you two still together?' he asks.

I spot a look in his eyes – a look of pure disappointment – and I don't think he's disappointed that he didn't get to sleep with me, I think he's disappointed in me, like I haven't been completely honest with him.

'No – of course not,' I insist. 'Let me make the tea, and I'll tell you everything.'

I make a pot of tea and place it on the dining table, along with a plate of chocolate and hazelnut biscotti.

'She's breaking out the fancy biscuits, this can't be good news,' he jokes.

I tell him everything – the truth, the whole truth, and nothing but the truth. He listens to my babbling attentively, occasionally sipping his tea.

'So now he's here, living in the garden in his campervan, smoking God knows what, trying to terrify poor Frankie about the foods he eats. He just knocked on the door this morning and waltzed in, in his underwear, and started telling me how to live my life.'

'Was he always like that?' Alfie asks.

'I guess I used to be more eager to please him,' I admit. 'And I thought he was making me a better person, but he was just making me a female version of him. Of course I wish Frankie had grown up with a dad, but I feel so relieved that I never went travelling with him because, where would I be now? In my thirties, homeless, skint . . .'

'Try not to focus on what could've been,' he says. 'Just focus on right now.'

I nod. He's right.

'I'm really sorry about yesterday,' I say.

'Let's just . . . focus on the funny side of it,' he says with an awkward laugh.

'OK,' I reply. 'I just . . . I don't want this to affect us.'

'That's what I wanted to talk to you about,' Alfie starts. I can see something in his eyes, a sort of anxiety . . . I've seen it before in the eyes of men who have found out I have a kid (or realised they fancied my mum more). I know exactly what's coming.

'I know things are really difficult for you at the moment and I'm sure this has only made them harder. The last thing you need is me, making things even more complicated. It'd be great if we could be friends, and I'll still help you with the deli. I have a few things in mind, and a few jobs to do today, if you want to join me?'

I smile my best fake smile and nod. He might be insisting that this is for my own good, but I think it's for his. Well, who would want to get involved with a single mum who has just seemingly moved her slacker ex in? I want to say that maybe he is a player, that maybe he isn't the great guy I thought he was . . . but I really can't blame him for running a mile.

'Sure,' I reply. 'I'd like that.'

'I've only got a few short jobs to do. If you want to come with me, I'll show you a few of the places that make Marram Bay special. See if we can't make you fall in love with the place.'

'You're certainly welcome to try,' I tell him. Although I can't help but feel like today would've been much more fun if we hadn't decided that friends is all we can be.

Chapter 24

If I'd known that one of Alfie's quick jobs involved dropping some off apple cider jam at the vets', I might have said no. Charlie, apparently, wanted a few jars to give 'her friend' for her birthday – what twenty-something gives jam as a gift?

I don't like Charlie, she seems phoney to me. Not just because she seemed kind of bitchy when I met her, and it's not even because Channy told me Charlie has been trying to get her claws into Alfie since he moved back to town all rich and good-looking. It's mostly because I am sure she's spreading rumours about me. I mean, what are the chances that a rumour should start doing the rounds that Frankie's dad was in prison, just hours after she speculated as much? If she's been working Alfie for so long, she probably sees me as some kind of threat. She'd hate me even more if she knew that Alfie and I had kissed . . . she has nothing to worry about now though, does she?

'I passed your cottage early this morning, Lily,' Charlie said to me as the three of us made small talk.

'Oh,' I replied, not all that interested in getting into conversation.

'Yes, it was the strangest thing. My eye was caught by the orange van parked outside. When I looked closely, I realised there was a strange man urinating outside it.'

I'll kill him.

'That's Frankie's dad,' Alfie chimed in.

'Oh, wow,' Charlie replied.

'Oh, that Nathan,' I said with a faux laugh. 'He doesn't realise he's not in the jungle any more. He's been abroad, doing his bit to change the world. Building houses in Third World countries, improving the environment – for the animals and to address climate change. Not in prison, like the rumours suggest.'

I don't know why I make excuses for him and tell these exaggerated stories to make him sound like such a hero. Truthfully, I have no idea where he's been. I thought I knew in recent years, based on his postcards, but after realising they didn't always come from the place where he was, I don't really know where he's been or what he's been doing. I suppose I'm embarrassed and think that if I make Nathan sound like a warrior for peace and happiness it will reflect more kindly on me.

'So what are you two getting up to today?' she asked.

'I'm taking Lily all around Marram Bay, showing her the sights,' Alfie told her.

'Sounds like a cute little date,' she replied. Alfie just laughed this off, much to my delight and her annoyance.

Alfie said that today was going to be all about showing me the cool and quirky things that make Marram Bay such a unique tourist hot spot – after all, the UK is rich in cute coastal towns, so something has to make it special.

The first thing he showed me was an alternative route to the seafront, rather than heading down Main Street or the adjacent road. Instead, if you travel along the road a little, you'll find a small yet beautiful park. Sure, it was pretty, with its stunning flowerbeds and cute little kids play area, but as we got closer I realised it sat at the top of a manmade, zigzagged cobbled road that led down the steep hill to the seafront. Alfie explained to me that it used to be that cars couldn't drive down the hill, so they made this bizarre yet beautiful road to make it easier. As you drive (or walk down the steps running alongside it) on the windy road, each stretch that connects the six hairpin turns is lined with big, beautiful flowerbeds, overflowing with greenery and brightly coloured flowers. I imagine the beauty is to offset the 5 mph speed limit, but with so much to look at, and the sea straight ahead, there's a lot to take in. Rows of buildings encase the road, with little shops, a tearoom and holiday homes. It doesn't feel like something that belongs in this country, it's like what you would see on holiday. I can see exactly why people in the UK would opt for a staycation here.

At the bottom, between the road and the seafront, is a large grassy area. Alfie explained that every November, they have the Winter Wonderland Festival – yet another thing that attracts tourists. They have stalls, rides and games, a bit like a funfair. Alfie tells me that the best thing about it is usually the street food – he even suggested we might have a stand for the deli there. I'm sure the locals would *love* that. He also told me about this cute little shop, just outside of town, that sells Christmas things, except it's open all year round. Frankie loves Christmas, so I can't wait to take him there.

After that we walked to what Alfie calls the very touristy seafront bit. Over there we found the Treasure Island arcade. I was just expecting your usual tacky seaside arcade, with coin pushers and slot machines – which they do have – but here, in the front it's an arcade for kids, but in the back it's a speakeasy where parents can go and get a drink, or people can just go for a night out. I did wonder why there was a doorman outside – I just figured it was a really rough arcade.

Now, we're over on Hope Island, in a restaurant called Yorkshi – a place that specialises in Yorkshire sushi, whatever that is. When Alfie told me where we were going I must've looked very worried – conjuring up images of weird seafood dishes in my head – but he assured me that it was really just classic Yorkshire dishes presented in a sushi-style. You know it's a fancy place because they offer a tasting menu, rather than a real menu, bring out cute little dish after cute little dish. I take a few pictures on my phone to preserve the clever beauty of each dish, which makes Alfie laugh.

First up we had Yorkshire pudding inari – little Yorkshire pudding pockets filled with roast beef and gravy. We also had fish and chip nigiri, full English rolls, and Wensleydale and smoked salmon rolls.

Dessert has just been placed in front of us: a selection of sweet treats all made up with fruit to look like the real thing. I pick up a cone-shaped rice pudding and strawberry jam one and pop it in my mouth.

'Oh my God, this place is amazing,' I say, which I realise is an unladylike thing to do, given that I haven't swallowed it yet, but I can't hide how much I'm enjoying it.

Alfie laughs.

'I'm glad you like it. I've been meaning to bring you here for the past week, it's hard not to love it. I nearly brought you here on Monday, but decided to do the picnic instead.'

Conversation grinds to a halt, I imagine because Alfie is thinking what I'm thinking – that the picnic was amazing, and there was something between us, and now it's ruined.

'Are you warming to Marram Bay?' he asks eventually.

'I am,' I admit. 'It really is beautiful and quirky – everything I hoped it would be. But the people . . .'

'People change, Blossom,' he points out. 'I was thinking, maybe be on the lookout for little ways to help people, show them what a good person you are, and that you have their backs. The people will see that you love it here, and that you're making an effort, and they will embrace you eventually, I promise, OK?'

'OK,' I reply, but there's only one person in this town that I want to embrace me and he's sitting at this table.

Chapter 25

Another day, another awkward 'family' breakfast at Apple Blossom Cottage. When I got home from my day out with Alfie, Nathan told me that he and Viv had been shopping, and that he was going to make us all a special breakfast in the morning. I'd be lying if I said I was happy about this, not just because I know that it won't be a bacon sandwich, but because I almost resent him for making an effort, because you can't just drop in after not caring for nearly a decade and be crowned Dad of the Year.

I feel a real sense of smugness when Nathan's breakfast bombs. Well, quinoa cereal with blueberries, almonds and strawberry 'milk' was never going to be a hit with us.

'It's interesting,' my mum says. 'Very interesting.'

'Thanks,' Nathan replies, finding a compliment where there isn't one. 'The strawberry milk is the best bit, and it's just strawberries, sweetener and good old water – which means no poor cows were tortured in the making of it.'

Just this poor cow, who had to watch him making it this morning, wearing nothing but his underpants.

I look over at Frankie who is politely pretending to eat it. I remind myself to sneak him something to eat before he leaves for school, before starting an inevitable – yet oh-so awkward

– conversation with Nathan.

'So, I was thinking maybe we have a new house rule, that everyone has to dress for breakfast,' I suggest.

'You're in your dressing gown,' Nathan points out through a mouthful of breakfast. He's holding his bowl close to his face and he spoons his food in at an alarming speed.

'Well, yeah, what I mean is just . . . not being nearly naked at the table, I suppose,' I clarify. 'I don't know if you're having trouble adapting to life back in our culture or what, but . . .'

'But what?' he asks.

'But you're acting kind of inappropriately. You're sitting here in your pants, eating your breakfast like you're scared someone is going to take it off you – you're peeing in the garden.'

I hear Frankie snigger.

'Lil, you know me, I like to be naked, so the undercrackers are a compromise.'

'How kind of you,' I say sarcastically.

'I'm eating like this because I'm hungry, because this is the first real meal I've had since I arrived here, because you have a fridge, freezer and cupboards filled with nothing but cruelty. And I'm peeing in the garden because you won't let me live in the house.'

'How about I give you permission to call me and wake me up if you need the toilet in the night, save you from resorting to doing it in the garden?'

'Don't have a phone,' he says.

'Of course you don't.'

'Don't have any money to get one.'

'You could get a job,' I suggest.

'You need someone at the deli, right?' he says, and he's being deadly serious.

'Do you have any experience selling meat?' I ask sarcastically.

'No.'

'Could you recommend a cheese to go with a bottle of Rioja?' I persist.

'Of course not,' he replies.

'Well then sorry, buddy, but the job isn't yours. I'm desperate for staff, but not so much that I'd employ someone who will actively encourage people not to buy things.'

'Fair point,' he replies. 'Guess I'll head into town today and see what I can find.'

'Good idea,' I reply.

After nearly a decade apart, it might not be fair to say that I know Nathan all that well any more, but I did once upon a time. Sure, he had jobs back then, but only casual gigs to pay the rent on his flat. He would only work zero effort jobs with no responsibility and that was that. He worked to live – but only as much as he needed to. I've always been a little different, I fantasised about having a career and a job where I felt like I made a difference. Sure, running a deli isn't changing the world, but it makes people happy, and I like putting my passion for food to good use. Even when the plan was to travel, we were going to work for charitable organisations, and work hard and, when we got enough money together, I wanted to set up centres for women in places where providing support for women wasn't high up on the agenda. Nathan always used to say we'd never be able to do that, but I figured he just didn't have the drive, so he didn't believe in us. I'll never know what could have been now.

None of this prior knowledge of Nathan gives me especially high hopes that he will find a job – and then, of course, there's the fact that he knows me, and no one likes me.

'I thought we could go for a kickabout after school, Frank,' Nathan suggests.

'I don't really like football,' Frankie admits.

'Don't really like football?' Nathan booms, causing poor little Frankie to jump out of his skin.

'All right, calm down,' I insist. 'Not all men like football.'

'When I was coaching kids football in Togo they lived for the beautiful game, and here you are, surrounded by fields with easy access to balls, and you don't want to know.'

'Ignore him,' I tell Frankie. 'Your dad has ridiculously old-fashioned views for a liberal.'

I remember back when we lived together, Nathan invited some friends over to hang out. The men were watching football in the living room and the women were banished to the kitchen, but it turned out one of the women loved football, so she went to sit with the men. She asked what the score was, and the men looked at her like she was crazy and asked her why she wanted to know. By watching football rather than complaining and insisting they turned it off, she was confusing the men. She told them she liked football.

'Go on then, what's offside?' Nathan persisted – like a firm grasp of football is exclusively reliant on an understanding of the offside rule. He didn't expect her to know, but she did (come on, it's not rocket science – even I could have answered that question) and suddenly, the menfolk were in awe – a female person who knows what offside is? How adorable!

It annoys me that men are allowed to like manly stuff without it being cute, or seeming like they're only doing it to impress the opposite sex. Men like Nathan think it's adorable when females like video games, action movies, sci-fi TV shows, sports, etc.

This makes me think of Alfie and his dad, who didn't think he was manly enough because he didn't like sports and farming. I don't want to show Nathan up in front of his son, but I'll take Frankie to one side later and explain to him that it's OK for boys not to like football. Maybe I'll ask Alfie to have a word with him, because Frankie respects him, and he's obviously turned out just fine.

'You want to give it a go?' Nathan suggests. 'It can't hurt to try, can it? Maybe you can grow up big and strong like your dad, travelling the world, teaching other little boys to play football.'

'OK,' Frankie replies, a little glimmer of excitement in his eyes. I've noticed that he spends a lot of time staring at Nathan, a mixture of curiosity and – dare I say it – adoration. Frankie is fascinated by people with interesting stories, like Henry and his war stories, and now it turns out he's got a dad who is full of it – I mean full of *them*.

'Or you could end up selling cheese, like your mum,' he adds. I don't rise to it.

'Are you two OK to pick Frankie up from school today?' I ask Viv and Nathan – mostly Viv, but I really am trying to make an effort with Nathan.

'Of course,' she replies.

'Thanks, I'm going to drop him off and then check in at the deli, make sure the fitters left everything tidy. Still no news on the licence, so I'll give my boss a call, see what he says. In fact, we'd better get off now, Frankie,' I say, giving him a wink that only he can see.

If we set off now, we'll have enough time to drop in on Henry and Clara and see if they're open for breakfast because, I don't know about Frankie, but I'm starving! Of course, it's nice that Nathan is making an effort, but we can't starve just because we don't like his cooking. Anyway, what Nathan doesn't know won't hurt him, will it?

Chapter 26

It's 5 p.m. when I finally lock up the deli, after spending three hours here, all on my own, trying to figure stuff out.

The good news is that I spoke to Eric, and it seems like we're going to get the liquor licence we need, so that's great, that means we can plan the opening now. The bad news is that he asked me if I had come up with a name yet – obviously they need to get the signs made – but I just don't have anything, nothing feels right. Another week or so, tops, is all he's giving me, and then I suppose he'll do it himself. There are plenty of beautiful, cool, original names he could come up with, but he really wanted me to find something perfect for here specifically.

That's the good and the bad covered – now for the ugly news, because I can think of no other way to describe it.

The first call I received was from Nathan – via my mum's phone, obviously, telling me that his job hunt had been unsuccessful. I gently suggested to him that maybe this had something to do with his look. Well, the dishevelled-hippy-traveller look doesn't really smack of a strong work ethic, does it? Employers think twice about hiring people with unwashed hair and clothing made of hemp, it's just the way it is.

Nathan, surprisingly, was open to the idea of a haircut.

'I've had some good times with this hair,' he said wistfully. 'But maybe it is time for something new.'

I was taken aback.

'Brilliant,' I replied, because the sooner he gets a job, the sooner he can find his own place to live.

'I could take Frankie with me, get him a trim?' he suggested. I thought about it for a second, wondering whether that was a good idea. Every time he seems like he's making an effort, I feel a sort of sympathy for him, because this situation is far from ideal, and trust is almost impossible to gain back once it is lost.

Seeing as Nathan really was trying, I said yes.

I received another call, not long after, which made me realise that Nathan taking Frankie for a haircut was the least of my worries.

I was excited when I saw that it was Alfie calling.

'Hello,' I said brightly.

'Hey,' he replied. 'I've just had a run-in with your ex.'

'Oh God, what happened?'

'I'd walked down to the gate with Pugsley, just as Nathan and Frankie were walking past. Frankie came running over to see me with Nathan close behind him. We were just chatting when your ex pipes up, telling me I don't deserve animals because I mistreat them. I asked him what he meant and he started banging on about dairy farms – he's got a real bee in his bonnet about dairy farms.'

'Alfie, I am so, so sorry,' I said, as though that would do anything.

'I told him "I don't run a dairy farm, pal, I grow apples. I made cider and jam." Even Frankie chimed in to tell him that I didn't have any cows, before listing the animals I do have. Nathan looked a bit embarrassed, like he didn't want to be wrong, so he started muttering about using fruit to make alcohol being unethical. When I told him that didn't make any sense, he told me karma would see me right.'

Oh my God, he sounds like a psychopath. Obviously he doesn't think alcohol is unethical, he just didn't want to admit he was wrong – he's always been stubborn.

'Alfie, I'm sorry. Obviously he's having problems with me and he's taking them out on you.'

'Is he jealous?' he asked. 'Of us? Because of what he saw?'

'No, no, no,' I insisted. 'He's just here for Frankie – or, more likely, somewhere to live. There's nothing between us.'

'You might want to make sure he realises that,' he replied.

Furious, I finished up my work, giving myself a chance to calm down, and now I'm headed back to the cottage.

I park my car alongside his van, peeping inside to see if he's there but he isn't, so he must be in the house.

Before I get to the front door, Viv comes out to meet me. She stands in the doorway, hugging herself with her arms, as I walk up the path.

'I saw your new diary sitting on the side today,' she says. 'I had a peep inside and saw that you hadn't written in it.'

'You came out here to confess to reading my empty diary?' I laugh, but then I go cold. 'Did you read my diary when I was younger?'

'Of course not,' she insists.

'I think I'd like to remove them from your house,' I say. 'Just in case.'

'Oh, OK, fine, I threw them out years ago.'

'You threw them out?' I squeak.

'Yes, well, I needed the space for my romance novels, and they were full of "deforestation" this, "icecaps are melting" that – and we're fine, the world hasn't ended. I didn't think you'd care.'

I'm so glad I never wrote anything truly private in them.

I laugh it off – well, does it really matter now?

'I forgive you,' I say, making a move for the door.

'Erm, in the spirit of forgiveness,' she starts. 'Just remember, that it takes a big person to forgive, and that everything is going to be fine.'

'If you're talking about Nathan having a go at Alfie in the street, I already know,' I tell her, pushing past her. 'I don't know why he's being such a wa . . . What have you done to your hair?'

I am two steps through the door when I clap eyes on Nathan, sitting on the sofa with his feet up, watching TV, his newly shaved mohawk sitting on top of his head.

'Do you like it?' he asks, turning his head proudly from left to right, to give me a glimpse from all angles.

'I hate it,' I reply. 'Looking like a hippy wasn't getting you a job so you thought the punk-rocker look might work?'

'It's modern and stylish,' he insists. 'Frankie loves his.'

'Hilarious,' I reply. Frankie has had wild, curly brown hair pretty much since the day he was born, except it's grown wilder and curlier as he's grown up. When Frankie goes to the barber, it's to trim his fringe from his eyes. This isn't something I make him do, it's how he likes his hair. He looks completely adorable though. I slip off my jacket, making eye contact with my mum as I hang it up. There's this look in her eyes . . . sadness tinged with terror, if I had to guess.

'No,' I blurt, suddenly not so sure Nathan is joking. 'Frankie doesn't have that haircut, does he?'

'Lily, listen,' she starts, but I'm already marching towards Frankie's bedroom.

I open the door just as I hear my mum reminding me that 'hair grows' and there, sitting on the bed, colouring in a picture of a footballer, is my son, smiling up at me, with a shaved mohawk to match his dad's.

'Do you like my hair?' he asks excitedly. 'It's just like Dad's. And we went to the field and we played football and he says I'm really good at it. We're gonna play again.'

I purse my lips and try not to cry.

'I'm gonna go start dinner,' I tell him, my voice cracking a little.

'OK,' he chimes.

I close his bedroom door behind me and march over to where Nathan is sitting. He's scratching down his pants and laughing wildly at something on the TV until he realises how angry I am. He jumps up and runs over to Viv, hiding behind her.

'Lil, what's wrong?' he asks.

'Don't you "Lil" me,' I say angrily, trying to get around my mum. 'And stop using my 51-year-old mother as a shield.'

'Lily,' she snaps angrily. 'Don't be shouting my age like that.'

'Lil, please, he wanted to be just like me – and he's so happy with it,' Nathan insists.

I stop trying to attack him. To be honest, I doubt I would've done anything, even if he didn't have his human shield for protection. My mum is right, it is just hair, even if his curly hair was impossibly cute, but I don't know what I hate more, the fact that he has this stupid haircut or the fact that, with it, he looks just like Nathan.

'He'll get kicked out of school with hair like that,' I tell Nathan, because it's true. 'It's got to go.'

'That's one lame school,' he replies.

I massage my temples until we're disturbed by a knock at the door.

'Alfie,' Viv says brightly. 'Is everything OK?'

'No,' he replies, marching in. 'I need a word with *him*.'

Alfie squares up to Nathan, who looks dwarfed next to Alfie's muscular frame. Nathan may be skinny and kind of short, but he's fearless when it comes to fighting.

'What's the problem?' he asks him.

'What have you done with my dog?' Alfie asks him.

I gasp.

'Nathan?'

'I haven't done anything, Lil,' he insists. 'Last time I saw the dog – that you don't deserve – was when I saw you earlier today.'

'See, there it is, saying things like that . . . and suddenly, Pugsley is missing.'

'He's a dog, they wander off,' Nathan says flippantly. 'He'll be back.'

'It seems like you think everything just wanders off and comes back when it feels like it,' Alfie points out. 'But Pugsley is a good boy, he doesn't go off on his own.'

'I haven't seen him,' Nathan insists.

'Listen, I'll help you look,' I tell Alfie, grabbing my keys. He dashes out the door and jumps in his car before speeding off.

'Nathan, if you've touched his dog . . .' I start.

'What am I going to do with a dog?' he replies. 'You're the one who eats animals.'

Ignoring him, I head out to my car and set off in the opposite direction to Alfie. He's gone towards the school, so I head towards town.

Poor little Pugsley, I wonder where he's wandered off to. I drive slowly and carefully, frantically looking out of both windows as I go. I see a Labrador, who looks like he's taking himself for a walk, his leash clipped to his collar, but held in his own mouth. I crawl all the way to Main Street but there's no sign of Pugsley. Poor Alfie must be going out of his mind, I can't even imagine how he's feeling. Pugsley is his only companion in that big, lonely house. I don't know what he'd do without him.

I exhale deeply, frustrated that I haven't been much help. I decide to drive back to Alfie's, to regroup, but as I head back towards home I notice a Volvo 4x4 parked outside the convenience shop, with Pugsley in the back, yapping at the window. I park up and jump out, hurrying over to the car. I try the door but it's locked.

'Don't worry, baby, I'm gonna get you out,' I reassure him, calling Alfie.

'Alfie, I've found him,' I say. 'He's in a car, outside the convenience shop.'

'I'll be right there,' he says.

In a matter of minutes, Alfie is here, parking up behind the Volvo.

He pulls a puzzled face as he walks over. 'This is Charlie's car,' he says.

'Charlie's car?' I reply. 'Why does she have your dog?'

'I don't know,' he replies. 'But she was at the house not long ago.'

Charlie walks out of the shop with a bag in each hand. As she spots us standing there, next to her car, the easy smile that is always plastered across her face falls.

'Alfie,' she says. 'I was just coming to see you.'

'I've been frantically looking for Pugsley – why do you have him?'

'I left your place and, I don't know, I guess he chased my car? I got here, stopped at the shop and there he was. I noticed you were a bit down in the dumps so I thought I'd come here, buy a few bits to make you dinner. I figured I'd just bring Pugsley back with me. Sorry, I should have called.'

I frown. A likely story.

'You know how much he loves me,' she continues, unlocking her car.

Alfie lifts Pugsley out and holds him close.

'You gave me such a scare,' he tells him before kissing him on the face a few times. 'Cheers, Charlie.'

'Oh, it was nothing,' she insists. 'I was on my way back to make you dinner anyway.'

'Thanks.' He smiles.

Ergh, she's so obviously done this on purpose and I hate that he's too sweet to realise. I can't say anything though, can I? How could I prove it?

'Well, I'll get going,' I say.

'Thanks for helping,' Alfie tells me.

I bat my hand.

'Didn't really do anything,' I say. 'See you later.'

They both say goodbye to me. As I walk towards my car I can hear Alfie excitedly asking Charlie what she's making for dinner – it's a surprise, apparently.

I get in my car and turn the key, only for it to fail to start. Oh, don't do this to me now. Is that what I get for doing a good deed? My car breaks down?

Alfie puts Pugsley in his car before coming over.

'Again?' he says. 'I'll take it back to my mechanic tomorrow, this shouldn't be happening.'

'Thank you,' I reply softly.

'I can give you a lift back,' he suggests. 'Come on.'

As much as I'd rather walk back, I accept the lift.

'Charlie, I need to drop Lily off on the way, her car's knackered,' he calls over.

'OK,' she replies. 'I'll follow you.'

Perfect dog-rescuing Charlie with her perfect surprise dinners and her perfect functioning car.

'It's so unlike Pugsley to run off,' Alfie tells me as we make the short journey home. 'He's never been one for chasing cars either.'

I shrug.

'Are you OK?' he asks me.

'Oh, just Nathan, doing everything he can to make life difficult,' I reply.

'I'm sorry to hear that,' he replies. 'The good news is, I've been thinking about some people who might be a good fit for the deli.'

He pulls up outside Apple Blossom Cottage.

'Oh really?' I reply.

'Yeah,' he says. 'We can go through them tomorrow though, you look exhausted.'

'Thanks,' I reply, opening the car door. 'Well, have a good night with Charlie.'

I close the door behind me a little too quickly for Alfie's liking. He gets out of the car too and hurries around to me.

'You OK?' he asks, placing his hands on my shoulders.

'Just the usual stress,' I say. 'I'll be fine.'

Charlie pulls up behind us and gets out of the car.

'Everything OK?' she asks.

Before anyone has chance to say anything, Nathan and Frankie emerge from Nathan's campervan.

We all stare for a moment, at Frankie's perfectly bald head.

'There,' Nathan says. 'I fixed him. You happy now?'

Oh, I'm ecstatic!

Chapter 27

It's my turn to pick Frankie up from school today. With no work to be getting on with – other than the impossible task of naming the deli (I'm thinking of calling it The Stomach Ulcer) – I've been going a little crazy, seeing so much of Nathan. The only thing worse than seeing so much of Nathan, is seeing so much of Frankie hanging out with him, looking at him with adoration in his eyes, thinking he's the coolest person in the world.

When they came home from school yesterday, they'd roped Viv into buying the supplies they needed for Nathan to build Frankie a tree house in the back garden. He was telling Frankie all about the huts he would build for people who didn't have homes, and when Frankie said they sounded cool, he offered to build him one. I didn't say anything at the time, but when they came home yesterday with supplies, I took my mum to one side and begged her not to give Nathan money, because he's taking the mick, living here, not paying his way, demanding special food and near-exclusive use of the TV. He has a newfound passion for daytime TV that is driving me absolutely mad. He just lounges in front of the TV, heckling the people on the screen – as though they can hear him – passing judgement on their lives. It's unbelievable.

So now he's building Frankie this tree house, which will be

great if he gets it finished. The Nathan I knew had never finished a thing in his life, but if he's been building houses out of wood on his travels, then at least he knows what he's doing.

Today was the day he was going to make a start. When I said I was leaving to go and pick Frankie up he jumped up from the sofa and headed out into the back garden to get cracking – finally.

I left a little bit earlier today, unwilling to spend a second more in his company, especially seeing as my mum has been out all day – God knows where.

I'm sitting on one of the benches outside school, ignoring my surroundings, just enjoying the scenery. It doesn't bother me now, that the other mums don't talk to me. To be honest, it's easier when they don't. More peaceful.

It's been a strange couple of days, really. I haven't seen Alfie, Nathan is always there, wherever I turn, and as for Frankie's bald head, well, I don't have a panic attack every time I see it now, which is progress, but I'm also worried this is my new normal. This isn't the life I hoped for when I moved here.

Mrs Snowball appears in the school doorway, which is strange, given that now is about the time the Little Acorns usually make a break for it.

'Mums and dads, if you have a moment, could you gather in the hall, please?' she bellows across the small playground.

Oh, here we go. Of course there's an assembly with Mrs Snowball on the day *I* pick Frankie up. I shuffle in with the others, showing no real urgency and, as Mrs Snowball addresses us, I glance around the room. There's a wall of family portraits that the kids have drawn so I look around to find Frankie's. It takes me a moment to find it but there it is, Frankie holding hands with Viv and me. It's cute.

'It's important that we contain this,' Mrs Snowball says. 'Or before we know it, we'll all have headlice.'

My ears prick up when I realise what she's talking about.

'So, just a few tips to help prevent the spread from child to child,' she continues. 'Keep long hair tied back until the case has cleared up and apply a little tea tree oil to your child's hair to discourage the lice. Check your child's hair for lice – and eggs – and remember: shaving your child's head to rid them of lice is entirely unnecessary . . . like using a bomb to get rid of a spider in your bath.'

Everyone turns to look at me.

'Frankie doesn't have nits,' I announce defensively.

'Because you shaved his head,' one of the mums I don't know suggests.

'No, he didn't before either. His dad took him for a haircut and I didn't think it was appropriate for school, so he shaved his head, that's all.'

'So Frankie *does* have a dad?' Mary-Ann asks.

'No, the stork brought him,' I say sarcastically.

'I thought he had two mums,' Mary-Ann says, pointing to the drawing on the wall.

'No,' Mrs Snowball interjects. 'That's Lily's sister, Vivien.'

Oh, it's just so like my mum to pass herself off as my sister.

'She's the one who flirted with my husband when he picked Josh up on Wednesday,' I hear someone mutter.

'So his dad is the man who had long hair?' Jessica asks.

'Yes.'

'I heard he's been living rough in the wilderness for the past twelve years,' I hear a man behind me whisper to someone else. 'Maybe that's when he got the nits.'

I turn around, unsure who I'm addressing because I only heard his voice, so I tell everyone.

'If he'd been in the wilderness for twelve years he would have struggled to father my child,' I point out. 'And for the tenth time: Frankie does not and has not had nits.'

'I thought she was seeing Alfie Barton,' someone whispers behind me.

'He dumped her,' another whisper replies.

'I heard a different story entirely,' Avril pipes up. I furrow my brow because it's not like Avril to come to my defence.

'I was at the vets this morning,' she starts and I wonder whether she was there for her pet or herself. 'And I heard a rumour that you shaved his head so we'd all think he was ill, so we'd stop giving you a hard time about the deli.'

Gasps echo around the room.

My eyebrows shoot up.

'What?' I can't help but laugh. 'That's ridiculous. And you heard this at the vets? From Charlie then?'

'I don't disclose my sources,' she replies.

'OK, OK, everyone settle down. I didn't call this meeting for a witch hunt, just to alert everyone to the fact that we may or may not have a louse infestation in this school. I'm not saying any child is known to have lice and I'm sure there is no truth in the story that Lily shaved her child's head for sympathy – that's just ridiculous.'

'Thank you,' I say.

Mrs Snowball claps her hands.

'OK, meeting over,' she announces with a big smile. 'And don't forget we've got the autumn show coming up and the kids have all been working so hard on their performances. I'll go and fetch the children from their classrooms and you can all get home.'

As I wait for Frankie I notice a few stares and hear a few whispers. It concerns me, how rumours are started and shared in this town. People seem to take the smallest element of a truth and run with it, until a monster of a story has formed that can't be beaten.

Poor Frankie doesn't need kids avoiding him because they think he's got nits, and I could definitely do without people thinking I'm actually evil. Opening a deli in a small town isn't evil, despite what they say, but pretending a child is ill for sympathy is abhorrent.

'Mum,' Frankie says excitedly as he charges over to me.

'Hey, kiddo, good day?'

He pulls a funny face.

'Same,' I laugh. 'But your dad is building your tree house as we speak, and we're gonna stop at the shops on the way home and get some stuff for dinner.'

'Cool,' he replies. 'I can't wait until my tree house is ready. Can I sleep in it?'

'Oh, I don't know about that,' I say, ushering him out of the building.

'Dad told me that he slept in a tree when he was in Canada and it wasn't even a tree house, it was just a tree. He said that he was exploring, and he saw a bear, and the bear saw him,' he tells me, pausing for just a second while I buckle him into the car. 'And he told me that you're supposed to sing to them, to stop them killing you, so he sang "Earth Song", but it didn't work, so he had to climb a tree and wait for the bear to go, except he didn't go for ages, so he had to sleep in the tree.'

'Oh really?' I say, pretending to sound fascinated, but I highly doubt that happened.

'Yeah, he's really cool,' Frankie tells me.

'Isn't he just,' I reply. I don't vocalise to my son that, after hearing so many of Nathan's stories since he got back, I'm starting to wonder if any of them are true. The only one that I do believe, without a doubt in my mind, is the first one he told me, about being sacked from the farm. Working on a farm in Australia isn't exactly changing the world, is it?

I park up outside the shop and we head inside. I grab a basket and fill it with the few bits we need for dinner as Frankie follows me.

'Dad said he could help me stop eating animals,' Frankie says. 'I don't like the food he eats, but he says we can find ones that I do like.'

'Frankie, you're a just a kid. It's OK for you to eat whatever you want and then make up your own mind when you're an adult with all the facts.'

'But Dad says what we eat is bad.'

'He also says that playing video games instead of football is going to turn your brain and your body to mush – but that's not right either,' I point out.

With everything we need I join the queue, only to spot Mary-Ann in front of me. I keep quiet, hoping she won't notice me, the awkward events from school playing on my mind still.

'It's £11.95,' the man behind the counter tells her with a smile.

Mary-Ann takes a card from her purse and places it in the machine before punching her pin in.

'Oops, could you try again, please?' the man instructs.

'Erm, yes,' she says awkwardly, doing as he asks. It doesn't work though.

'Am I typing my pin wrong?' she asks.

'No, I don't think so, it says there's a problem with the transaction,' he tells her.

Mary-Ann glances around to see if anyone is in the shop to witness this and that's when her eyes find mine and she grimaces.

'Can you try it again, please?' she asks, panic in her voice.

The shopkeeper tries one more time, still with no luck.

That's when Alfie's words pop back into my head – when he suggested I do nice things for the locals to try and get them onside.

'I've got this,' I say.

'What? Don't be crazy,' Mary-Ann says.

'It's no big deal, you can give me it later,' I insist, putting my card forward. 'You know what these machines are like.'

Mary-Ann watches me silently as I pay for her shopping.

'Thank you,' she says sincerely.

I bat my hand.

'It's nothing.'

She smiles at me and picks up her bags before leaving.

'That's your good deed for the day,' the shopkeeper tells me.

'No good deed goes unpunished,' I remind him. He nods in agreement.

'Right, kiddo, let's go home and see how this tree house is doing.'

As we walk out of the shop, we bump into Henry outside.

'Hello, strangers,' he says. 'We've not seen you in a while.'

'Hello,' I reply.

'Henry,' Frankie chirps, running over to him to tell him all about his dad's return.

'Sounds like you've had a hectic week,' he says.

'You have no idea,' I reply.

'Seen much of Alfie?'

'Not really,' I reply with a sigh.

'Well, if you ever need us to look after this one, just give us a shout,' he says as he heads for the shop. 'Give Alfie a call, see if he's available.'

I smile and nod, but I know that, as far as I'm concerned, Alfie is completely unavailable.

Chapter 28

I stare out of the kitchen window, watching Frankie in his tree house as he plays with his new pet. I mean, it's not really a pet, it's a frog he found hopping around by the pond that he's holding ever so gently in his hand. I can't hear, but I can see his lips moving, so I imagine he's telling the little reptile all sorts. It's also not a real tree house because, having realised it was going to be harder work than he thought, Nathan resolved to prop pieces of wood up against the tree, so he's just sitting underneath that – even *I* could have done that.

It's a Saturday morning. Nathan has gone for a run, my mum is in the living room painting her nails an alarmingly bright shade of pink, and I'm here, cradling a cold cup of tea, watching my son make the best of a pretty rubbish situation. Of course he thanked Nathan for the tree house – and he probably meant it when he said it was great, because his dad made it for him. Nathan assures us that he's going to do it properly over the coming weeks, but we'll see.

There's a knock at the door. It's amazing how often people knock on this door, given that we're in the middle of nowhere.

'I'll go,' my mum says, hopping to her feet with an agility grandmas don't usually boast, which reminds me . . .

'Did you tell people at school we were sisters?' I ask her as she heads for the door.

'They believed me,' she says with a wink. 'If I were you, I'd admit it's because I look young. Better than the alternative.'

I frown.

'Alfie,' she squeaks as she opens the door. She leans forward and gives him a kiss on the cheek, which makes him blush.

'Hello, Viv,' he says. 'Just here to see if I can take your Lily out for the day.'

'You can take my Lily anywhere you like,' she tells him. 'Can't he, Lily?'

'Where are we going?' I ask.

'I have the answer to a few of your problems,' he tells me.

'Oh my God, time travel,' I say sarcastically.

He laughs. 'Not quite, but it'll do the trick.'

'OK, great,' I say. 'Viv, are you OK looking after Frankie?'

'Of course,' she replies. 'I think the boys are planning on doing more work on the tree house today anyway.'

Alfie peers outside.

'They might want to try building it in the tree,' he suggests.

'I don't think Nathan is up to it,' I say. 'He's trying though.'

'Well, you know, I'm great with stuff like that so if there's anything I can do or . . . if Nathan needs a hand, just let me know.'

I am almost certain Alfie would rather do anything than spend time with Nathan, so I appreciate the offer.

I knock on the kitchen window to get Frankie's attention before waving goodbye.

'Right, lead the way,' I say, following Alfie towards the front door.

As we're getting into Alfie's car, a sweaty Nathan comes bounding over.

'You never apologised to me for accusing me of stealing your dog,' he says to Alfie.

'You never apologised to me for leaving me to raise our child alone for eight years – shall we call it quits?' I say, giving him a look with my eyes that suggests he shut up. 'Frankie is outside waiting for you, he's ready to do more work on the tree house.'

'I'm pretty beat from my run,' he says, stretching his quads. 'Do you think he'll take a rain check?'

I don't answer him, I just close the car door.

'Poor kid has already waited eight years, what's another day, eh?'

'I suppose he seems like he's trying,' Alfie says hopefully.

'Yeah, he seems like he's trying, but also, he seems like he's not really trying at all. You'd think he'd be jumping through hoops to try and make things right but he's all talk, far-fetched stories and empty gestures. Frankie thinks he's amazing though. He's all about his dad, he barely has time for me these days. I've raised him single-handedly – my entire life, since the day he was born, has been all about him – and here Nathan is, getting all the glory with his cheap moves and his crap tree house.'

'Hey, Frankie knows you do everything for him,' Alfie tells me. 'His dad is just this new, exciting thing. And, you know, he could always be worse.'

'He could, sorry,' I say. 'So where are we going?'

'We are going to visit my friend Biagio,' he says, parking his car outside a row of terraced houses. 'Biagio is practically a local celebrity around here. He moved over from Italy when he was younger, got married and opened up the ice cream hut on the beach. I remember when I was younger, I'd love going to see him for a 99. He was this loud, passionate, friendly person and he made every customer feel like the most important person in the world, like one of his best friends. Off the record, a couple of years ago the gambling problem no one knew he had came to a head and he lost his business, his wife left him . . . The official word is that he gave up his job for health reasons. He's doing OK now, but he's bored. Not only would it do him good to get a job, but the man can sell food – and I mean *really* sell food – and everyone loves him. He'd be a real asset.'

'And you think he'll work for me?'

'We're here to find out,' he replied with a wiggle of his eyebrows.

We walk up to Biagio's bright green front door. Just a few seconds after Alfie presses the doorbell, we're greeted by a short, smiley Italian man.

'Alfie,' he sings, grabbing him, practically standing on his tiptoes to reach up and kiss him on the cheek – everyone is getting to kiss him but me today and this feels so unfair.

'*Ciao, bella,*' Biagio says as he pulls me close, kissing me on both cheeks. 'Alfie's told me so much about you.'

Biagio's English is perfect but his Italian accent is strong and charming. The way he sings his words, packing them with enthusiasm – it really stands out amid all the low-pitched Yorkshire accents I've been trying to get used to lately.

'Come in, sit down,' he says. 'Alfie said you were coming so I made a little antipasti.'

He shows us into his kitchen, where the table is laid out with meats, cheeses, olives and bread.

'A little?' I laugh. 'There's so much food – it looks amazing.'

'*Mangia, mangia,*' he says.

We all take a seat at the table and chat. I ask Biagio questions about his life, he asks me questions about mine. We make small talk about the town until Alfie gets down to business.

'Biagio, I was telling Lily that you might be looking for work,' he says. 'I told her you've been a bit bored since you stopped selling ice cream.'

'I lived to sell ice cream,' he tells me, his hands together. 'It's a simple job, but the one I was born to do. I got to talk to people, spend my days on the beach . . .'

'Well, I don't know if Alfie has told you but I'm opening up a new deli on Main Street, and we're looking for staff. Someone who knows food well, someone who is great with customers – you seem like a great fit.'

Biagio shrugs.

'I may be a good fit for the job – and the job may be a good fit for me . . . but is the deli a good fit for the town? Who knows?!'

'Well, I'm working hard to show people that we are. I understand your reservations, what with everyone being so wary of the deli, but . . . I'm throwing a tasting party on Monday evening, why don't you come along?'

'I didn't know that,' Alfie says. 'That's a great idea.'

'Didn't I tell you?'

Probably because I just came up with it. Well, it was an idea I'd been thinking of, to invite a few people in to taste-test some of our foods, but throwing a party ASAP sounds like a great way to get Biagio and the locals in to see the place now it's finished.

'OK, sure. I'll be there on Monday night and we'll see if your food is as fantastic as mine, eh?'

I laugh.

'This will be hard to beat,' I tell him. 'But I'll give it my best shot.'

After more kisses we head for the door.

'He seems really nice,' I tell Alfie.

'He is, he just had a spell of bad luck. Seriously though, you're not just doing him a favour, he will be great for business.'

It certainly would be nice, to have such a fun, friendly, passionate employee – if only to balance out Channy, who's only in it for the money.

'So how long have you been planning this tasting party?' he asks once we're back on the road.

'It's a relatively new idea,' I say.

'You came up with it when you said it, didn't you?' he laughs.

'OK, yes, but it's not a lot of work. I just need to make the place look beautiful, have my bosses send me some supplies on Monday, and then get it all set up by the evening. It'll be great. The hardest part will be getting people to turn up,' I point out.

'You know I'll help you,' he says.

'Thank you,' I reply.

'What are friends for, Blossom?'

I feel my smile fall. There's something about when he reminds me we're just friends that breaks my heart.

Chapter 29

It's been a hectic Monday, getting everything ready for the tasting party, and with so much to do something was bound to go wrong . . . except it hasn't. The deli is looking great, Channy has been working hard and all of the food Eric and Amanda sent not only arrived on time, but is also all ready to serve. All that is left to do is go home and get ready, after I pick Frankie up from school.

I'm a little late – of course I am – but I'm relieved to see that, when I arrive at school, Frankie isn't the only one in the playground, Jessica Dawson's son is there too.

'Hello,' I say brightly as I head over to the pair of them. I can't help but smile as I see the two of them sitting together, building some kind of structure on the wooden table in the playground. They've got a collection of stones, twigs and leaves which they are painstakingly balancing on top of each other in a way that I'm sure makes sense to them. It's just nice to see Frankie socialising with one of the other kids.

'You're late,' Frankie says. 'Dad is never late.'

I could argue that he's eight years late, but I don't.

'Who's this?' I ask, still smiling.

'I'm Simon,' the small boy says quietly. 'Have you seen my mum?'

I feel my eyebrows shoot up. I thought I was the only mum who was late.

'I haven't.' I watch as Simon's face falls, the thought that his mum may have forgotten him laying heavy on his mind. 'But she called me and asked me and Frankie to hang out with you until she got here.'

'Oh, OK,' he replies, turning his attention back to his sculpture.

I sit and watch the pair of them as they build and chat, and I can't help but notice that all Frankie talks about is Nathan.

'When my dad finishes my tree house, you can come over and play in it, can't he, Mum?' Frankie says.

'If he finishes it,' I can't help but start, but this criticism goes over the kids' heads. 'Of course he can.'

'My dad is so cool. He has all these stories from loads of different places. He says one day he'll take me travelling and I can't wait.'

'My dad sells meat,' Simon replies.

'My dad *hates* meat,' Frankie tells him emphatically. 'He says we shouldn't eat it but I don't think I could eat what he eats because it's just plants, but he says he'll help me learn to like it too, which is great, because I love animals too.'

As I watch my son chatter away, it strikes me now more than ever just how similar he is to his dad, and the thought of Nathan giving Frankie ideas about taking him travelling and feeding him kale just fills me with fear. My son doesn't think I'm the cool parent anymore, he's obsessed with his dad.

'Simon,' I hear Jessica pant as she runs up the school steps.

'Hello,' I say, before she has chance to say anything else. 'I told Simon how you suggested he hang out with Frankie and me for a while before you picked him up, just so they could get to know each other.'

I watch as Jessica processes what I'm saying.

'Yes!' she says, enthusiastic with relief. 'I did say that. I just need a quick word with Lily before we go.'

Jessica ushers me to one side, away from the boys.

'I just . . . I just forgot,' she babbles.

I shrug. 'I left Frankie in a shopping trolley in Tesco when he was a toddler. Only for about thirty seconds, but even so – this is nothing.'

'Thank you for covering for me,' she says, and she sounds like she means it. 'If he thought I'd forgotten him – or if the other mums caught wind.'

'We all make mistakes,' I tell her. 'Anyway, they seem to be really getting along.'

'They do,' she says, nodding in agreement.

'Hey, are you free tonight?' I ask. I didn't set this up – how could I have? – but this seems like a good opportunity.

'I am,' she replies cautiously.

'I'm having a food tasting event at the deli. It would be so great if you could be there, and if you could bring some of the other mums . . .'

Jessica looks at me for a moment and it suddenly occurs to me that she might think I'm trying to blackmail her.

'OK, sure,' she replies with a smile. 'I appreciate you helping me out, I owe you.'

'Awesome,' I reply. 'Tell everyone it's at the yet-to-be-named deli, at 7 p.m.'

'Looking forward to it,' she replies, and I think she might mean it. 'Come on, Simon, let's go.'

'See you tomorrow,' Simon tells Frankie as he hops down from the bench.

'Bye,' Frankie says ecstatically.

'You made a friend,' I say, offering him a high-five once Jessica and Simon are out of earshot.

'I did,' he replies, running past me. 'I can't wait to go home and tell Dad!'

Back home the first thing Frankie does is charge inside to find Nathan. He finds him, of course, sitting on the sofa watching TV.

Nathan would always criticise people who watched too much TV but he seems to be finding it preferable to finding a job since he came back. His latest passion is watching *Come Dine with Me* and blindly rooting for the vegetarian or vegan participant on moral grounds. He might like to give it a go, he mentioned yesterday, if I would let him use the kitchen. I didn't even humour him because you just know that, if he did apply, and his kooky personality got him accepted, I'd probably end up cooking for his guests – or my mum would. My mum who is currently ironing his freshly washed clothes for him. I keep telling her that, as much as I appreciate her helping out, she shouldn't be doing everything for Nathan, because it only encourages him to do even less.

'Remind me why I can't come to the party tonight, Lil,' Nathan says as he rubs Frankie's bald head like a crystal ball.

'Because you're looking after Frankie,' I point out.

'But I want to come along. The locals love me!'

'No, they don't,' I correct him. 'Some of them think you're fresh out of prison after murdering someone, others think you've been living in the jungle and have caused a nit outbreak at school.'

'All rumours,' he points out.

'And then, of course, there's your beef with Alfie – no pun intended – and the local vet did see you peeing in the garden.'

'And you said we could do some work on the tree house tonight,' Frankie says enthusiastically.

I look over at him, my eyes wide with anticipation. I wonder what his excuse will be tonight, because he always seems to have one.

I watch Nathan rack his brains for a moment.

'Probably best to get things fixed in place ASAP,' I say. 'We're expecting storms next week.'

'Really?' Nathan says in disbelief.

'Really,' I reply. 'I heard it on the news today.'

This is entirely true. The weather forecast said we're going to be in some kind of low-pressure zone, with the Yorkshire coast bearing the brunt of the strong winds and heavy rain that are coming our way.

'OK, sure,' Nathan tells Frankie. 'After *Hollyoaks*.'

Frankie frowns, but only for a second. He's getting what he wants.

'I saw your outfit for tonight on the bed,' my mum says, sidling up alongside me. She gives me a wiggle of her eyebrows.

'That's just my optimistic plan A,' I tell her quietly. 'I've got a plan B, just in case I look awful.'

'You're going to look amazing,' she assures me. 'So am I.'

'I expect no less from my sister,' I joke.

'I'm sure Alfie will be pleased to see you,' she says, delivering an elbow to my ribcage to emphasise her point.

'I'm sure Alfie will be pleased to see you,' Nathan says mockingly. 'What is it with women and that bloody farmer?'

'Nathan, he's *gorgeous*,' Viv insists. Nathan frowns at her. 'And so are you,' she adds. 'In your own special way.'

An almost enviable level of ego allows Nathan to see a compliment in that. He smiles.

'Do you want Alfie to be your boyfriend?' Frankie asks, taking his eyes off *Come Dine with Me* for a second – a show he's never previously been remotely interested in.

''Course she doesn't,' Nathan insists. 'Do you?'

I look over at them, an almost carbon copy of one another were it not for the twenty-three years that separate them. It's almost like Nathan is a scary vision of what Frankie could turn out like when he's older, if he doesn't make the right choices, and I can already see him doing almost everything he can to be just like his dad.

'Alfie is my friend,' I tell him, because that is technically true.

'Dad could be your boyfriend again,' Frankie suggests.

I clear my throat, suddenly so uncomfortable.

Nathan looks over at me, waiting to see how I reply.

'We're just friends too,' I tell him. 'You know I don't have time for boyfriends.'

Of course it's only natural for Frankie to want his parents to get back together, and for us all to be a happy family, but he's just way too young to understand why this is a terrible idea. Other than the fact that I don't love Nathan – which is arguably the most important – I just couldn't live with him. I couldn't go back to how things were, I don't have the time or the energy to look after him too, and then there's how I feel about Alfie . . .

'I'd better go get ready,' I say. 'Lots of setting up to do.'

'I'm looking forward to helping out,' Viv says.

My mum has very kindly offered to help out this evening, seeing as it's just me and Channy working. Alfie will be there for support, and he's invited loads of people, so hopefully some of them show up.

I'm scared to say it, but I'm excited. This feels like the first bit of progress I've made with the deli – well, not progress as such, but the possibility for progress. At this stage, I'll take what I can get.

Chapter 30

Stepping behind the counter, I pull my dress back down over my arse. I bought it because it looked great on the woman modelling it online. However the model, unlike me, is significantly lacking in any lumps or bumps, which gave the dress she is wearing an extra three or four inches on mine. My dress has a lot of uneven terrain to contend with and, as such, is appearing like more of a mini than it was intended. Of course I didn't really realise this until I left the house. It did that thing outfits somehow manage to do, where it behaved from the house to the car, and then the second I reached my destination, boom, I'm in self-conscious city.

Viv assures me that I look great, but Viv's outfit is a beast all of its own. My mum is wearing a pair of super-tight black PVC trousers with a black lace top, and she looks amazing in it, it's just maybe a little bit much for a small-town deli food tasting.

I am also wearing black, which Nathan happily made fun of as we left the cottage.

'You two look like you're going out on the pull,' he laughed. 'Or to a wake.'

I'm wearing a slinky wrap dress that rides up when I move, courtesy of my butt moving as I walk. If I can stand still I'm fine, it stays in position, but as I move around my hemline starts creeping back up again. My very high heels are ensuring I take small, ladylike steps, which seems to slow the process down a little, thankfully. I'm dreading the moment when I need to bend over for something.

Wardrobe malfunctions aside, the evening seems to be going well, which has taken me by surprise.

When I arrived back at the deli, all dolled up and ready to be disappointed, all of our hard work getting the place ready today was so clearly noticeable. Outside, the deli looked spotless, the flowers all looked amazing, all of the little twinkly lights we put up were visible as the sun started to set – it was everything I had in my mind when Eric and Amanda sent me here and all I could think was that it was such a shame not many people would see it . . . but then people started turning up. I don't know if they turned up out of curiosity, for the free food, or because they genuinely wanted to, but the place is packed and, unless this is some kind of coordinated act of sabotage, things really might be on the up.

Luckily my bosses had large containers of ready prepared food for the evening, so all I need to do is serve it, which has taken away a lot of the stress of throwing this party.

I've spotted a lot of familiar faces already – mums from the school, local business people and, just like he said he would be, Biagio is here. As I approach Avril, Jessica and Mary-Ann, armed with a plate of food for them to try, I notice Biagio heading over.

'These are fennel, sea salt and cracked black pepper cracker breads with—'

'You have to guess what kind of cheese it is,' Biagio interrupts me.

The women stare at him, puzzled, but happily take a cracker bread from the plate.

'Oh, wow,' Jessica says through a mouthful of food.

'It's not like anything we make,' Mary-Ann adds, and she sounds relieved, I suppose because she's the local dairy farmer. This must show her that we're not trying to step on her toes.

'We've actually spent a lot of time in France,' Avril starts, lightly dabbing a serviette around her mouth. 'So I know a thing or two about European foods, and this is definitely French.'

'No, no, no,' Biagio protests, sounding more Italian with each word. 'It's Italian. It's burrata – mozzarella on the outside, Stracciatella and cream on the inside. Delicious.'

'You know your cheese,' I tell him, impressed.

'Would you like me to hand some out?' he asks.

I feel a big, stupid grin slowly creep across my face – I'm just so overwhelmed. If he wants to help out, he must be considering working here.

'Yes please,' I reply.

'I already handed out a few fruit tarts. I told people they're all part of your five-a-day. Entertain your guests,' he insists. 'I'll help with the food.'

'Lily,' I hear Alfie call from behind me.

Alfie had texted me and warned me that he was going to be a little late, as Leonardo the alpaca seemed a little off colour, so he'd asked Charlie to stop by on their way to the deli. There was something about his use of 'their way', like they came as a pair, that just filled me with jealousy.

I turn around and see him standing behind me. He has his usually wild locks slicked back and, teamed with his black trousers and a crisp white shirt, he looks positively dashing – nothing at all like a farmer.

'Hey,' I say brightly. I hurry over, my hands pulling on my hem as subtly as possible, and kiss him on the cheek to greet him. This isn't something we do and I immediately wonder why I did it.

'Lily, you look . . .' He pauses to find the words and with each second I grow more self-conscious. 'Incredible.'

I finally exhale and smile.

'Oh, thank you,' I say bashfully, and for a moment I feel like the prettiest woman in the room.

'Hey,' Charlie says, stepping out from behind Alfie. 'I didn't expect so many people to be here – and I didn't think I'd need to dress up, plus I was just at Alfie's checking on Leonardo, so I hope it's OK I came like this.'

You could be forgiven for thinking Charlie had turned up in a white vet coat, covered in cow dung, but she's wearing a pair of black PVC trousers, not unlike my mum's, and a plunging V-neck black vest. She looks incredible, with her face perfectly highlighted and her impossibly long eyelashes. In fact, she and Alfie almost look like they've coordinated outfits, making them look like they belong together – well, not *together* together, but like they belong next to each other, at least.

'You look great,' I tell her.

'Says you,' she replies, her big, toothy smile beaming brightly. 'I wish I were brave enough to dress like that.'

Her words, whether they were intended to hurt my feelings or not, send a rush of blood to my head. I smile.

'I just need to check on something in the kitchen,' I say, hurrying away. I manage to make it through the door just as a tear escapes my eye. I hurriedly wipe it away, just as my mum walks in.

'Darling, what's wrong?' she asks.

'Nothing,' I insist. I should know better than to think I can lie to my mum.

'Something is wrong,' she says. 'That's the fastest I've seen you walk in that dress all night, and there's no fire in here . . .'

I laugh as another tear escapes.

'I think Charlie might've just insulted me – or maybe I just imagined it, I don't know.'

'What did she say?' Viv asks.

'She said she wishes she was brave enough to wear this dress . . . it's just the way she said it.'

'Are you really going to let some little girl, who constantly plays "hard to want" around Alfie, upset you?' my mum asks.

'Apparently,' I reply. I laugh, but my true feelings cause my voice to crackle.

My mum puts an arm around me.

'You look amazing,' she tells me. 'I don't know why she would suggest you were brave for dressing like this but . . . look, do I really need to tell you that looks don't matter?'

'I know they don't but . . . y'know,' I reply.

'Listen to me,' Viv starts, squeezing me tightly. 'You might think Charlie looks better than you do but so what? She's not going to look like that forever, and you're not going to look like this forever. You're going to get old. Really old. You're gonna go all saggy and wrinkly and grey and you're gonna go through the menopause and you're gonna start wearing really big knickers and slippers and watching *Loose Women* and saying things like "it looks like it's trying to rain" and "Margaret's prolapsed again" – and you're not the only one. I'm going to get there, Charlie is going to get there, and no shallow man is going to stick around for any of that anyway, they'll be off, trying to find some young thing to replace you. But a real man doesn't care about any of that, a real man cares about what's going on inside. I've seen the way you and Alfie look at each other and you've only known each other five minutes – she's been trying to get her claws into him for five years, if what Channy tells me is true, and where has it got her?'

I smile. There is no one like your mum for putting things into perspective. I knew all this – of course I did – but it's easy to forget sometimes.

'You're right,' I tell her.

'I'm always right,' she replies. 'I also wear these trousers better than her, the girl doesn't have an arse.'

I laugh.

'Now get back out there and own tonight,' Viv insists.

'I will,' I say, hopping to my feet. 'Is my make-up OK?'

'Still perfect,' she replies. 'Remember who you are, OK?'

I give her one meaningful nod before turning on my heels, grabbing a tray of Belgian chocolate brownies as I head back out there.

My mum is right, I need to remember who I am. I'm Lily Holmes and I am awesome – and I look great in this dress, whether it rides up when I walk or not. Maybe Charlie is smaller and slimmer than me, with a more impressive job and zero baggage, but she isn't me and she never will be.

Now I'm walking around with a real spring in my step, dress be damned.

'You OK?' Alfie asks. 'You hurried off a little quickly . . .'

'Oh, I'm fine,' I assure him with an air of unwavering confidence, despite noticing Charlie still lingering at his side. 'I just remembered the brownies in the oven.'

I hold up the tray of Belgian chocolate brownies. Of course, they came ready prepared, so this is a lie, but it beats telling the truth.

'Would you like one?'

Alfie raises his eyebrows with delight, the rich smell of chocolate drifting up towards him.

'I'd love one,' he says eagerly.

'Oh, not for me,' Charlie says, practically turning her nose up at them. 'Some of us can't get away with eating stuff like that.'

I shrug.

Luckily before I can reply, Jessica beckons me over.

'Did you say you baked?' Jessica asks.

'Yes, brownies,' I reply, offering the tray to them. 'Help yourselves.'

The ladies each take a brownie and eat them in near silence – something I find is often a good sign when it comes to food, because it usually means people are too busy enjoying what they're eating to focus on anything else.

'So, you like to bake?' Avril says.

'Love to,' I reply, hoping to find some common ground, even if it's not strictly true. Well, I'm sure I'd love baking if I knew how and had lots of spare time.

'Ask her,' Jessica encourages.

'As part of the start of autumn festivities, we're having a bake sale at school, and we could do with an extra baker's contributions. Would you be interested?' Avril asks. I can hear a cautious reluctance in her voice, but that only makes me more convinced that this is my shot at proving I am one of them.

'Oh, yes,' I say, trying to sound enthusiastic and not at all like I'm lying or panicking. 'When is it?'

'The day after tomorrow,' Avril says. 'We're bringing everything in the morning, so that the kids can set it up throughout the day, ready for after school. Will that be a problem?'

'No,' I say with a casual bat of my hand. 'I'll whip a few things up tomorrow.'

'Well, OK then,' Avril says. 'Great.'

'Great,' I reply.

I'm about to walk away when Avril places a hand on my arm.

'You know, we can see that you're making an effort to fit in,' she says. 'And the food tonight is great.'

'Also,' Jessica chimes in, 'Simon has asked if Frankie wants to come to his birthday party.'

Jessica removes a small blue envelope from her handbag and hands it to me.

'Thank you,' I say, trying to sound casual, but getting the blessing of the head of the PTA is like getting the blessing of the Godfather, and Frankie will be over the moon that one of the kids is including him.

I hurry over to Alfie, pulling him to one side.

'You'll never guess what just happened,' I tell him. 'Avril said she liked the food, and she said she could tell that I was making an effort to fit in.'

'Aww, have you finally made friends with the cool kids?' Alfie teases playfully.

'Yes,' I laugh. 'Frankie too, he's been invited to a party.'

'That's great, Apple Blossom Girl. Sounds like you're getting everything you want.'

Not quite everything I want.

'I just love that I've acquired this nickname – Apple Blossom Girl. Apple Blossom Girl, living in Apple Blossom Cottage – we may as well call this place Apple Blossom Deli, because that's all it's going to be known as.'

Alfie laughs. 'There are worse things to be called . . .'

'And I'm sure I've been called those too,' I reply.

I furrow my brow as a brainwave washes over me.

'What *about* Apple Blossom Deli for the name – seriously?' I suggest after a few seconds. 'It's beautiful, it sounds good, and it's definitely personal.'

'You know what, I love it,' he replies. 'It fits in with the town and the name has already caught on for you – there's no reason it won't take for the deli too.'

'I can run it by my bosses and, if they like it, we can get the signs made up, ready for opening.'

'Erm, Alfie . . . sorry, Lily,' Charlie interrupts. 'I was just thinking – and I know it's not like me to make a mistake, and I'm sure I haven't – but I think I might have given Leonardo the wrong injection. Just for my peace of mind, can we go check on him?'

'Yeah,' Alfie says, a worried expression consuming his face. 'Sorry, Lily. I'll be back.'

'It's OK,' I insist – but it isn't. 'It's nearly kicking-out time anyway.'

If I thought for a second that something might actually be wrong with Leonardo, I'd probably drive Alfie up there myself, but this just seems like another one of Charlie's little games.

He returns the kiss on the cheek I gave him earlier before hurriedly heading for the door.

'See you, Lily,' Charlie says with a smile.

'Bye.'

I slowly follow them towards the door, watching to see where they head. If they came in one car, does that mean Alfie will be driving her home later? Or if they're friends – does she stay there? She implies that she does, seeing as how they're BFFs.

I can't actually see where they've gone, so I step outside into the fairy-lit garden to glance around. There's still no sign of them, but then I hear a quiet mumble from around the corner. My curiosity getting the better of me, I peep around the building and there, in the shadows, I spot two people kissing. It's dark, but what little light is getting around there I can see bouncing off Charlie's PVC trousers. I can't help but gasp with shock.

'Lily, sorry,' I hear the man say. I'm standing in the light, so he can see exactly who I am. I can't see him, but I recognise his voice. It's not Alfie, it's Biagio.

'No, I'm sorry,' I say. 'I didn't . . .'

Something suddenly occurs to me. Charlie wasn't the only person wearing shiny trousers tonight.

'Mum?' I ask, as though there might be a doubt in my mind.

'Hello, darling,' she says. 'Still going well?'

'Oh, marvellous,' I tell her, slightly traumatised to catch my mum getting off with someone, like outside a school disco. 'I'll see you later.'

I hurry back inside, back where things are going well. Things inside the deli might be starting to improve, but outside they're only getting worse.

Chapter 31

'Year 9,' my mum says as she watches me carefully spooning equal-sized dollops of cupcake batter into bun cases. 'That's the last time I saw you bake anything.'

'That's probably because that was the last time I baked,' I admit. 'And look how that turned out.'

'Those biscuits weren't that bad,' she says as she washes dishes in the sink next to me.

'Mum, they were supposed to be buns,' I remind her. 'I never put any baking powder in them.'

'You should've made dairy-free cakes, set an example,' Nathan calls over from the sofa.

'It's hard enough as it is,' I call back. 'And is it not bedtime?'

'I'm watching *A Place in the Sun*,' he protests, until I point out to him that I was referring to Frankie, who is falling asleep next to him.

My mum has to take a phone call (no doubt from her new fancy man, who we're still yet to discuss) so I ask Nathan if he could put Frankie to bed, but he explains to me that we can't pause live TV, and he really wants to see how this one plays out. I can't believe I've ended up stuck with him here, spending his days on the sofa either watching TV, annoying me, or a combination of both. In his defence, while we were at the deli last night, he did go outside with Frankie and make a real start on the tree house . . . sort of . . . there's something in the tree now at least, anyway. He's building it in the tree next to the kitchen – something to do with his idea for a zip line, which I promptly vetoed. It doesn't look like he's done much work on it, but it's a start, I suppose.

I end up putting Frankie to bed while Nathan has the ever so simple task of keeping an eye on the cupcakes as they bake. I asked him to give me a shout when the time was up, safe in the knowledge that in this rubbish old gas oven, it would probably take longer than it would in an electric fan oven.

I tuck Frankie in and listen to him gush about his dad, how he's starting to be included at school, and share his concerns for his frog, which has gone missing from the garden. I thought the frog might have taken a backseat to Nathan, so it's nice to know he still thinks about it.

After Frankie falls asleep, I just watch him for a few minutes, stroking his little bald head, feeling a combination of wonder and terror over how quickly he's growing up.

It's the smell of burning that snaps me from my thoughts. I hurry into the kitchen where I find my cakes burning in the oven, and my no good ex still watching TV.

'Nathan, you said you'd watch them,' I say as I hurriedly take them out, as though that would do anything to undo the damage that has already been done. Realising he has messed up, he rushes over and fusses around the cakes, suddenly trying to seem useful, but not actually doing anything other than making excuses.

Looking down at the near-black cakes, despite it being quite late in the evening, I realise that I have no choice but to start again.

'The Lil I knew never cared about baking, or impressing people,' Nathan insists.

'Well, people change,' I tell him. 'Most people, anyway.'

If there's one thing that has been crystal clear since Nathan arrived, it's that he hasn't changed at all.

'I still see the same Lil I fell in love with, deep down in there somewhere,' he tells me. I don't realise he has edged closer towards me until I turn to look at him in disbelief, and notice him right next to me. Close to me. Very close to me, in fact.

'What are you doing?' I ask, but Nathan doesn't answer. Instead, he grabs my head with both hands and tries to kiss me. It's uncomfortable and unwanted, so I shove him away from me as hard as I can, causing him to stumble backwards. He manages to save himself from falling, but not without knocking things off the worktop.

'I, er, I think I'll go to the van . . . get some sleep,' he says awkwardly, his cheeks slightly flushed from his misjudged pass at me.

'Yeah, good idea,' I reply angrily.

I don't think I can feel angrier until I notice the open packet of baking powder, bobbing upside down in the sink full of soapy water.

'Did you need that?' Nathan asks, although I'm sure he knows the answer. 'I'll go get you some more.'

'From where?' I reply, pointing at the clock. It's late at night, everywhere will be closed.

Nathan quickly hurries off to the safety of his van, leaving me alone in the kitchen, so angry about so many things. Not only has he completely sabotaged my baking efforts – and not even on purpose, just by being himself – but then he tried to kiss me . . . I just don't know what he was thinking. Since his return, at no point have I said or done anything to give him any indication that there is anything romantic between us. His pass was completely out of line and, to make sure he realises this, I'm going to have to have an awkward conversation with him about it at some point, which I am not looking forward to, but I can only sort one mess at a time. With Nathan hiding in his van, I turn my attention to solving my baking crisis.

As I stress over my problems, I spot the answer to my prayers across the kitchen. Packets and packets of biscuits and cakes sent from my bosses. Everything looks so professional and perfect though, there's no way anyone will believe I made them, so I attempt to make them look a little more rustic and homemade. I cut up sponge cake and cover it with buttercream, I empty out a packet of biscuits into a sandwich box and shake it up a little, just to make them look a little rough around the edges, and, telling myself that the more I contribute, the more I'll help the autumn bake sale, I even open up a packet of brownies, cut them in half and then sprinkle them with icing sugar to make them seem different to the ones we had at the party, just in case anyone thought I might have brought the leftovers or – God forbid – not made them at all.

Chapter 32

I had faith in my plan last night, but not in my improvising abilities, which is why I dropped Frankie off at school this morning with sandwich boxes filled with sweet treats, before quickly making my exit. I was worried that if anyone saw them, they might compliment me on them and ask for the recipe or something. So I left them with Frankie, safe in the knowledge that by the time I came back this afternoon, my store-bought baking would be blending in amongst all the home-baked stuff, and no one would be any the wiser. Except that isn't how it's played out . . .

When I arrive at the school in the afternoon, I can't help but notice that my contributions are nowhere to be seen. I've done a full lap of the room but I can't spot any sign of them.

'Where are yours, Mum?' Frankie asks me.

'Perhaps they've all been sold already,' I wonder out loud. Well, they were made by professionals after all.

I feel my palms start to sweat as I begin to worry. They invited me to take part, so why wouldn't they want to sell them? Was there something wrong with them? Are they on to me? I don't see how they could be, but something isn't right here.

'Lily, wow, I've never noticed your tattoo before,' Avril says, sneaking up behind me. She's referring to the silhouette of a flock of birds on my back that I had done back in my hippy phase.

'Oh, yeah,' I reply. 'Do you have any?'

'Oh, gosh no,' she replies, a little too quickly for my liking. 'You know you have them for life, right?'

'You have children,' I laugh. 'They're pretty permanent fixtures too.'

'Indeed,' she says, unamused. 'Anyway, I'm here to ask about the allergens in your baking.'

'Hmm?' I reply, causing her to repeat herself.

'We couldn't put your baking out because you weren't here to tell us the allergens, so we didn't know which table to put them on.'

'It's fine,' I insist, making sure she realises I'm not at all offended. I mentally high-five myself for not coming in this morning, I hadn't even considered allergens, so I would've had no idea what to say.

'So?'

'So?' I repeat, still smiling with relief.

'So, tell us now and we'll lay them out.'

Oh, *sugar*.

'Well, they all have flour in them,' I say. 'And, er, dairy.'

I'm pretty sure that's right.

'OK,' she replies. 'What about nuts?'

'Nope, no nuts,' I reply, but then I realise that, I don't actually know that for sure. Sure, on the surface, it might not seem like any of the products have nuts in them, but don't things sometimes say they were made in the same place as where nuts were handled? 'Wait, no, maybe.'

'Maybe?' Avril replies, puzzled.

The bake sale is buzzing with life around us but, thankfully, the only person listening to this conversation is Frankie. I didn't tell him that I was passing deli products off as my own baking, but he knows his mum, and I think he might be working it out for himself. I place an arm around him and give him a squeeze.

'Which ones have nuts in?' she asks.

'Maybe all of them,' I reply honestly.

'Lily, you either put nuts in or you didn't,' she laughs. 'So which ones?'

There are no lies that can get me out of this situation that won't see a child with a nut allergy potentially exposed to nuts, and I can't risk that.

'You didn't make these, did you?' she asks.

I'm frozen on the spot, unable to speak. Avril has me banged to rights.

'You didn't make these, did you?' she says, louder this time. Now we've attracted the attention of parents, kids and teachers throughout the room. Now everyone is frozen on the spot, silent, looking over at me.

'What's the problem?' Mrs Snowball asks, hurrying over in her usual busy bee manner.

'Lily can't tell me whether or not her baking contains nuts and I think it's because she didn't make any of it,' Avril says, addressing the room. I feel Frankie cling to my arm protectively.

'Lily, you're not trying to pass off cakes that you didn't make as your own, are you?' Mrs Snowball asks.

'I . . .' There's nothing I can do but tell the truth, is there? 'I *did* bake but, due to circumstances beyond my control, it got ruined last night and I just didn't want to let everyone down.'

'Lily, not only is it spectacularly dangerous, to potentially feed children foods they may be allergic to, but it's incredibly dishonest of you to pass this food off as your own.'

I feel my cheeks warming with embarrassment as I'm ticked off in front of everyone.

'You should've just said you couldn't do it,' Avril insists.

'I'm sorry, I wanted to be helpful,' I reply.

'To get us all on board with your deli, I'll bet,' Avril says. Her hostility may have faded at the party but it's back tenfold now.

'Wait, is that why you helped me out in the shop?' Mary-Ann chimes in.

'Of course not,' I reply. 'I just wanted to help.'

'And why you helped me?' Jessica adds. 'So that I'd feel like I had to come to the party?'

'No, no, you've got me all wrong,' I insist, but standing here, surrounded by angry faces, I realise that I'm wasting my breath.

'The raffle,' Mrs Snowball shouts excitedly. 'Let's do the raffle.'

She hurries over to the stage, taking the gaze of most of the room with her.

I know that helping out Mary-Ann and Jessica may have benefited me, but that's not why I did it. I wanted to help. And I did try and bake, I really did. It was relying on bloody Nathan to help me last night that was my downfall, but even if I did throw him under the bus, is that a good enough excuse? And Frankie loves his dad, what would he think if he saw me passing the blame on to him?

'Now, this raffle might just be our biggest yet,' Mrs Snowball says, to an echo of woos around the room. 'We've got a three-course meal in the private room at The Hopeful Ghost tonight, a hamper full of delicious foods from a range of local shops, and, the pièce de résistance, a brand-new 42-inch TV, generously donated by an anonymous parent.'

Mrs Snowball winks at Avril, who bats her hand and flashes a faux-embarrassed smile. Anonymous indeed.

'Come on, kiddo, let's get out of here while they're distracted,' I whisper to Frankie, ushering him towards the door.

'I hope you've all got your tickets ready,' Mrs Snowball says, plunging her hand into a small red bag. She rummages around in there before pulling one out. 'And the winner is . . . ticket number 202. Anyone? Anyone?'

We're just about through the door when Frankie pipes up: 'We won, Mum! We won!'

I look at my son who is holding the raffle ticket I'd forgotten we were pressured into buying a couple of days ago. I only bought it so that we didn't look bad, so I told Frankie he could have it.

'Mum, we won,' he says again.

I glance around to see everyone staring at us, once again, only this time with a bitter resentment beneath their glares.

'Of course we did,' I reply.

Carrying a 42-inch TV to your car, alone, is no easy feat, and it's a task that is somehow made harder when you're being watched by an angry mob of parents who are secretly hoping you'll drop it – preferably on your own foot. The hamper was pretty heavy too, I had to take things to the car in two trips.

I can tell people are angry because I won – I didn't want to win, I wish I hadn't – and I did consider refusing it, but I imagined that would somehow make people mad too. I am well and truly back in everyone's bad books, and just when I thought I'd made so much progress too. It was hard getting into their good books before but it's going to be even harder now.

'Nathan, can you get something from the car for me please?' I ask as I walk in, dumping the hamper down on the floor.

'After this,' he says, unable to remove his eyes from the TV. 'What is it?'

'It's an even bigger TV,' I tell him and he's suddenly interested.

'Hmm?' he says, his eyes wide.

'Hmm,' I confirm.

Nathan jumps to his feet and runs out to the car like a kid on Christmas morning.

'I'll go help,' Frankie says, running out after him.

'Where's Viv?' I ask once they're back inside, as I take things from the hamper and put them in the right place in the kitchen.

'She's out with her fancy man and she said not to wait up,' Nathan says. 'Good news for you, right?'

'Is it?' I reply.

'Yeah, he was saying how he wants to work in the deli,' Nathan informs me as he unboxes the new TV. 'We could sell the old TV and buy a sofa bed for in here, so I don't have to sleep in the van anymore.'

I ignore his comment about the sofa because there is no way he is moving in properly. Sure, he's pretty much living here seeing as how he's using the facilities and spending his every waking moment on the sofa, but the fact that he sleeps outside is – I think – the boundary that stops him feeling like he's got his feet under the table, that will keep him motivated to find work and a place of his own. If I buy him a bed, that will be it, he'll be happy enough living here, sponging off us, getting in the way, rubbing me up the wrong way.

'Biagio said he'd work for me?'

'Yeah,' he replies. 'That's great, right?'

'It might be too little too late,' I admit. 'And if Viv breaks his heart . . .'

My mum isn't one to take a long-term lover.

'You're never happy, Lil, are you?'

'Are you kidding me?' I reply. 'I'm not happy because the whole baking thing was a disaster – everyone knows I faked it. Any headway I'd made has been erased. I'd say I'm back to square one, except I think I'm in a worse position now.'

'You got this rad TV though,' he replies. 'So it's not all bad.'

'Way to look at the silver lining,' I reply sarcastically.

'How about we have a boys' night?' Nathan suggests to Frankie. 'We could watch *Blackfish*.'

'Yes,' Frankie chirps.

'Erm, no,' I say. 'He's not watching that.'

'Why not?' Nathan asks.

'Because he's 8.'

'You can never be too young to learn about the dangers of keeping killer whales in captivity.'

'But you can be too young to watch something like that and escape without being traumatised,' I point out.

'OK, fine, we'll watching something kid-friendly, I'll pop us some popcorn – how about that?'

'Yeah,' Frankie enthuses. 'Can we, Mum?'

'OK, sure,' I reply. 'I need to pop out tonight anyway. Just promise me you'll keep him out of trouble.'

'When is Frankie ever trouble?' Nathan replies.

'I was talking to Frankie,' I point out, grabbing my phone as I head into my bedroom, closing the door behind me.

'Hello, Blossom,' Alfie answers cheerily. 'How's it going?'

'Ohhh.' I laugh. 'Not amazing. Would you be interested in dinner this evening?'

'I would,' he replies. 'Did you have anything in mind?'

'I actually won a three-course meal at The Hopeful Ghost tonight, if you fancy it?'

'You won it?' he echoes. 'OK, sure. I'll get ready then pick you up?'

After making a plan I begin rushing around my room, trying to transform myself from a stressed-out single mum into a sexy single lady – well, the closest thing I can get to the latter.

I step into a red off-the-shoulder cocktail dress, teamed with a black leather jacket – because now that it's autumn it's finally starting to feel a little chilly on an evening now – before climbing into a pair of red heels and slicking on some red lipstick. I blend my black smoky eyes out a little as I look in the mirror, wondering whether this outfit is a bit much for a dinner at the local, but as I look at the time I realise it's too late to change now.

'Where are you going?' Nathan asks angrily as I kiss Frankie on the cheek before heading for the door.

'Out,' I tell him. 'And, what was it my mum said? Don't wait up.'

Chapter 33

Winning this dinner tonight is worth more than any TV, because I'm at The Hopeful Ghost, with Alfie, with their private function room to ourselves. I might have worried that I was overdressed but as soon as I got in Alfie's car and saw that he was wearing a navy suit, I relaxed. He's clearly made an effort tonight too.

The food here at The Hopeful Ghost is great. It's just good, old-fashioned pub grub, but it's done so well.

To start with, I opted for the haddock fishcakes, topped with a poached egg and hollandaise sauce, which was absolutely delicious – so delicious that I cleared my plate, which was why, when they placed my main down in front of me, I was worried I might not be able to eat it. The roast beef was cooked to perfection, the vegetables were spot on, and the giant Yorkshire pudding – puffed up like a cloud – was perhaps the best bit.

My dessert, baked chocolate chip cookie dough with peanut butter ice cream, has just been placed down in front of me and, despite thinking I was full, the sight of it has caused my stomach to somehow make way for more.

As soon as we arrived, I filled Alfie in on the latest drama in the life of Lily Holmes, and after a brief chuckle at the absurdity of the chain of events that saw me resume my public enemy number one title, he assured me that everything was going to be OK. His optimism is touching, but I'm not sure I have his faith.

After polishing off as much of my dessert as possible, I finish off my Westwood Farm cider.

'God, these are good,' I tell him.

'Thanks,' he replies. 'I'm hoping to sell them farther afield, you can only get them locally at the moment. Watch this space.'

I'm not just saying this because he's my friend, his ciders really are amazing and they should be sold all over the country. I feel like they'd be really at home in a YumYum deli, alongside our other speciality alcoholic drinks. I'm going to give Eric a call in the morning and mention it to him.

'The deli is pretty much ready to open now – the only thing we'll be missing is customers.'

'I believe in you and I believe in the deli,' he says and, again, I wish I had his faith. 'Why don't we go for a walk? I could do with it, after everything I just ate, and maybe we'll come up with something that might help.'

'That would be great,' I reply. 'I'm in no rush to go home.'

Alfie smiles. 'You know, I think that might be the first time you've called this place home.'

'Really?' I reply.

'Yeah, you always refer to it as "the cottage",' he points out. 'Do you think you might be finally fitting in?'

'If you'd asked me that this time yesterday, I probably would've said yes,' I say. 'But now, everything feels messy again.'

As we leave the pub and walk along the seafront, I take Alfie by the arm. This is mainly to steady myself on the bumpy path, but there's also this overwhelming urge to be close to him.

'It's chilly tonight, isn't it?' I say, offering up an alternative reason for holding on to him.

'It is,' he replies. 'I'd say it was a welcome break, after some of the roasting nights we've had this summer, but apparently it feels so much colder because of the wind, ahead of the storm coming tomorrow.'

'I heard about it on the news,' I tell him. 'Am I going to be OK in the cottage or am I going to wake up in Oz?'

Alfie laughs.

'You know where I am if you need me,' he says. 'But I'm sure Nathan will know what to do, given his experience.'

'Oh, yes, of course, his experience,' I reply. I'm growing increasingly convinced he doesn't actually have any real experience in anything, and I have a few pieces of wood haphazardly placed in a tree to show for it.

'We haven't walked this way before,' I say. We've been on a few walks together and we've been around looking at the sights, but this part of the beach is new to me.

Alfie leads me to a small cove. A private little nook in a coastline I thought I'd seen every inch of. It's dark here, and oddly quiet – I suppose because we're away from the roads, and the public hot spots.

Using our phone torches for light, we walk across the small patch of sand, sandwiched between sea and grass. Alfie leads me towards a weather-beaten old bench with a rusted plaque screwed onto the backrest. I hold my torch closer to it, leaning in to get a better look.

'In loving memory of Donald and Joan Barton,' I read out loud. 'Were they related to you?'

Alfie nods as we sit down.

'My grandparents,' he tells me. 'You know that my relationship with my dad wasn't great, and that my mum's relationship with my dad wasn't great either. I don't think anyone who knows about my parents' marriage is surprised I'm 35 years old and unmarried, because growing up in that kind of environment isn't exactly an advert for it. But my grandparents were a different story. They met when they were kids, they got married, had my dad and lived happily together until my granddad died. My grandma, who was seemingly healthy, died of a heart attack a few weeks later. Now, I'm not saying she died of a broken heart, but that's what everyone said at the time. What I do know is that they devoted their lives to one another and that's why I'm not put off love and relationships, because some of them work and some of them don't. But the great ones are really something special, you know?'

'I know,' I reply with a smile.

'Bad experiences put us off things, but everything has the potential to be something great. Don't let a little setback convince you that you can't be happy here. The headway you made with the mums at school is a sign you should keep at it, because it is possible.'

'I know, I know. I just feel like this is a big sign that I should give up.'

'This isn't a sign,' he laughs, wrapping an arm around me. 'Signs are more obvious.'

As I turn to look at Alfie and smile, I notice that he's already looking at me. Our faces are just inches apart and all I want to do is kiss him, because he's wonderful, because he looks after me, because my feelings for him just won't go away. Is he giving me a sign that I should kiss him? Or are signs really much more obvious than this?

I feel my breathing quicken as we look into each other's eyes. As much as I want to kiss him, I should respect what he said about wanting to be friends, and not wanting to get involved with me while things are so messy. I should . . . it would be awful of me if I didn't . . . and yet . . .

I've barely moved my face an inch towards his when his phone rings from inside his pocket. I quickly pull back.

'It won't be anything important,' he insists.

'No, no, it's fine, answer it,' I say, feeling a little saved by the bell. If I had tried to kiss him, and friends was still all he wanted to be, I would've ruined everything.

'It's just Charlie,' he says. 'I'll call her back later.'

'No worries,' I say, wiggling free from his arm.

If there really are unexplained signs in the universe, this seems like a pretty blatant one.

Chapter 34

Today I am working from home, and by working from home I mean I'm sitting on the unusually vacant sofa with my notebook (that is now officially just a notebook and not a diary, because I never actually wrote anything in it) doodling the name of the deli – kind of like a young girl would do with her crush's surname.

It's much colder today, especially now that the storm is starting to pick up outside, so I'm curled up with a big pot of tea, a leftover brownie and a blanket wrapped around my legs.

Life doesn't stop because of a bit of bad weather (rainstorms and soon to be 50 mph winds, specifically), especially here on the coast where everyone seems used to it, so after a session here trying to come up with names, I need to pop to the deli to accept a delivery, then I need to rush over to the school where Frankie and his schoolmates will be singing for the mums and dads as part of their autumn celebration. I hated doing stuff like that when I was at school but, now that it's my kid taking part in them, I can't get enough of them.

'Look at you,' I say to my mum as she walks out of *our* bedroom. I guess I'm used to sharing my space with her now, I don't really think twice about it. It's just the new normal, sharing my bed with my mum. I suppose we need to talk about what's happening long-term, I'm just scared to do it in front of Nathan in case he thinks he's included.

'Just something I threw together,' my mum says, giving me a twirl. She's wearing a red jumpsuit that you might think is too young for someone her age, but she looks amazing in it.

'Are we going to talk about you and Biagio?' I ask.

'Lily, I really like him,' she gushes.

'You really like everyone,' I laugh. 'But thank you for convincing him to come and work for me, he called yesterday to tell me. I called Eric and Amanda and told them all about him, how well the tasting party went, what kind of new things we should stock – I didn't mention the whole Great British Fake Off debacle. So they're delighted.'

Viv laughs.

'Everything will be fine,' she assures me. 'And . . . I don't know, it's just different with Biagio. It's true what they say about Italians being the best lovers.'

'Ah, Viv, please, you'll put me off my brownie.'

'Sewage backing up out of the toilet wouldn't put you off a brownie,' she reminds me. I scrunch my face up in disgust but realise she may have a point. I do love chocolate.

'He's nice to me,' she says, softening a little, letting her usual sassy guard down. 'I feel like he cares about me, and about what is on the inside.'

'That's really nice,' I tell her. 'Well, go, have a lovely lunch with him, try and keep it PG if you're going to a restaurant.'

'I will,' she laughs. 'See you at the concert.'

'See you,' I say.

I feel like 'concert' is a term too grand to describe forty kids singing in a small hall, but it's nice to see her excited about it too. Even Nathan is coming, despite the fact that it clashes with *Escape to the Country*, which Frankie is more excited about than anything. He went off to school this morning with a real spring in his step, after spending extra time in the bathroom getting ready so that he would look his best for his performance. He was over the moon to learn that he's invited to Simon's birthday party, and it sounds like the kids at school are starting to embrace him, even if the adults still aren't crazy about me.

Nathan comes charging into the cottage like a baby elephant, dropping a pile of papers down on the table in front of me.

'New Delhi!' he bellows.

'That's probably a bit too meta for somewhere like here,' I tell him. 'Plus, I already came up with a name: Apple Blossom Deli. I forgot to tell you.'

I didn't forget to tell him, it just didn't seem important to keep him in the loop.

'What?' he asks, puzzled.

'Calling the new deli, New Deli. I think it's a bit too meta for the area, everything is kind of traditional and—'

'No idea what you're talking about,' he interrupts me. 'What I'm talking about is the job I just got offered in New Delhi, starting ASAP, they're paying for flights over later today. Pack your bags, go get Frankie from school, let's do this.'

His excited ranting stuns me into silence for a moment. Eventually, his words set in.

'What? You want us to go to New Delhi with you? Like, move there?'

'Yes,' he says excitedly. 'I've got a job offer – and it's a real charity gig this time, not like before. Look, I admit, you were right, I'd run out of money, I was struggling to find work to keep up the lifestyle, but now I have something. It's part of a big programme that supports disadvantaged children – and there's even work in elephant camps, can you imagine? Working with elephants. Frankie will love it.'

I walk over to Nathan and give him a reluctant sniff.

'I'm not high,' he laughs. 'Look at the paperwork. I just went to the library, checked my emails, saw the offer – everything is in place.'

'I live here,' I say slowly. 'Frankie lives here. He goes to school here. I have a job here.'

'But no one likes you,' he says, a little too enthusiastically. 'The deli is gonna flop, Frankie doesn't like that stupid school really. Lil, the other day he was telling me about his best friend – some guy called Henry? He's like 70 years old.'

'Erm, he's in his sixties,' I correct him. 'Nathan, we haven't been here long. There's no reason for me to just up and leave and – with you. Why would I move to India with you?'

'So we can be a family again,' he says, rubbing my shoulders. 'Look, I'll admit it, seeing you with that farmer, it makes me jealous. We're meant to be together, me and you, not you and him. And we have Frankie together, and doesn't he deserve parents who are together and love each other?'

'He would have that if you hadn't left before he was born,' I tell him, wiggling his hands off me. 'Oh God, is that why you tried to kiss me? Nathan, there's nothing between us. You know that as well as I do.'

'Just, give it a chance,' he says, taking my chin between his thumb and his index finger. 'Give family a chance. Give love a chance.'

'Nathan, seriously, get off me,' I say, swatting his hand away.

I sit back down on the sofa and put my head in my hands. I feel Nathan sit down next to me.

'Well, OK, maybe the romance will take time, but don't you want the adventure? What we always talked about? And Frankie would love it!'

'Nathan, no,' I tell him firmly. Looking him in the eye so he knows I'm serious. 'Even if I didn't have a job to do here. No.'

'I could just take Frankie,' he suggests, and I feel my entire body flinch. Over my dead body he's taking my kid away from me.

'He doesn't even have a passport,' I lie. I'm not sure if that was a suggestion or a threat, but I'm not risking it.

'Oh,' he replies. 'I could go and you guys could meet me once you've finished setting the deli up?'

'Or you could not go,' I suggest. 'You could stay here for your son and get a real job.'

Nathan thinks for a moment. I can see the mental anguish on his face and I realise that he's considering going anyway, with or without us.

'Nathan, don't you dare,' I say. 'You can't just drop back into his life and then piss off again after just a few weeks. He loves you. He loves you as much as he loves me. You're too important to him now.'

'So come with me,' he says.

'Or what, you'll just go? You'll leave your son? When I look at Frankie I'm just overwhelmed by how much I love him. I could never leave him. Everything I do is for him. I can't believe I made such a perfect little person.'

'We made him together,' Nathan reminds me. 'That's why you should come with me.'

'No, that's not what I mean,' I say. 'Anyone can have sex and get pregnant – that's just how you make a baby. What I'm talking about is what a smart, thoughtful, funny, caring young man he's become, and that's nothing to do with you, that's how I raised him. *I* made him. Me alone, and I'm so proud of him. I don't want to take him to another continent, to teach him how to feed elephants. I want him to get the best education. I want him to go to university – if he wants to – to be whatever he wants. You just want him to be a mini you.'

'Because there's something so wrong with that?'

'Absolutely, yes,' I say. 'You want to take an 8-year-old out of school, to live in India, while you wash elephants.'

'Lil, listen to me, I'm trying to be reasonable here. I'm going – I can't turn this job down. It's everything I've dreamt of! I'm trying to do the right thing by taking you guys with me.'

'Nathan, we're not coming. And if you were any sort of man, you would stay here and continue to build a relationship with the son you only met *this month*.'

I watch the cogs turning in his head, until Nathan confirms my worst fear: he's not thinking about what he should do, he's thinking about how to tell me.

'Lil, I'm taking this job, and I'm going today.'

'And how are you going to explain this to your son?' I ask him.

'I'll have to leave within the hour,' he tells me. 'Maybe you could explain it to him? Daddy has important work to do abroad, you know, like you said before?'

I shake my head.

'Nathan, I know doing the right thing doesn't come naturally to you, so I'm going to really spell this out for you. If you were any kind of man, you wouldn't go at all. If you had just a shred of decency, you'd turn up to his concert this afternoon and then you'd tell him yourself that you're leaving him, so soon after coming into his life. It's not my job to do your dirty work for you.'

'I'm not sure I can do it,' he says.

'I'll be there,' I say.

'No, I mean because I'll miss my flight. I need to hit the road, to make my flight from Heathrow.'

I can't help but laugh.

'Nathan, you're going to ruin his life,' I tell him plainly. 'It's that simple. You can't abandon him again.'

He nods thoughtfully.

'Look, I need to go to work for a delivery. Sit here, think things over more carefully, come to the concert, watch him sing, look him in the eye and then see if you still want to give him up, just so you can travel, OK?'

He puffs air from his cheeks.

'Yeah, OK,' he replies.

'OK, so I'll see you later?'

'Yeah, OK,' he says again.

I stand up, grab my coat and my bag and head for the door.

'Please, think carefully,' I remind him. 'He's not just a kid, he's a person. And one day he's going to be a grown man and he's going to understand every decision you've made, and not necessarily in a good way.'

He nods.

As I hurry through the strong wind and rain and get into my car, I have this horrible feeling in the pit of my stomach. He'll do the right thing, I tell myself. He has to.

Chapter 35

You'll never know pride quite like it, until you see your child on a stage (well, standing on a small platform, the school hall isn't big enough for a stage), singing their little heart out.

Frankie is up there, belting out songs about autumn that I'd hazard a guess someone wrote just for the occasion, like his life depends on it. That's my boy, doing his absolute best, completely oblivious to the fact that it's just Viv and me sitting in the audience. Did I think there was a chance Nathan might not show up? Honestly? I really thought he'd be here. I know that he's walked out on the two of us before but I thought things would be different this time, because this time he knows just how amazing Frankie is – how could anyone leave him? There's still a chance though, that he might have changed his mind. Maybe he's back at home, cancelling his plans, telling whatever organisation has recruited him that, sorry, he can't make it, because there might be loads of kids who need help in India, but there's already one very important kid right here who needs him more.

After his performance I clap and whoop loud enough for two parents – more than used to taking on both roles – and, of course, Viv's right there with me. But after he comes running over the first thing he does is ask where his dad is and my heart sinks. I make an excuse, nothing committal, just to get him into the car and head home. Well, there's no point hanging around at the school because I'm still getting the cold shoulder from everyone after yesterday.

But we've just pulled up outside and, although it's hard to see with the rain beating down on the car windscreen, there is no mistaking the fact that his campervan has gone. As we hurry from the car to the house, trying to get out of the gale force winds, no one else notices the letter sitting on the coffee table, addressed to me in Nathan's handwriting.

'Go get dry and put some clean clothes on, kiddo,' I tell him.

'OK,' he replies, heading for his room. 'Where is Dad?'

'I, erm, I'll figure that out while you're getting changed,' I call back.

Viv spots the letter in my hand. On the way to the school I told her all about Nathan's big job offer and I think she, like me, hoped that he wouldn't take it.

'That spineless bastard,' she curses quietly. 'Leaving you a letter instead of sticking around for his son or having the balls to tell him that he was leaving.'

I sigh as I open it.

'Dear Lil,' I read aloud, quietly, so only Viv can hear. 'If you're reading this letter I'm sure you will have figured out that I've gone. I wanted to come and say goodbye, I really did, but I would've missed my plane and I couldn't have afforded to buy another ticket myself. You know how important travelling is to me, and how important it is for me to make a difference around the world. I've told Frankie all about it and I hope that one day he will not only forgive me, but that he'll come and join me – you too, Lil. I know you don't want to, but please explain to him why I had to take off so quickly. All my love, Nathan.'

'Spineless,' Viv says again. 'Absolutely spineless.'

I feel tears fall from my eyes, which I quickly wipe away.

'Mum, how am I going to tell him that his dad has left him?'

I ask, my voice quivering with emotion.

'Come on,' she says. 'We'll do it together.'

'Am I in trouble?' Frankie asks, seeing us both walk into his room with ominous looks on our faces.

'Are you ever in trouble?' I reply with a smile. 'Take a seat.'

We all sit down on the bed together, and as Frankie looks at me, waiting to hear what I have to say, my heart breaks all over again and tears escape my eyes again.

'Mum, what's wrong?' he asks me. 'Is Dad OK?'

'That's the thing,' I start. 'Your dad is absolutely fine but, er, he's had to go.'

'Go where?' he asks.

'To India,' I tell him honestly. 'They needed someone to do some important work, looking after kids and—'

'Is he coming back?'

'I don't know,' I tell him softly. 'Not for a long time, I don't think.'

'This is because you made him sleep outside,' he says angrily – an emotion I'm not used to seeing from my son.

'That is not why,' Viv says sternly. 'Your dad chose to go, because he wanted to.'

'But he said we were best friends . . .'

I watch as my son's bottom lip starts to shake. I could kill Nathan for doing this to him, I am so mad at him. I'm also mad at myself, for giving him a chance. I should have told him to do one the second he turned up on our doorstep.

'Frankie, listen to me,' I start, but we're interrupted by a loud smashing noise. We all hurry into the living room, where the strong winds have brought part of a tree crashing in through the window, taking it out along with part of the wall and the roof. As rainwater pours in, I hurry over to move anything that could get damaged. That's when I spot that bloody, unfinished tree house – or should I say, the large bits of wood he left up in the tree, that have just come crashing through the cottage.

'Frankie, hurry into your room and grab a few things, we'll have to go to a B&B. You too, Viv, and pack some stuff for me please.'

They do as they're told, hurrying off to grab their things, while I move things from the living room to my bedroom. Anything electrical, or breakable, or anything that could be ruined by the wind and water beating around inside the remaining strong walls, I grab and move out of the way. Luckily my bedroom door locks with a key, so I can keep our things safe in there while we're at the B&B tonight. Although if the crime rate here is a low as Eric told me when he was pitching Marram Bay to me, that shouldn't be a problem.

With everything locked away and our overnight bags packed we hurry out to the car, just as Alfie happens to be passing in his Range Rover. Spotting us, he quickly pulls over.

'You're not heading for a day at the beach in this, are you?' he shouts over the weather.

'We're going to try and find a B&B for the night – a tree just fell into the cottage, the back wall is destroyed.'

Alfie's face falls.

'Come and stay with me,' he insists.

'It's fine, really,' I say.

'Don't be daft,' he replies. 'Get in.'

'Come on, darling, don't be rude,' my mum says, ushering Frankie towards Alfie's car.

I do as she says, hopping in the front seat next to Alfie. Once we're all in and the doors are closed, I exhale deeply.

'Thank you,' I say.

'I couldn't leave you out there in this, could I?' he replies. 'I can't believe a tree blew into your house.'

'Yeah, I don't suppose the unfinished tree house helped,' I say quietly. 'It acted like a sail.'

'Ah,' he replies. 'You know Nathan is welcome to come and stay as well. Probably not safe for him in the van tonight.'

I feel a knot in my throat as I smile. If ever I wondered whether or not Alfie was a good man, this just confirmed it. I know how he feels about Nathan and yet he'd still be willing to let him stay in his house.

'Nathan's gone,' I say, practically in a whisper.

I glance to the back of the car, where Frankie is glaring angrily. I'm not sure if he's glaring at me, or it's just a general look of upset, but I don't like it.

'Oh, OK,' he says, leaving it at that.

Alfie doesn't just drive up the driveway, he pulls right up to the front door so that we can get out without having to walk in the rain. Then he goes and puts his car in the garage and runs back. He lets us inside and sits us down on the sofa before making us all a cup of tea. Pugsley watches over us attentively while his master is busy making our drinks.

'That'll warm you up,' he says.

I cradle my cup in my cold hands, still freezing from moving things around in the blustery living room.

'Are you sure you don't mind us staying here?' I say.

'Of course not,' he replies. 'I told you, I like the company. Plus, I've got a job for Frankie, if he fancies earning his keep.'

Frankie – his thoughts clearly weighing heavy on his mind – gives Alfie a disinterested smile.

'Wait here,' Alfie says with a cheeky smile. He disappears into a room before returning seconds later with the tiniest kitten in his hand. He has it held close to his body, and the little cutie is snuggling into his neck.

'This is Kitty,' Alfie says. 'I'd noticed a stray tabby on the farm recently. Next thing I knew she'd had kittens, underneath a pile of logs down the bottom of the field. But this little one had a bad infection in her eye so I took her to Charlie who gave me some medicine for her. The plan was to return her to her mum, but she's gone. I felt bad, so I've been feeding her myself. I could do with a hand looking after her tonight . . .'

I look over at Frankie, who finally has a little light in his eyes.

'I'll do it,' he says.

'Here you go,' Alfie says, handing Kitty over. 'Make sure you support her body or she'll get scared and cling on with her claws. No one wants that. She might seem like a sweet little thing now, but you should see her at playtime.'

There is something so attractive about a big strong man holding a cute tiny animal. I suppose it shows a nurturing, caring, affectionate, responsible side – all of which are excellent qualities. I'm not sure Nathan possessed any of those, which, I guess, is why I've found myself alone, yet again.

'She's so, so cute,' Frankie says, having fallen in love at first sight.

'I'll need to find a home for her,' Alfie tells me. 'I'd keep her but Pugsley isn't happy about sharing me.'

'Can we have her, Mum?' Frankie asks.

'We'll see,' I laugh. 'We don't really have a home at the moment.'

'You're all welcome to stay here while the cottage is being fixed,' he says.

'Thank you,' I reply, but the truth is that I've got something else in mind.

'Shall I make us some tea?' Alfie asks. I look down at my cup.

'Dinner,' he says. 'Sorry, I forget you're southerners.'

Gosh, I love that little chuckle he does after he makes a joke.

'I'll help you,' I say.

'I suppose I'll just take it easy and keep an eye on these three,' Viv says, nodding towards Frankie, Pugsley and Kitty as she makes herself more comfortable on the sofa. She'll be asleep in less than ten minutes, I guarantee it.

As we prepare dinner in Alfie's stunning kitchen, I quietly fill him in on what happened with Nathan.

'Man, that's rough,' he says. 'I wasn't exactly his biggest fan, but I didn't think he'd take off again.'

'I suppose he was only here because he ran out of money,' I say. I look over at Frankie, who is currently amusing Kitty with a piece of string, to make sure that he isn't listening. 'Soon as he got a better offer, he took off. He never wanted to be a dad – I thought that he'd grown up and matured, he'd seen the error of his ways. And then I thought that none of that mattered, because now that he'd met Frankie, why would he ever want to leave him again?'

Alfie squeezes my hand.

'Frankie deserves better. How's he coping with it?'

'Not well,' I tell him. 'The problem is, we were just talking about it when the tree came crashing in. And now we're here and . . . he just seems so angry at me.'

'It's just displaced anger,' he assures me. 'Because Nathan isn't here.'

'I think he thinks I'm the reason he's gone,' I say, swallowing hard to fight off whatever emotional outburst is trying to creep up on me.

'Even if that were true,' Alfie starts, 'in a few years he's going to be old enough to understand what a waste of space his dad is, and that he left because he's selfish. It doesn't matter how hard you try to protect him, one day he's going to realise that his dad going off to muck out elephant enclosures – which, I can't believe is what he's ditched you guys for – isn't a very valid reason.'

I sigh. 'I know.'

'Let's put dinner in, I'll show you all where you can sleep and then after dinner, once Frankie is tucked up in bed with Kitty, maybe you can try and talk to him again?'

'Yeah,' I reply. 'Maybe that's for the best.'

'Lucky for you, I have lots of space and lots of guestrooms,' he says. 'Although I'm not sure what for. I think the architect who designed the place figured I was more popular than I am.'

'You really don't need to go to any trouble for us,' I tell him. 'It's just one night.'

'I told you, you can all stay here while the repairs are being done.'

'I know – that's so kind of you but, you know how we were talking about signs? Well, I think a tree crashing through the window and destroying the cottage is a pretty strong sign that we just shouldn't be here.'

'Come on, Lily, I wasn't serious about that,' he insists, a little worry in his voice. 'You can't give up now.'

'I think Kitty needs something,' Frankie interrupts us.

'Probably some water,' Alfie says, snapping back to his usual, charming self around Frankie. 'Come with me, I'll show you where her things are. She might be ready for her litter tray too.'

I watch as Alfie leads Frankie and Kitty away. Why couldn't I have got pregnant with someone more like Alfie, someone who is great with kids, someone caring? Frankie must be so confused. No wonder he thinks I'm the reason his dad has gone – what's the alternative? That his dad doesn't love him enough to stay?

From the drama with the deli to the upset at school to the cottage finally crumbling around us . . . there really is nothing to stay here for and the sooner we get back to London, the better.

Chapter 36

There are so many things that I love about Alfie Barton. I love his passion for cooking, and the way that everything he has cooked for me so far has been incredible. I love the little wrinkles that frame his gorgeous brown eyes, that only become more apparent when he smiles. I love how much he cares about animals, to the point where he is taking in homeless cats and raising them as his own. I love how he is with Frankie – especially today, when he needs it most. I could almost be tempted to say that I just love him . . . but that would be crazy, right? And even if it wasn't crazy, it's hugely inconvenient, given that I plan to pack up and head back to London tomorrow.

Sitting here on the sofa, with Alfie's arm around me, drinking a nice, warm cup of tea, watching his roaring fire, I couldn't feel more comfortable. Viv and Frankie have both gone to bed so we can talk more freely now.

'Are you sure moving back to London is the right thing to do?' he asks, gently massaging my shoulder.

'Coming here was just such a mistake,' I tell him. 'I was excited about the idea of a better job so I just uprooted my family – how does that make me any different to Nathan?'

'There's a difference between moving to India and moving

to Yorkshire,' he says. 'It's not that much of a culture change up here, is it?'

'Only that you call dinner, tea,' I joke. 'And that you dress up like it's the Second World War for fun.'

'Er, Yorkshire puddings versus jellied eels? No contest.'

'Well, you've got me there,' I laugh.

I feel his arm around me tighten, pulling me a little closer.

'We've just both had so much to contend with since we got here,' I say. 'I think he'll deal with this better back home, in an environment he's used to, surrounded by people who love him.'

'Hmm.'

I know it seems like we're giving up. But I'm not sure how long I'll have a job if the deli flops, no one likes us, we're homeless. It's not a sign of weakness, to give up. I think it takes strength to know when to fold.

'Well, regardless of whether the deli stays here or not, I spoke to my bosses this morning. They were telling me they'd be granted a licence and it made me think of your drinks . . . anyway, I pitched them your products and they just loved them, they want to stock them in all of their delis, all over the country.'

'Lily, that's incredible!' He beams. 'I've been working so hard on getting the brand out there. It's easy, here in Marram Bay where everyone knows me, but getting the rest of the world to catch on – well, this is exactly what I need. Someone to take a chance on me. Thank you.'

'You deserve it,' I tell him. He really does.

'You know, if the locals knew you'd done this for me, their opinion of you would change. That's such a generous thing to do, it's great for Marram Bay business.'

'Too little too late,' I say.

I realise I've placed a hand on his thigh – on some kind of autopilot, I certainly didn't realise I had – and tense up.

'Sleep on it,' he suggests. 'You might see things clearer once the storm is over.'

'I've made up my mind, Alfie,' I say. 'There's nothing to stay here for.'

'Not even this?' he asks, placing a hand on my cheek, turning my head to face his. I can't help but notice how his touch differs to Nathan's earlier. Nathan was too rough, too sleazy. Alfie, though, has this soft touch that gives me goosebumps on every inch of my body.

I close my eyes as Alfie's lips meet mine, but it's not the eager, passionate kiss we shared before, it's slow and soft and I can't get enough of it.

'I don't want you to go,' he says between kisses.

'I know,' I reply.

'I don't want you to leave me,' he says, making his intentions even clearer.

I want to tell him that I don't want to leave him either, that I want to stay here with him forever, but I just don't see how we can be happy here.

'Let's go upstairs,' I suggest quietly, my eyes still closed, too scared to look at him, in case he says no.

'OK,' he replies, pulling me to my feet.

This isn't me. I don't do this. But this doesn't feel like my home or my life and tomorrow it will all just seem like a bad dream. A bad dream with one part worth remembering.

Chapter 37

Waking up in Alfie's bed, cuddled up close to him with my head on his hairy chest, I could almost be tempted to stay here forever – not just in Marram Bay, but here in this bed. I feel so protected and safe with him. He's still sleeping so I stroke his chest. It's been so long since I felt this way about anyone and it terrifies me. I would love to give staying another chance, but I promised Frankie that if things didn't get better, I would take him back to London, and I'm keeping that promise. I haven't done anything with only me in mind since Frankie was born – even moving here was supposed to give him a better life – and I'm not about to start now. What he needs right now is familiarity and stability, and he can't get that here. Still, it's nice to lie here, pretending this is my wonderful life. I'll just drink it up for five more minutes before . . .

'Lily, Lily!' I hear my mum screaming.

Alfie wakes up suddenly, jumping up from under me. I'd say it was nice while it lasted but I've never heard my mum sound so worried, so I grab my dress from the floor and run downstairs to find her.

'What's wrong?' I ask, Alfie close behind me, hopping into his trackies.

'It's Frankie, he's gone,' she sobs. 'And the front door is wide open.'

'Don't worry, we'll find him,' Alfie assures me. 'Go check the cottage, maybe he went back there.'

'OK,' I say, dashing back for my shoes. 'Do you think he's run away again?' I call out from the bedroom.

'I think he might have,' Alfie calls back. 'And I think he's taken Kitty with him.'

I should have known that he'd try and run away again, like he did last time he was upset. Is this going to be his new thing? Just darting from his problems? Just like his dad? I remind myself that I'm just upset and scared, and that I just need to focus on finding him and then everything will be OK.

I run down the hill from Alfie's farm to the cottage, with a level of athleticism I never realised I had. It's amazing, what we're capable of when we need to be.

I run into the living room, check the bedrooms and the bathroom – I even check the garden, but there's no sign of him. Now that the storm has passed, I can see just how damaged the kitchen is. If ever there was a metaphor for my life, this cottage is it. Knackered, beaten, broken and empty.

I hop into my car, which doesn't start until my fourth attempt, but I'm just so grateful that it does. I try and think about where he might be going – last time he said he was going back to London, but there are no signposts or anything around here, just country roads and fields. I consider an 8-year-old's logic – if the way into Marram Bay is this way, then he might think the other way is the way out of town, and the way back home.

I drive along slowly, terrified he'll be in the long grass at the side of the road somewhere and I'll miss him. I keep going – I don't know how long for – because I don't know what time he snuck out, so I don't know how far he could've got. I pull over, searching for my phone to call Alfie and see if he's found him on the farm, but I must have left it there. *Shit!*

Maybe it will be like before, he'll just be out on the farm, looking at the alpacas, showing them to Kitty. It's a good sign, right? That he has the kitten with him?

Maybe I should give up searching this road, because there's no real evidence he went this way. Maybe I should go back to Alfie's and call the police. Yes, that's what I'll do. Eight-year-olds shouldn't just wander off on their own, I need to call them, we need to get a search going as soon as possible.

I make a U-turn and head back for the farm and, this time around, the journey feels like it takes much longer than it did in reverse. I cover a bit of ground I haven't yet, just in case he might have taken a different route, but there's no sign of him at all.

I'm about to drive straight past the cottage, when I notice a crowd of people standing outside.

'Alfie?' I say, getting out of the car. 'Have you found him?'

'Not yet,' he says. 'But everyone has come out to help.'

I glance around and, despite it being early in the morning, I can account for almost everyone I've met since the day I arrived here.

'People have brought you clean clothes, blankets and food. Jeff is out back, patching the back of the cottage up until you can get it fixed. Everyone else is here and ready to search, so come on, let's go.'

'Why would they do this?' I ask him quietly. I don't want to seem ungrateful, it's just confusing.

'Because you're one of us,' he tells me. 'Because you're having a hard time, because your kid is missing, and because I asked them to. I don't think it hurt that I posted all about you getting the delis to sell my products last night either.'

'Thank you,' I say, squeezing him tightly.

'OK, get in my car,' he insists. 'I've got a few ideas about where we can look.'

Alfie, noticing how worried I am, stops in his tracks to comfort me.

'We're going to find him,' he insists firmly, holding me by my sides. 'I promise you, we're going to find him.'

I nod, but I'm still terrified. My mind is jumping to all sorts of horrible conclusions.

As I climb into Alfie's car I notice another pull up outside the cottage. Avril gets out.

'Wait,' I say, quickly opening the door again, as I notice her lift something out of the back of her car. It's Kitty, closely followed by Frankie.

'Alfie, he's there,' I squeak, jumping out and running over to him. 'Frankie, oh my God, Frankie. Shit!'

'Swears,' he says as I grab him and damn near squeeze the life out of him.

'My God, it's so good to hear you tell me off,' I say, twirling him around.

'Mrs Snowball says that saying "God" like that is just as bad as swearing, that it's taking the Lord's name in vain,' he says.

I put him down and place my hands on his face.

'You ran away again – you promised me you wouldn't.'

I don't wait for an answer, I turn to Avril and hug her tightly. 'Thank you so much, where did you find him?'

'Outside Clara's,' she says. 'Waiting for them to open, but they were both still in bed. He said they wanted chicken nuggets. I don't think they were waiting there for long.'

I realise by 'they' she means Frankie and Kitty.

Frankie may have only been out on his own for an hour, but the time I spent looking for him is easily the most terrified I have ever felt in my life. It's going to be a long time before I let him out of my sight – and maybe my arms – again.

'I can't even imagine how scared you must've been,' Avril says. 'I was just in the right place at the right time. I saw Alfie's post in the group about Frankie being missing. Maybe we should let you in the group – you know, for security reasons.'

I hear what she's saying.

'Thank you,' I say again. 'Thank you.'

'You gave us quite a scare, kiddo,' Alfie says. It touches me, to hear him use my nickname for Frankie.

'Come with me,' I say, leading him towards Alfie's car. 'Do you mind if we have a quick chat?'

'Go for it,' he says, taking Kitty from Frankie. 'I'll look after her while you talk. Give me a wave if you want me.'

'Thank you, everyone. For everything. Thank you so much,' I say to the crowd of people who all came out just to help us.

I climb into the back of Alfie's car with Frankie and take him by the hand.

'I know you're upset about your dad leaving – I am too. And I'm sorry we didn't really get to talk about it last night, with everything that happened. The fact is, I could tell you all sorts of stories, about how your dad has important work to do around the world, which is what he wanted me to tell you, but one day you're going to be old enough to figure out for yourself that that just isn't true.'

'Doesn't he love me?' Frankie asks, his bottom lip quivering. I feel my heart just crumbling to dust inside my chest.

'He does love you,' I tell him. 'He just doesn't show it properly. He has the love, he just lacks things like responsibility and he's selfish. The truth is, he wasn't ready to be a dad when you were born, and he's still not ready now. But that's a problem with him, not you. You are amazing.'

He nods.

'One day, when you're older, if he comes back, you can decide whether or not you want a relationship with him. Maybe he'll stay longer next time, maybe he won't. But all you need to remember is that you have a mum who loves you, and a gran who loves you.' I look outside the car window where I spot Alfie watching us. 'I think Alfie loves you too.'

'Do you love Alfie?' Frankie asks. His question takes me aback.

'I do have very strong feelings for him,' I admit. 'He's a good man.'

'Then why do we have to leave?' he asks me.

'Leave? You ran away,' I remind him. 'Don't you want to leave?'

'I heard you, last night. You said we were going back to London. I don't want to go back, I want to stay here with Alfie and Kitty and all my friends at school.'

Before I have a chance to say anything, Viv gets in the other side of the car.

'You had us worried sick,' she tells him, before her anger dissolves and she grabs him and hugs him, holding him tightly.

'I'm sorry, Viv,' he says, his voice muffled by her body.

'He ran away because he overheard me saying that we were moving back to London,' I tell her.

'You're not, are you?' Viv says. 'And just when I was thinking of moving here too.'

'What?'

'Biagio has asked me if I want to move in with him. I mean, it's lovely living with you two, but I can't be sharing a bed with my daughter, not when I'm pushing forty.'

Frankie and I both giggle at her blatant lie.

'Is it not a bit soon to be moving in with him?' I ask her.

'Darling, when you know, you know,' she tells me. 'You'll never need convincing of anything that you feel sure of. I know who I care about, I know what I'm comfortable with and I know what I want. Always go with your gut, my girl.'

I think for a moment, although I'm not sure why. I want Alfie. I want to stay here and I want to make a go of it with him, with the deli – sure, things will be tough while we figure out what to do about the cottage, and the deli . . .

I wave at Alfie, beckoning him over.

'Shift up,' he says, opening my side of the car. I do, and he squashes in the back with us. Well, I say he squashes, it's not exactly cramped in the back of a Range Rover.

'So, we think we might stay here,' I tell him. 'All three of us. Viv is moving in with her fancy man, apparently.'

'Good for you,' he tells her with a chuckle.

'Well, I definitely have room for two at my place,' he says. 'And I still need someone to look after Kitty – although, she's not old enough to eat chicken nuggets yet, mate.'

'Can we live with Alfie, Mum?' Frankie begs.

'Thank you,' I tell Alfie. 'If we could stay until the cottage is sorted.'

'We'll see,' he replies. 'Maybe I'll convince you to stay a bit longer.'

I smile.

'I can't believe everyone came out to help,' I say, blown away by the support. 'No one thought I'd faked the kidnap of my child for sympathy then?'

'I told you, people were impressed you said you'd stock my products,' he tells me with a laugh. 'You just needed to prove that you loved the town, so that the town could love you back. Apple Blossom Girl did a good thing and people saw that.'

We hold eye contact again. That long, lingering eye contact I've gotten so used to sharing with him. It's so calm, yet so full of possibilities, and when I have his attention like this, my breathing always quickens.

'Let's leave these two alone for a second,' Viv suggests. 'They can figure out who is going to sleep where and we can go and make sure Kitty is OK.'

'OK,' Frankie replies, holding onto the word a little longer than usual, in an almost knowing way.

Once it's just the two of us, I shift up a little to give Alfie more space, but he follows me.

'So, you're staying,' he says.

'I am,' I reply.

'And you're going to move in with me.'

'For now,' I laugh.

'You've tried my shower, right? No one leaves that shower.'

'That is true, you do have a good shower.'

'And my bed,' he says, running a hand up the side of my face and into my hair where he holds the back of my head. 'My bed is pretty good, right?'

'It's a pretty good bed,' I tell him coyly. 'I'll give it another go.'

Alfie pulls me close and kisses me.

'I love you,' he whispers. 'I think I loved you the second I laid eyes on you. Or maybe since the second time I laid eyes on you. The first time you were surrounded by cow crap and very angry.'

I laugh and I feel a tear escape one of my eyes, which Alfie quickly wipes away.

'I love you too,' I tell him. 'Always have. But, listen, it's not an easy job, taking on someone else's kid, you have to be sure.'

'That's true,' he says, thinking carefully for a moment. 'But so long as you promise to be a good mum to my dog, cat, alpaca, ducks – and Phillip, of course, he's a handful – then I think we might just be able to make it work.'

Alfie not even thinking twice about the fact that I come with Frankie tells me everything I need to know about him. He's a good man and staying here with him is absolutely the right thing to do.

Chapter 38

Ding.

I'm not sure why I opted to have a bell fitted on the deli door. I suppose it was in case a customer came in while I was in the back room.

I don't think I'd anticipated just how much custom we'd be getting, and while the constant noise could be viewed as annoying by some, to me it serves as a victory bell, a little chime of success. That I'm not sure I'll ever get bored of hearing.

'All of our cream cakes are one of your five-a-day,' Biagio assures a couple of middle-aged lady customers. They laugh giddily, immediately won over by his outgoing Italian charms, but it's been two months since the deli opened, and Biagio only has eyes for Viv.

I look over at my mum, sitting at a table, sipping a cup of tea, smiling wildly as she watches her man in action. I've always thought of my mum as being an optimistic, happy person, but now that I think about it, maybe we all put on a happy face for our kids from time to time, and I'm not sure that's something we mums will ever stop doing – nor do I think we ever should. But it's only now, seeing how she is around Biagio, that I realise just how truly happy she is with him, and it's a side of her I've never seen, not with any of her boyfriends (or the occasional one of mine). She looks – if possible – even younger and healthier and it makes my heart want to burst. My mum always has been, and always will be, the most important woman in my life, and her happiness means everything to me.

'Wow, what are those?' I ask Channy as she carries in a plate of delicious-looking *somethings*.

'I was mucking around with a coconut macaroon recipe,' she explains. 'These are chocolate orange ones – I dunno, I just liked the idea. Try one?'

'I've never turned down chocolate,' I laugh, but this is Channy's first week with Biagio training her in the kitchen, so I'm yet to try anything she's made yet.

'Oh my gosh, they're amazing,' I admit.

'Yeah?' she replies, with a hopeful humbleness. 'Really?'

'Really,' I tell her. 'Ask the others, I'm sure they'll agree. Maybe see if a few customers want to sample them. If they're good, we could sell them.'

'Chanaroons,' she says excitedly, trying the name out for size. 'Maybe this is my thing?'

'Maybe it is,' I reply. After all, this is exactly what happened to me. I was at a crossroads in my life, I wound up at the deli and, for some reason, it just felt right. I knew that this was my calling, and while it might not be as impressive as raising elephants, or as worthy as teaching kids English, it makes me happy and allows me to take care of my son, and I like to think that's a worthy cause too.

Speaking of Nathan, I received a postcard from him yesterday – the first time we've heard from him since he took off again. This time, I didn't hide it away in a panic, shoving it at the back of a wardrobe or stuffing it in the secret pocket of my handbag, I simply read his note, which boasted all the warmth of a newsletter, before placing it down on the sideboard by the front door. I told Frankie it was there, and that he can read it when and if he chooses. I won't ever stop him having a relationship with his dad, but it will be on Frankie's terms if he does.

Right on cue, Frankie comes charging through the door, throwing his arms around my leg as I clear tables.

'Mum, can I go to Bart's house for tea tomorrow?'

'Tea?' I laugh, amused to hear how quickly he's picked up the local dialect. 'Of course you can.'

'That'll give us some time alone together,' I hear Alfie say, creeping up behind me, wrapping his arms around my waist.

'That would be nice,' I say, leaning back into him.

Alfie kisses my cheek affectionately.

'Hey, how's Pugsley doing?' I ask. Alfie took him to the vet today because he's been snoring a lot louder than usual lately.

'He's fine – just one of the joys of owning a pug,' he laughs, before his face falls. 'We saw Jim, instead of Charlie. I've been getting the feeling she's been cold with me, since we got together . . .'

It hadn't escaped my attention that Alfie's friendship with Charlie seemed to stop just as our relationship started.

'I think everyone but you knew that she was trying to pull you,' Channy says. I didn't realise she was listening in, and I shoot her a glance to try and halt her honesty.

Alfie rubs his chin.

'She wasn't a real friend then, was she?' he reasons. 'So that's no loss.'

I smile. 'I'm just glad you're OK, and that Pugsley is OK.'

'Yeah, he's fine,' he says, hugging me again. 'We just might need to get some ear plugs.'

'With an 8-year-old, a zoo of animals and a multitude of weird gadgets, a snoring dog is the least of our worries,' I laugh. 'It's a madhouse, isn't it?'

'It's exactly what I want,' he replies, kissing me on the cheek. 'How about I take Frankie home and make a start on tea?'

'God, you're amazing,' I blurt.

'I feel like a housewife,' he laughs. 'What would my dad say?'

'He'd be proud of you,' I insist. 'How could he not be?'

Alfie kisses me again.

'Love you,' he says.

'Love you too,' I reply.

'Come on, kiddo,' Alfie calls. Frankie, who was chatting with Viv, charges over to him.

'Bye, Mum.'

'Bye,' I call after him.

I feel so completely comfortable with Alfie looking after Frankie. They make such a cute double act and seem to really love spending time together. We feel like a proper little family – something I'd never felt before. Living here, with my son, my amazing boyfriend, our pets, and with my loved-up mum nearby, doing a job that I love, with no secrets hanging over me . . . I finally feel like I have it all.

My mum was right when she told me: when you know, you know. I know that here is my home now. I might not be travelling the world, living out of a suitcase, planting trees and feeding elephants, but life here is an adventure all of its own, and I can't wait to see what it has in store for me next.

Here Comes the Ex

Luca is used to being 'the single one' – which is partly why she is dreading going to the wedding of an old university friend. Surrounded by faces she hasn't seen in 10 years, Luca can feel herself being sucked back into the immature, decade-old gossip that no one seems to have forgotten.

But when Tom walks in, Luca's heart stops. He was her crush, her 'almost boyfriend' – but then he broke her heart at a party ten years ago. And now here he is, hotter than ever, and standing next to the girl he broke Luca's heart with.

As the day unfolds and the champagne continues to flow, it's clear that Tom can't take his eyes off her. Are some people best left in the past, or is Luca's luck in love finally about to change?

Love on Tour

Nicole Wilde's life is one of sell-out gigs, sleeping on tour buses, and partying with the band all night long. But she's not in the band. She's a music journalist, paid to do a job many would kill for.

Nicole has had a crush on rockstar Luke Fox since she was a teenager. When she's invited to tour with his band, she knows nothing can happen. She's spent too much time with musicians to seriously consider a romantic relationship with one of them – and with her best friend Dylan King caught up in yet another scandal, she's far too busy for love.

Watching fans throw themselves at Luke, Nicole settles for friendship. But as the tour goes on, will she allow it to turn into something more?

Drive Me Crazy

In reality it was a business trip, prettied up as a romantic mini break, but the man behind the wheel was meant to be Candice Hart's boss and (married but separated, I swear!) lover. Not Danny the new guy!

Not only is Candice faced with a new driver, but the office's far too handsome hipster expects her to share the cramped space inside his 'fully' restored VW Beetle, aka The Love Bug, and put up with his constant opinions about her life . . .

Before long she is tired of playing the 'good girl' and, with Danny's help, is determined to finally show the world the real Candice Hart!

Acknowledgements

Thanks so much to Sophia, George and the rest of the team at HQ for all of their hard work on my books. You're doing such a fantastic job.

Thank you to my lovely readers for taking the time to read and review my books. It means so much to me.

Finally, thank you to my incredible family (Joe, Joey, James, Kim, Pino, Aud & Darcy) for all of their support – I couldn't do it without you.

Dear Reader,

We hope you enjoyed reading this book. If you did, we'd be so appreciative if you left a review. It really helps us and the author to bring more books like this to you.

Here at HQ Digital we are dedicated to publishing fiction that will keep you turning the pages into the early hours. Don't want to miss a thing? To find out more about our books, promotions, discover exclusive content and enter competitions you can keep in touch in the following ways:

JOIN OUR COMMUNITY:

Sign up to our new email newsletter: http://smarturl.it/SignUpHQ

Read our new blog www.hqstories.co.uk

𝕏 https://twitter.com/HQStories
f www.facebook.com/HQStories

BUDDING WRITER?

We're also looking for authors to join the HQ Digital family! Find out more here:

https://www.hqstories.co.uk/want-to-write-for-us/

Thanks for reading, from the HQ Digital team